A CLASS APART

"Paul." Sepia winced as she heard herself call his name. She didn't want to ask him this and hoped he would get inside before she gave in to the urge, but no dice. She had to do it. She had to know.

"Yeah?" he asked, turning around.

"I was upset this morning when I found out you left."

Paul cleared his throat. "I had to go in because of the shooting. It's in Cromwell, but Luke is lead invest—"

"I know you had to go, Paul, but why didn't you tell me you were leaving? It would have taken a second and would have been nice."

Paul's expression stilled and grew serious. "The truth?"

"Yes." Had she repulsed him so much by coming on to him that he couldn't face her? That's what she was worried about.

"The truth is, I wanted to tell you. I just couldn't risk it."

"Risk what?"

"Risk going into your bedroom. I don't think I would ever have left."

Sepia was speechless as he turned and went inside. What a hit-and-run that man was.

ANGELA WINTERS

A CLASS APART

ARABESQUE

★BET BOOKS™

BET Publications, LLC
http://www.bet.com
http://www.arabesquebooks.com

ARABESQUE BOOKS are published by

BET Publications, LLC
c/o BET BOOKS
One BET Plaza
1900 W Place NE
Washington, DC 20018-1211

All Kensington Titles, Imprints, and Distributed Lines are
available at special quantity discounts for bulk purchases for
sales promotions, premiums, fund-raising, and educational or
institutional use. Special book excerpts or customized printings can also be created to fit specific needs. For details, write
or phone the office of the Kensington special sales manager:
Kensington Publishing Corp., 850 Third Avenue, New York,
NY 10022, attn: Special Sales Department, Phone: 1-800-221-
2647.

First Printing: July 2004
10 9 8 7 6 5 4 3 2 1

Printed in the United States of America

This book is dedicated to all those aspiring writers who send me e-mails every day asking for advice and sharing their dreams with me. Keep writing, keep reading and keep dreaming!

One

This guy was leading them on a cat-and-mouse chase in the dark and Officer Paul Healy knew how this type of scenario usually ended. Someone was going to get shot and he had to make sure it wasn't him or his partner. He rushed down the dark, unsteady staircase at the risk of his life. Two steps had already collapsed underneath him. He'd caught himself just in time to keep from falling through, never letting go of the gun in his ready hands. The missteps had given the suspect more of a head start than Paul was comfortable with.

It was after midnight and the last thing he wanted was to be in one of the many abandoned buildings in Crawford's projects, chasing down a gang member. But he was a cop and the Ravens were becoming fierce enough to rival any gang in neighboring Washington, D.C. If anyone got a tip of a drug deal or any gathering of Raven members, you didn't turn it down. Especially not now with the whole town beating the police department down for showing up ten minutes late and a dead body or two down.

Paul could barely see, but his ten years on the force would not allow him a second of fear. Besides, if he couldn't see, neither could the other man. There was only one left. When they'd shown up, one got away, but the other ran into this broken-down shack and they were gonna get him.

Paul stopped, listening to the sound of his own breathing. Silence. Whoever this punk was, he was standing still. But where? Paul's partner, David Parks, was at the bottom of the steps, waiting for him. That was the plan. Couldn't fail. He had to come up or down. All the windows were boarded up.

The silence bothered him. Was David on his game? He'd been acting so weird lately; Paul couldn't ignore the concerns even though he wished they weren't there. He and David had been partners for five years. He had to believe David wouldn't let him down.

Wait.

Paul held his breath. He could swear he heard something. Was it the wind? Or a whisper? Voices? Then nothing. Something was wrong.

Thump! Tumble.

Someone had hit the floor.

"David!" Paul came rushing down the last two flights of stairs, gun raised.

He felt the panic rise in his throat as he saw David on the floor, rubbing the back of his head, trying to get up.

"I'm all right," David said in a grumbling voice. "He hit me with his gun. He got away."

"Damn!" Paul rushed down the hallway and out the front door. Left, right. Nothing. He was gone, and a sense of dread fell over Paul. He hated to fail. It just didn't happen to him.

He looked across the street at one of the few project buildings that were still livable. He saw figures looming behind barred-up windows, staring at him. He was an imposing figure, six feet tall, coffee colored, with dark eyes and dark hair. He was muscular and dominant. The community usually admired these physical qualities in their protectors, but he sensed no admiration tonight. They knew what went on in this building and as they saw him exit, realizing he was empty-handed, they turned from their windows and their lights went dim. What good was he?

How could he ever make detective in three months now?

Paul lowered his gun as he heard David shuffling behind him. When David came out into the night, lit only by the moon because all of the streetlights in this project center were knocked out, shame consumed his expression. Being the friend that he was, Paul felt compelled to console him and let him know all that mattered was that he was okay. But right now, he was a cop and they had failed, adding on to the string of failures the department had been experiencing with the Ravens.

David rubbed his head. He was biracial, but his features were mostly Caucasian. His skin was barely yellow, his eyes green, his lips and nose so small they were almost feminine. He was only twenty-eight, but he looked ten years older.

"I'm sorry," David said, as if knowing what was coming.

"Sorry doesn't cut it," Paul answered. "I know you're going through some stuff, man, but you're letting it interfere with your job."

"It wasn't about that. He just came out of nowhere."

"Are you kidding me?" Paul asked, not believing what he was hearing. "He came down the steps, right in front of you."

"I turned around. I'm . . . I thought I heard something down the hallway. It only took a second and I felt this—"

"I don't want to hear it, David. You should have heard him, felt him. You're a better cop than that."

David leaned against the wall, shaking his head. "I . . . I can't explain it."

Two police cars rolled up and parked behind theirs.

"Well, you better figure out how to explain it," Paul said as he began walking toward his fellow officers. "Because it starts now."

"Paul," David called to him, desperation evident in his voice.

David looked back at his partner, unable to fight the pity he felt for the guy. Money problems, marriage problems, and now this, their second failure in one week to capture a Raven member in the progress of a crime.

"You got my back, man, right?" David's brows centered in a question.

Paul sighed, turning back to David. He stood across from him, placing his hand firmly on David's shoulder. He looked directly into his eyes. "You're my partner. I always got your back."

"Ms. Davis, how nice to see you."

The host at Frasé, the finest French restaurant in Maryland and the only French restaurant open for breakfast, rushed from behind the podium to greet Sepia Davis. His smile was from ear to ear.

"Hello, Aaron." Sepia held her hand out as he

kissed it. Aaron was an eternal flirt, especially when it came to what he referred to as "ladies of distinction." He knew who the power families were and paid them special attention when they came to Frasé, at the manager's orders. "I'm here to—"

"Meet Mrs. Ryan," he completed for her, sliding the edges of his sandy blond hair behind his ears. "She is waiting for you. Please follow me."

Sepia did as she was told and followed him through the restaurant that was unusually busy for a weekday morning. She nodded to the people she knew, and she knew them all. Frasé was a reservations-only restaurant and it was a favorite of the black upper crust of Cromwell, Maryland. The same people all the time.

Cromwell was one of the wealthiest suburbs of Washington, D.C., just minutes from the district and at the edge of the Potomac. It was predominantly African-American and overwhelmingly wealthy. There were some growing middle-class citizens living in condos and town houses, but the majority of Cromwell was the new rich and old rich black folks living in Mcmansions and full-out estates. The eternal battle that waged elsewhere was less so in Cromwell. The old rich had their own things that the others couldn't have. It had always been that way, but they blended well with the new rich. After all, they were all rich and money could build many a bridge.

Sepia Davis, thirty years old and a best-selling romance author, was from the old rich, and not a day had gone by in her childhood when she wasn't reminded of how special that made her. She had embraced it for so long, but in these last few years as she blossomed from a spoiled rich girl to a woman with some pain to pepper her spirit, all of those old speeches from Dr. and Mrs. Davis had lost some of their luster.

Still, they were her people and she was theirs, so she smiled at them as they waved to her and smiled back. They admired her perfection, dressed in her sexy casual designer clothes, her caramel complexion gleaming from regular spa treatments. Her chestnut hair, done every week and cut barely an inch from her head, was wavy and held a shine that rivaled her eyes in sparkle. Nothing about her told you that she had just broken off an engagement, was making a major change in her career, and was at a crossroads in finding herself.

As she thanked Aaron and slid into her booth, Sepia warmed at the sight of her editor, Margo Ryan, who was waiting dutifully for her, all decked out in red Donna Karan to match her flaming red hair. Margo always looked like a million bucks first thing in the morning. Sepia would always hate her for that, although she truly adored her.

"You're late," Margo said, "but you're looking lovely, so I forgive you."

"What are you up to, Margo?" Sepia placed her packaged, completed novel on the table. She had done the third and final edit on *Love's Promise* and would be grateful to be rid of it.

"Me?"

"Yes, you. It's nice to see you, by the way."

"Yes, let's get the niceties out of the way, dear. Great to see you too." She took a sip of her coffee. "Now what are you accusing me of?"

"Coming to Maryland to collect my manuscript." Sepia's large eyes squinted as she studied her friend's innocent gaze. "I could just have easily mailed it to you in New York as I have with the last ten manuscripts. You're up to something. Is this about our phone conversation last week?"

Sepia hadn't been able to decipher Margo's reaction over the phone when she'd told her that she wasn't going to write romance anymore. That she wanted to make a change in her career after *Love's Promise.* There was a "that's interesting" and a "we'll talk later." Then Margo had called two days ago and said she would be in D.C. and wanted to drop by to get the manuscript. They hadn't been face-to-face in over a year when Sepia's last book, *Love's Revenge,* was released and they went on the book-signing tour.

"Don't flatter yourself," Margo said. "I'm a wife and mother of three ungrateful teenagers. I just wanted to get away."

"I'm not buying it." Sepia felt a tinge inside at the mention of "wife and mother." Would she ever get the chance to describe herself as such?

Margo sighed. "You want the truth?"

"Nothing but." Sepia leaned back as the waiter came and took her order. Croissants and coffee. She wasn't a breakfast kind of girl.

"How are your parents, by the way?" Margo held her hands out, observing her finely manicured nails. "Back from Aruba?"

"Antigua and they're great." Sepia hadn't been speaking to her parents too much since she'd broken off the engagement with Jason Allen a month ago. "What is it?"

Margo nodded to the carefully packaged manuscript on the table. "Is that *Love's Promise*?"

"Of course." Sepia slid all four hundred pages across the table at her. "What's wrong, Margo?"

"Oh, Sepia." She sighed heavily. "It's a big deal to jump genres. You know that."

"I know." Sepia smiled. She was confident in her own decision, but she needed her editor on her side. "But I'm done with romance. I enjoyed it and it's made me a lot of money."

"It made you famous."

"But it's over. My romance with romance has ended."

"Is this about Jason?"

Sepia frowned and Margo cringed, seeming to immediately regret her words.

"No, Margo. I've been mulling this over for months now. There is this woman inside me and she keeps yelling at me to let her out."

"You writers and your voices." She nodded a thank-you as the waiter brought their warm and buttery croissants. "You're all a bunch of weirdos."

"Yes, we are." Sepia couldn't help but laugh. "But I let that woman inside me out, and Marissa Grace must be heard."

"This is her name? Marissa Grace. Your new . . . character."

"My new heroine." Sepia smiled proudly. "She's a cop on the force. I've already outlined the crimes she'll be solving in my first two books. She's witty and injured and feisty and determined. The readers will love her."

"Does she fall in love?" Margo asked hopefully.

Sepia shrugged. "She has sex, if that counts."

"It's a start."

"This is not a romance series, Margo. Marissa is only concerned about getting respect from the guys on the force and making detective. Her sex life is a means of entertainment for her right now."

"She's a whore?"

"No." Sepia looked around, certain that someone had heard that. "She's free. People confuse the two at times."

"Sepia, darling, I don't mean to insult you, but you know nothing about the blue-collar world of policing. All your private schooling, Ivy League education, and society breeding makes you completely unrelatable to what a woman cop would go through."

Sepia was insulted, but she wouldn't show it. "There's much more to me than my privilege."

"I'm sorry, dear. I know, but . . . a cop?"

"I'm immersing myself in that world."

"Internet research isn't going to—"

"I've been doing more than that. I've been interviewing female cops. I'm even going for a ride-along tomorrow morning."

Margo looked horrified. "Sepia, that's dangerous."

"I know, but I have to get into that life if I'm going to make this character real, and I'm going to do that. I won't shortchange my readers."

"Your readers want romance."

"I think they want me. They can read romance anytime, Margo. The reason my books go into multiple printings and make best-seller lists is that readers like the way I write about women and what we feel."

At least she could write about it, even if she couldn't live it. Her own love life went from being a mess to nonexistent, but that was neither here nor there. Right now, nothing mattered but this new book.

Margo mumbled as she chewed. "You are my best writer."

Sepia smiled. "Hands down."

"Fine then." Margo placed *Love's Promise* in her Gucci bag and turned back to Sepia with a confident smile on her face.

"Is that it?" Sepia asked.

"I came down here because I wanted to see the look on your face when you told me how much you wanted it. I wanted to see that unique fire you have, and you have it. I'm sure it'll be a success."

"You won't regret this," Sepia said, gleaming.

"I better not. The marketing group will have to completely work over your release. I'll have the contract out to your agent next week."

"She's waiting for your call." Sepia leaned back, feeling herself finally catch up with the day as her eyes came to life.

So it was official. Her career was making a major shift. Away from the guaranteed sales of the romance genre that she had come to be so well known for to the mystery genre. Mystery was much more competitive and challenging in different ways. Just like Sepia liked it. *Patricia Cornwell, J.D. Robb, be forewarned. There's a sister coming to town.*

"You're quite pleased with yourself," Margo said, observing Sepia's relaxed smiled.

"I've needed to feel this way for some time. I—"

"Hey, guys."

Sepia and Margo looked up to find Louise Lyman, Sepia's best friend, standing at their table with eager, pleading eyes. She was dressed for work, the conservative world of D.C. lawyers, her long black hair pulled back in a tight bun, revealing a softly feminine cocoa-brown face made breathtaking with MAC's best.

"What are you doing here?" Sepia hadn't meant for the question to come out as it did. She loved

Louise and any time she could see her, which was generally all the time, she was happy. Just surprised.

"You told me about your breakfast with Margo." Louise looked in Margo's direction. "It's been some time."

The women shook hands and Sepia could sense the slight tension. Margo and Louise liked each other enough, but Louise was possessive of all of her friends. She didn't like to share Sepia with anyone.

"Can I join you?" Louise asked after she had already slid into Sepia's side of the booth.

Margo seemed uncertain, looking at Sepia, who nodded. "Of course you can. We're done with the business side of it, aren't we?"

"I'm done," Sepia slid her plate to Louise, who helped herself to what was left. "I talk about the book. My agent talks about business."

"If you'll excuse me," Margo said, sliding out, "I've got to go to the ladies' room. I'll be back."

Louise waited until Margo was out of earshot. "Did I say something?"

"What are you doing here, Louise?"

"I couldn't resist." She looked around with excitement in her eyes. "It's Frasé. Everyone who is anyone is here, and I'm nobody, so I can't get in unless I'm with you or Laurence."

Laurence was Louise's target of the moment. Laurence Weaver was one of the most eligible bachelors in Cromwell. He was from one of the finest families on the East Coast. The Weavers had a long line of lawyers, doctors, and business owners in Philadelphia, D.C., New York, and Atlanta. After a stint in the Midwest, Laurence returned to Cromwell ten years ago as a thirty-year-old investment firm president. Back then, every well-heeled sister in the D.C. metro area got in line to ring him in. Ten years later, none had made the cut.

Sepia had probably been the only woman not in that line. In the last ten years, Sepia had made a business out of long-term relationships that went nowhere. So, unavailability made it easy for her and Laurence to become friends. She cared for him, but she loved Louise, and she felt a stinging fear of regret that she had introduced the two.

"I can't pass up a chance to be seen here," Louise added, pulling her rolled newspaper out of her large purse. "How long can we stay?"

"You're the one with the nine-to-five," Sepia said. "Speaking of which, aren't you late for work?"

"I called in." Louise's shoulders hung low.

"Can lawyers do that? I didn't think you had the right?"

"I'm so sick of their bull . . ." Louise looked around. "I don't want to talk about it."

"But you will." Sepia turned to Louise, giving her her full attention. "Same old thing as always?"

"I'm a great lawyer."

"Of course you are."

"I don't know everyone that Cari Windsor has, but I know people."

"Someone get promoted over you?"

Louise looked at her, rolling her eyes. "I thought I could pass on the discrimination thing if I went to work for a black-owned firm. Only, there's another kind of discrimination that goes further than race."

"Class."

"I'm from the dreaded working class. I'll never live down that background at Sanders Law."

Sepia rubbed Louise's shoulder. She felt for her.

Louise had a chip on her shoulder about class. She wasn't born in the world that Cromwell represented, but she wanted in badly. She had made strides in the new rich world, but the old rich was still hesitant. Sepia tried to convince her that those people that mattered would accept her for who she was, but she knew that the rest of the world spoke otherwise. Which reminded of her why she might one day regret setting Louise up with Laurence. Louise had decided that marrying Laurence was her ticket in. She believed that a man could give her all of her dreams, and Sepia had learned the hard way that this was not possible.

"How is Laurence?"

"What's that's supposed to mean?" Louise's posture became defensive.

"I was trying to change the subject."

Louise sighed. "I'm sorry. I'm defensive right now. I think . . . Sometimes I feel like I'm walking up a steep hill that never ends."

"I love you." Sepia reached over, hugging Louise. "Laurence loves you."

"Don't get me started on him." Another roll of the eyes.

"Are we still on for tonight?"

"I guess." She flipped through the newspaper. Louise always went straight to the Style section. "He's been such an ass lately."

"Laurence couldn't possibly be."

"He's just been so caught up in the country club."

"Well, he is the club's general manager." Sepia hated trying to excuse Laurence, because she had told him he was overdoing it, but she knew Laurence had a passion for that club that nothing could calm.

The Cromwell Golf and Yacht Club was the new black-owned country club opening this upcoming weekend. Although it had been the dream of all Cromwell's citizens, it was Laurence's baby. It was born of his sweat and his heart. He had worked on establishing the club from the beginning, even while he was grieving the death of his parents a year ago. He had been obsessed and now that the opening was near, he was manic. Louise was getting the brunt of it.

"It will all be over after this weekend," Sepia assured her, even though she wasn't sure of that at all.

Louise rubbed her forefinger around the edges of the glass the waiter had just placed in front of her. "We got into it this morning."

"This morning?" So he was sleeping over during the week? That had to be progress.

"He was talking about the admissions process for the club. He had to decline four more people and he said this horrible thing."

"What?"

"He said he didn't know why people like that even applied in the first place. That they shouldn't even think they were worthy of fellowship with such superior people as the members of this club."

"He didn't mean anything." Sepia knew Laurence was a bit of a classist, but he was a really good guy. "It's the pressure."

"I'm back." Margo slid back into her seat with a refreshed smile on her face. "Is it safe?"

"We're just talking about love life problems," Sepia said.

Margo leaned forward, with a whisper. "You mean Jason?"

Sepia cringed. "No, not Jason. We don't talk about Jason, remember?"

"Oh, yes, I forgot." Margo nodded an apology, reaching for the remainder of the newspaper.

"We're talking about my pitiful love life," Louise said. "I do it as a charitable act so Sepia won't have to think about her love life, which is worse than mine."

Sepia smiled wryly. Louise could tease her. She was the only one who could. She had been there through the pain of breaking off the engagement, so she had earned the right to tease. It didn't hurt as much anymore anyway.

"For the love of God," Margo said, sliding the paper back to Louise. "How horrible."

"What?" Sepia leaned over as Louise opened the paper.

"You didn't hear it on the news this morning?" Louise asked, spreading it out. "Elliott Jackson was killed last night. Shot in the head, execution style."

Sepia grabbed the paper. "I can't believe it."

CONTROVERSIAL COMMUNITY LEADER MURDERED.

"Who is he?" Margo asked.

"Let's just say this," Louise said. "Those who live by the sword die by the sword."

"Louise," Sepia admonished. "He's dead. Come on."

Louise shrugged. "Elliott Jackson is a former gang member turned state congressman for Crawford."

"Where is Crawford?"

"Next door," Sepia said. "Crawford and Cromwell are like sister and brother. Tied together. Anything that happens in one town makes news in the other. We kind of bleed into each other."

"Good pun," Louise said.

"I didn't mean it," Sepia said, although she had to give herself kudos. She was awful. The man was dead and that was horrible. "I definitely wasn't a fan of Mr. Jackson, but this is bad."

"Elliott is more famous for his unique grammar," Louise said. "Every time he gets in front of the camera, you have to get your Ebonics dictionary out."

"And he was elected to Congress?" Margo asked.

"In Crawford, they'll elect anybody." Sepia regretted her words as Louise looked at her. Louise was from Crawford. "Sorry."

"Don't be sorry," Louise said. "I don't care. You see, Margo, I'm from Crawford and glad as hell to get out and never look back. It's a seedy town. What Sepia means when she said we bleed into each other, it's because all the people who live in Crawford service all the people who live in Cromwell."

"You knew this guy?" Margo asked.

"Hell no," Louise said. "I knew one of his baby's mamas. He has three baby's mamas and four babies. No wife."

"He ran with that posse," Sepia said, putting the paper down. "All of them former Ravens gang members themselves. Who knows what happened to him? They'll have so many suspects."

"Is that Marissa talking?" Margo asked with a sly smile.

Sepia smiled back as she rolled the paper up, intending to hold on to it. "She's a part of me."

Paul didn't want to hear it when he walked into the station for his next shift. The other officers knew and no one spoke to him. He was usually very popular in the Crawford Police Department, even after he was allowed a desk next to the detectives' division, something only reserved for the few. It wasn't his desk actually. It was shared by the top officers in the department, but this was his shift, so it was his desk.

No one else cared. They all believed he deserved it. He worked hard and when he was mad, he was mad, so they all knew when to back off, and today was that day. He had paperwork to file and a lot to explain.

When he reached his desk, Paul saw the white sheet of paper as bright as day, tacked to the back of his black chair. He ripped the paper off the chair, tearing it in half. *Lieutenant's Office—NOW!*

He looked around and David was nowhere to be found. Great.

Paul crumpled up the paper and tossed it in the garbage on his way to the toolshed. Lieutenant Dwayne Pitt was a hard ass, so Paul had no expectations that this would be anything but sheer hell.

What he hadn't expected was to see David sitting in one of the chairs facing Pitt, waiting for him.

"Sit down," Dwayne said in that raspy, trite voice he always had.

Paul took a seat next to David, who seemed hellbent on not making eye contact. "I'm sorry I'm late, I—"

"Shut up," Dwayne said. "I'm talking now. When I want you to talk, I'll tell you."

David shifted in his seat. Paul knew this stage. David was about to blow and that wasn't good.

"You missed the fireworks," Dwayne said. "I lit into your partner here. He took the heat all on his own. Said this was all his fault."

"We work together, sir," Paul said.

"Did I tell you to talk?"

Paul bit his lower lip. He didn't take orders well.

"We have a problem here, boys." He scratched at the cleanly shaven black beard. His eyes were intensely white and stood out against his black skin. "The mayor is on my ass now. Somehow he found out about last night."

"Screw the mayor!" David blurted out. "This is all political, man. It's all a bunch of bull."

He stood up and Paul reached for him to push him back down, but he moved out of his grasp.

"Sit down," Dwayne said. "You're already on desk duty. Don't make it worse."

"Desk duty?" Paul hadn't heard about this.

"Yeah," David said, turning to him. "They put me on the desk. Might as well cut off my—"

"Don't!" Dwayne said. "You're lucky to get this, considering everything else."

Paul looked from Dwayne to David, who shared a look that confused him. The tension was thick enough to cut with a knife and something was going on that he didn't know about. Paul hated that.

"You're dismissed, Officer Parks."

David waved his hand in the air and stormed out, slamming the door behind him. Paul didn't know what he could do for the guy if he was going to act this way. He wasn't going to give up on him though.

"Lieutenant," he said, "I'm sorry. You know he's going through some things."

"I know it all, Paul." Dwayne leaned back in his chair. "I know he's having problems with his wife."

"She's pregnant again, and . . ." Paul hated throwing David's business on the street, but he was trying to save his partner's career. "They're already strapped."

"Credit card debt and gambling."

Paul felt himself deflate. "Sir, I—"

"He's gambling on everything and he's got bookies. I know you know, Paul, so don't try to hide it."

"He's my partner, sir."

"He's going to pull you down with him, Paul."

"He's going through a bad patch."

"He's going through more than that."

Paul saw the look in Dwayne's eyes. "What did you talk about before I showed up?"

"You can't tell me you don't know."

"Sir, I—"

"Paul, you want that promotion to detective, don't you?"

Paul leaned forward. "More than anything, sir. I believe I've earned it."

"You have." He nodded. "But that doesn't mean you'll get it. Not if you're associated with a scandal."

"This problem with the Ravens. We'll figure this out. I've been talking to Luke, and—"

"You're not a detective yet, Paul. Don't bother with Luke and the investigation. You're a cop. You catch the bad guy when you see him."

"Yes, sir."

"The powers-that-be aren't inclined to promote anybody from this force because of the screwups we've had. It could hurt you."

Paul knew that. He thought about it every time he heard about another Raven gang member that got away or faked them out.

"But there is something you could do to help yourself."

Paul didn't like the look in Dwayne's eyes. Whatever it was, he wasn't going to like it. "I'm listening."

"I need you to fill in for Donna Pillant. She has

to take the day off tomorrow for a family emergency. Some crap with her kids."

"Fill in?" She was a cop just like him. What was he talking about?

"She had offered to do a drive-along with a—"

"No way." Paul stood up. "I hate those. I haven't done one of those in five years."

It was one of the tasks given to a rookie or someone who lost a bet.

"I know, but this is not just anybody. Do you know Sepia Davis?"

"Sepia who?"

"She's from Cromwell."

"Oh." That said a lot. Paul's ex-wife lived in Cromwell. She'd left him for a life in Cromwell. "She's one of those."

"Her father is best friends with the governor of Maryland And our chief of police. She's a big hotshot author. The sexy books, you know."

"No, I don't know, but what does she want to ride along for? She slummin'?"

"She's writing a book about a cop."

"Lieutenant, please."

"You need to do this. I can't have someone like Ms. Davis riding around with anyone."

"Oh, the delicate superior princess. Can't have any scrub touching her."

"I trust you. If she can't have Donna, then she'll have you."

"What about another female officer? She . . ." Paul suddenly remembered. Donna Pillant was the only female officer on the force. There was an issue there.

"Exactly," Dwayne said as if sensing Paul's realization. "You're the only one I trust."

"Lieutenant," Paul said, leaning over the desk,

"there aren't enough words in the world I can use to explain to you how much I don't want to do this."

"Think of three months from now, Paul. Think of what you'll look like if you did the governor and the chief of police a personal favor. I'll be sure to mention it."

Paul felt a little sick by this. Was he kissing up? Ten years of hard work and it came to this? He was a realist. No one got anywhere on hard work alone. How bad could it be?

"Fine," he said. "I'll take the princess on a roller-coaster ride."

"Keep her out of trouble, okay?"

"It's Crawford, sir."

"Keep her out of big trouble, then."

"I'll do my best."

"She'll be here at ten."

"I can't wait."

Paul turned to head out of the office, dread filling his stomach. She was just a spoiled rich elitist. Those people weren't made of any substance like the working man. Why Elaine had left him for that world, he couldn't figure . . . Who was he kidding? He knew exactly why she had left him. Money and prestige.

"Paul?" Dwayne called to him just as Paul reached the door.

Paul turned. "Yes?"

"Talk to your partner. At this point, you're the only one who can save him."

"I will."

Paul closed the door behind him, wondering what was going on. He hated not knowing things. Where was David?

"Who you looking for?"

Luke Drasutto was a grade-A detective with the Crawford Police Department and he was also Paul's mentor. In his late forties, Luke had a protruding belly from all the Italian meals he cooked. He had married a black woman, but instead of turning him on to soul food, he turned her on to Italian and together they expanded. He had dark black hair, with white at the temples. He was like the father that Paul never had. He was the man that had approached a brash, reckless rookie cop and turned him into one of the best policemen on the force.

"Hey, Luke. I'm looking for David."

"He just stormed out of here. Heard about last night."

"Hasn't everyone?"

"Sorry, man."

"We'll fix it. We'll catch some of these guys. How are your investigations going? Anything I can help with?"

Luke had been grooming Paul along by letting him in on some of the detective work. When he was off duty, Paul would hang out with Luke. He had nothing else to do, having no life of his own. The time had proved invaluable in his experience. Or so Paul had thought. Who knew anymore?

"I got pulled off everything to focus on this guy Elliott Jackson. We got people in an uproar over this."

"What for?"

"They think we're not paying attention because he was a former gang member."

"He just got shot last night. What do you have?"

"He was having some problems with one of his . . ."

"Babies' mamas," Paul said with a smile. "You can say it, Luke."

"I hate that phrase."

"Fine. If it feels better, one of the mothers of his children."

"Better." Luke sighed. "He had all the old rivalries with the people who got pissed at him for turning former members away from the gang to come work for him. Then you have the guys he rolls with."

"All with rap sheets a mile long." Paul thought about it. "Something is wrong here, though."

"What are you thinking?" Luke asked, interested.

"He was shot in the back of the head coming out of a crack house in downtown Crawford. It's too easy. It's too . . ."

"It's too something." Luke pat Paul on the arm. "I'm thinking on your level, man. I'll keep you updated."

Paul nodded thanks as Luke walked away. He was thinking about that murder, his promotion, David's problems, and now this debutante duty he was on. It all had him thinking about his ex-wife, Elaine. It had been five years since she left him to live life in the Cromwell world. He wasn't bitter anymore, but he wouldn't forget. He'd never forget. He hated everything Cromwell stood for.

Two

Sepia was in one of her moods as she stood in the lobby of the Crawford Police Department. She couldn't stop the nagging in the back of her head that told her there was so much missing in her life.

Last night, she had had dinner with Louise and Laurence. They had planned to meet at LaBrea's, a Mexican restaurant at the edge of Cromwell, for a nice dinner. It was anything but. Louise said she was sorry the second Sepia showed up at the restaurant, but before she could ask why, the answer greeted her with a smile.

Steven Glass, recently divorced father of two, was at least thirty-five, but looked much younger. He was incredibly handsome, but that was where his attributes ended. Sepia couldn't believe they were trying to set her up with this man. She knew, they all knew, that he was divorced because he cheated on his wife while she was pregnant.

Still, Sepia was the perfect lady all night. Well, almost all night. When Steven got caught up in his criticism of a young black woman and her children sitting at a nearby table, she couldn't hold it in any longer. Certain she was from Crawford, Steven quietly teased about her lack of a wedding ring, concluding that she was some hood rat whose babies had all different daddies, which led him to talk about Elliott Jackson, expressing something resembling happiness that he was gone.

Louise reeled her in, but the damage had been done. Sepia had lost her temper and ripped Steven a new one and had given Laurence a word or two for encouraging him. Everyone skipped dessert and that was that.

Now here she was, having waited for almost a half hour for her ride-along, letting her resentment brew. When did credentials become more important than character? Why would they think she would be interested in a man like that? What did they think she wanted? Certainly not Steven Glass.

Sepia tried to distract herself by taking in her surroundings. As officers passed by her in the lobby, they almost blurred together, but there was one standout. He was tall, dark, and incredibly handsome. As a writer, Sepia could have come up with something more original than that description, but it fit him perfectly. Despite the frown on his face, Sepia saw strength in the way he carried himself. He looked like a man who walked with a pride he had earned.

And he was walking right toward her.

It didn't make any sense, one woman being this fine. That was all Paul could say to himself when he saw Sepia standing in the lobby. It wasn't right. He remembered what Luke had told him once. There are beautiful women and there are women that send countries to war. She was dressed in a floral sundress in a pale shade of yellow that illuminated her skin. Everything perfectly in place, but still careless in some hidden way.

She stood like a woman who was used to being looked at. Like a woman who knew she was desired.

Paul had to remind himself what she really was. She was a princess who thought that a little ride in a car could make her understand what it meant to be a cop. What a joke.

"Ms. Davis?" he asked as he approached.

"Yes." Sepia held her hand out to him. Time seemed to stand still as she watched him reluctantly raise his hand to hers. The shake was quick and tepid. He didn't even want to touch her. "You are?"

"I'm Officer Paul Healy. I'm driving you around today."

"You're Donna's replacement?"

"I'm nobody's replacement," Paul said. "But I'm here."

What side of the bed did he fall off? "I wanted a wom—"

"A woman," he interrupted. "I know, but I can help you just as well."

"Are you sure?" she asked in response to his cold posture.

"What is that supposed to mean?"

Sepia waved her comments away. "I'm sorry, Officer, but it doesn't seem like you're very interested in this. When the lieutenant left a message on my voice mail yesterday, he said he had another officer who would be happy to have me ride along."

"That would be me," Paul said, not liking her tone at all.

"You don't seem happy at all."

"I'm the best you're going to get, Ms. Davis."

"Well, you're not good enough." Sepia placed a defiant hand on her hip. "I want to talk to the lieutenant."

"What is your problem, woman?" Paul didn't need her talking to Dwayne, but he wasn't going to let her talk to him like that. Not good enough? Hell no.

"Woman?" Oh, no, he did not just talk down to her. "Do you know me? Because you're talking to me like you know me, but I don't think you do."

Paul didn't need this crap. He'd gotten a call this morning from David's wife, Patsy, who told him through tears that David hadn't come home last night. There were Ravens running the streets terrorizing law-abiding citizens and here he was being talked down to by a society brat.

"I'm going on my drive, lady," Paul said, leaning toward her with authority. She smelled good. Fresh and sweet in a soft, underwhelming kind of way. "With or without you."

Sepia was speechless as he walked away. There was no way some beat cop was going to treat her like a child. She stormed to the front desk, not needing to get the attention of the desk sergeant, since he had been eavesdropping on them all along.

"I want to speak to Lieutenant Pitt," she said. "Now, please."

"He's out," he answered, seeming amused by her situation. "He's meeting with the mayor all day. "

"Well, then I want another—"

"Sorry, Ms. Davis."

"How do you know my name?"

"My wife reads your books," he said, stuffing half an onion bagel in his mouth. "You've made things a little hard on me. I can't compete with the men in those books."

Sepia had heard this before, and she wasn't moved. If a man wanted to hold on to his wife, he wasn't going to do it by blaming romance novelists for his inability to throw down in the bedroom.

"I want another—"

"I said sorry," he interrupted. "We have a serious problem on our hands. There isn't any officer free."

Sepia slammed her fist on the desk. It was very unladylike, but she didn't care. She wasn't going to let that cop with an attitude problem ruin this day for her.

Paul slammed on his brakes just in time. She walked right off the sidewalk into the street as his car exited the police garage. A few feet more and he would have hit her.

A smile slid across his mouth as she stood there, hands on hips. Her lips were pressed tight. He leaned back in his seat and folded his arms across his chest, staring her down. What did she think? He was going to jump out and run around to open the door for her?

Sepia told herself to calm down. This was no big deal. She was in a bad mood and probably misinterpreted him. Dwayne's message had said Donna was going to be replaced by his best officer.

"Can we call a truce?" she asked, sliding into the front seat and closing the door.

"Seat belt," Paul said, putting the car back in drive.

Sepia did as she was told just a tenth of a second before Paul drove off. "You have manners, don't you?"

"Yes, I do," he answered. "And we can call a truce if you're willing to follow some simple rules."

"Look, Officer, I—"

"Officer Healy. That's my name even though you never bothered to ask."

Sepia felt anger bite at her. "You didn't give me a chance to ask."

"Let's get back to the rules." Paul had a feeling she would have been fine never knowing his name.

"Wait a second!" He wasn't even letting her get a word in. "I—"

"Or we could pull over and I'll let you out next to your Mercedes." He stopped at the light, glancing over at her. She was pretty, he'd give her that. "Or is it a Lexus?"

"It's a Chrysler," Sepia retorted, "and I was just going to say that all I want to do today is observe. I'm not going to be like those ride-alongs that ask to get a piece of the action."

"Good," he answered. At least that was out of the way. "Because people like you don't know—"

"People like me?" He couldn't possibly have expected her to take that. "What exactly do you mean by people like me? Stuck-ups, snobs, elitists?"

Yes, but that wasn't what he would admit to. "I mean people who aren't familiar with the job of a cop. You tend to think it's not complicated. That we're just working-class stiffs with a gun that might stumble upon a crook every now and then."

"I don't think that," Sepia answered. "I'm sure what you do is important."

"That's not what I meant." Why was he so defensive with her? He knew. It was because she reminded him of his biggest failure: his marriage. "I just meant that this is dangerous, so just do what I tell you in case we come upon something."

Sepia couldn't help but get a little excited even

though she knew she would be smarter to be scared. "Like what?"

"Crawford is different than Cromwell, where you live."

"How did you know I live in Cromwell?"

Paul looked at her. She looked too smart to ask such a stupid question. This woman knew she had Cromwell written all over here.

She smiled, getting the picture. "Go on."

Paul couldn't help but smile, but only for a second. This was serious business. "We have a deadly gang problem here. Not like in the district, but it's getting there."

"I've been reading the papers."

Reading? Whatever. "Well, they're getting bold, even working in the daylight. Drug deals, prostitution, and murder."

"Is this what you do all day?" she asked. "Riding around the slums looking for scum?"

Enraged, Paul pulled the car against the sidewalk and slammed on the brakes. He looked at Sepia, whose eyes were so wide she looked like a cartoon. "Let's get one thing straight, Ms. Davis."

Sepia's hand gripped the handle on the door as she stared at him. He was angry and something in his eyes sent a chill down her spine. "What?"

"Don't refer to this town as slums, okay? There are some decent people here. Most of them are decent, hardworking, law-abiding, taxpaying citizens and they deserve more respect than to have their neighborhood called slums."

Sepia sighed, lowering her head a bit. He was right. "I don't know why I said it."

Paul bit his lip to shut himself up. He was ready to go on a tirade against her for putting down his town, but looking at her now, sitting across from him with her head down, she looked fragile and innocent. He had no desire to make her feel worse, even though she may have deserved it.

"It's okay," he said, returning to the streets. "Just ask me what you want to know."

Sepia looked at him, a little surprised at the tender tone in his voice. She watched his profile as he drove down the street, his eyes moving around. He was incredibly attractive, but this good guy, bad guy thing was confusing. Did he mean it?

"Okay," she said, taking her minirecorder out and placing it on her lap. "I just . . . I guess I . . . Look, I'm really sorry."

"I said okay." He turned to her, the sadness in her eyes reaching him enough to make him want to turn away. "Go on."

Sepia sighed. "Tell me what a cop's regular day is like."

"It's a hard one and it's thankless at times." Paul reflected on all his years on the force. All of his close calls. "You're a cop, a mediator, and a community leader. One second they see you as the only voice of reason and other times you represent oppression."

"Oppression? I know white cops have that perception problem, but black cops too?"

"It's the blue they see," Paul answered.

"How do you deal with it?"

"The best way we can. We try to get involved with the community a lot. Some days we spend just hanging out. People like you might . . ." He looked at her, catching the quick rise of her eyebrows. "I mean laypeople. You might think we're just hanging out, but part of our job is to be seen in the community in a relaxed, nonthreatening manner.

If the only time they see you is when you're hauling in one of the boys from their block, you become the devil."

"But you can't be friendly all the time," Sepia
said. "Especially you. You've got a hard edge to you."

"I do?" he asked.

"Please. You've got a don't-mess-with-me look all
about you and you know it."

"Didn't stop you." Paul smiled as she laughed.
Was he flirting with her? What was wrong with
him?

"I'm serious," she said, reaching across to briefly
touch his arm. It was a normal gesture she made
with anyone, but when she felt the taut muscle underneath his shirt, she quickly pulled away. "If
you're too nice, they think you're a pushover, right?"

Paul ignored that quick jolt from her touch. She
had very feminine ways about her that any man
would respond to. "It's a fence that we straddle
constantly and we have to know when it's the right
time to be what."

"What determines that?"

"The situation. I mean sometimes you go up
against people that are so scared they put everyone in danger. Or else you go against people who
are so void of a conscience that no conversation
will get them to reason."

Sepia was caught up, forgetting the questions
she had planned to ask. She just let him talk and
he seemed to enjoy it. As he told her of the danger
cops faced on a daily basis and the many hats they
were required to wear without a moment's warning or preparation, she came to understand something totally different than what she'd learned from
all of her research up until this point.

One thing she knew was that cops were underpaid and underappreciated. They got all of the blame and none of the glory. The television shows focused on the detectives, crime scene investigators, and prosecutors. The cops were the grunt workers, but they put their lives on the line every day for law and justice and paid the price. Not just from the danger on the street, but they paid with psychological problems and marital problems stemming from the stress of their jobs.

Sepia wasn't a psychiatrist, but she prided herself on being perceptive, and when Paul began talking about the psychological and marital problems cops had, his entire posture and tone changed to a very personal one.

"Who are you talking about?" Sepia asked as they stopped at a streetlight.

Paul turned to her, taken off guard by her question. "What do you mean?"

"I'm sorry." Sepia regretted asking the question. She had gotten so entranced by his words she forgot they didn't even know each other. "I was a psychology major in college. I can't help myself sometimes. It just seemed like you were getting very specific toward the end there."

"I didn't mean to." Paul was feeling a little uncomfortable now, which was an unusual position for him to be in.

"Have you had marital problems?" she asked, knowing it was none of her business.

"I'm not married," Paul said, driving on. "Not anymore."

Interesting, Sepia thought. "I was asking because you—"

"I know a lot of officers that have marital problems that are directly related to what they do, but I'm not going to be more specific than that."

Paul was thinking of David and wondering what he could do to help his partner. Deep down inside, he knew that was what he should be doing right now, and maybe he was taking that out on Sepia.

"Why are you divorced?" Sepia asked.

Paul looked at her with a confused frown and Sepia realized he must have thought her crazy to be so bold. "It's none of my business. Sorry."

"You're right, it isn't any of your business." Who did this woman think she was? "What other questions do you have?"

"I just asked because I'm trying to get into the personal life of a cop and how it affects them on the job and vice versa. Women are—"

"I'm not a woman," Paul said.

"I know that." She certainly knew that. "But . . . Well, men compartmentalize more than women do. We can't block things away from each other. Every aspect of our lives merges into each other. So, it would be more likely that—"

"I know what you're getting at," Paul said, "but it's better if you ask Donna about that."

"I was going to." Sepia turned the tape over in her recorder after it turned off. "I'll have to make another appointment with her."

"I'm not going to talk to you about my marriage, Ms. Davis, so please move on."

"Sepia," she said.

Paul felt himself soften a bit. He hadn't realized how tense he was. "Sepia, please move on."

"You aren't going to ask me what that means?"

Paul looked at her. "I know what Sepia means. Brown. A print or photograph of a brown color. Some of us cops read a thing or two."

That stung. This guy was too touchy, Sepia thought. He made her feel self-conscious about everything that came out of her mouth. She sat in silence for a while as he drove, looking out the window and seeing far too many working-age men not working, but hanging out. When jobs were hard to come by, cops had an even harder job.

"Officer Healy?"

Finally. Paul was wondering when she was going to talk again. He could feel her festering over there and he refused to feel sorry for her. "Yeah?"

"Do you even care why I'm here?"

Paul sighed. She was an emotional one, wasn't she? "You're writing a book."

"Have you ever read one of my books?" Sepia had a sudden urge to make him believe she was worth something. Make him believe she'd done some real work in her life.

"Are you kidding me?"

She smiled. "No, I'm not. I have a lot of male readers."

"They may be male, but are they men?"

"What does that mean?"

Paul laughed. "I'm sorry. That was crass. I just can't believe a red-blooded American man would read that stuff."

"Excuse me?"

"I'm sure it's good stuff, but not for men."

"It's great stuff," Sepia said with a trite tone. "And it's for anyone who believes in real love."

He looked at her again with a smile he hadn't meant to give. Real love hadn't worked out too well for him. "Do you?"

"Who's getting personal now?" she asked. Sepia couldn't have written a better smile than this man was giving her right now.

"Touché."

"The point I was trying to make, Officer Healy, was—"

"Paul." He returned his attention to the road. It was much safer, for more reasons than one.

"Paul, my point is, although I am very proud of all the books I've written, this book isn't going to be like any one of them. I want to get deep into this cop's psyche and define her as a professional. I want to know what it really means to be a cop."

"I'll tell you one thing," Paul said as he rolled into the parking lot of Sweet Dreams, his favorite greasy spoon. "You really want to know what it means to be a cop?"

With recorder in hand, Sepia eagerly leaned forward. "Yes?"

Her face only a foot from his, Paul realized how easy it would be to want to be around this woman despite her elitist faults.

"Cops really, really . . ." He smiled wider as she moved closer. "Drink a lot of coffee."

As he slid out of the car, Sepia gritted her teeth together. And here she was bending over backward to be nice to him.

She opened her car door and rushed out after him. He was already halfway across the parking lot when she grabbed him by the arm in an attempt to swing him around. Only she hadn't anticipated that on her best day she couldn't make his strong, much larger body do anything it didn't want to.

"Hey!" Paul swung around, glaring at her. "You can get into a lot of trouble for that. I am an officer of the law."

"A jerk is all you are." She pointed her finger in his face. "I don't deserve to be played with like that."

"That's a matter of opinion," he said with a grin.

"What do you think you're doing?" she asked. "I was guaranteed three hours of drive-along this morning."

"I'm taking a break. I don't think I can do you for three hours straight."

Sepia gasped at his choice of words. "I beg your pardon?"

"You know what I mean." He grinned at her discomfort. A woman like Sepia wasn't used to being talked to like this.

"I'll smack that grin off your face," she warned.

"Did they teach you to talk like that in finishing school?" Paul asked, liking this fire. She was a little scary when she got mad. More like crazy. "It's not very ladylike."

"For your information, not taking any crap from anyone *is* very ladylike and I'm not taking it from you."

Paul raised his arms innocently in the air. "I'm just trying to get a cup of coffee."

"Do you expect me to sit in that car and wait for you to have your drink and donut?"

"You can come in if you want."

"I will not." She looked at the place. The sign SWEET DREAMS only had every other letter actually there, was half hanging down, and the windows were filthy. "That place is a dump."

"Doesn't meet your country club standards?"

"I don't think it meets basic health or safety code standards."

"Suit yourself." Paul turned and headed for the shop. He needed a tall black one after a morning with her.

"I hope it falls down on your head!" Sepia yelled after him.

She wasn't going in no matter what. She would not follow him around like a puppy.

Sepia looked around her. The neighborhood was entirely too dangerous and there were all types lurking around looking at her. Sepia looked back at the dilapidated diner. No. There was no way she would give him the satisfaction. If he thought she would be the scared little princess, he was in for a surprise of his own.

Paul had kept a close eye on the lovely Ms. Davis from his seat at the counter in Sweet Dreams. He was amused by her stubbornness. She wouldn't even sit in the car where she might be safe. She stood outside, leaning against the front hood giving indignant stares to every man who passed her by and thought a second about hitting on her. None of them tried. She had that look about her that said, *Don't waste your time.* She was a head above and beyond anything these men were used to. In reality, Paul believed that these men were more scared of her than she was of them. After all, what was a woman that looked like that doing here? She had to be up to something and they didn't want any part of that.

Only ten minutes had gone by before Paul decided to cut his morning visit short. He realized that he enjoyed watching her entirely too much. She made him remember things about his marriage that he'd rather forget even though he knew he never could. Elaine had wanted so badly to be a part of that Cromwell world. She did so much to make Paul want it too and his refusal to do so tore them apart. When she'd left him, Paul allowed an anger inside him to build to a crescendo. Everything that represented Cromwell reminded him of his failure of a marriage.

"Enjoy your fresh air?" he asked as he approached the car. Her arms were folded across her chest as her eyes were almost slits at him.

"Yes," she answered, her sweet tone belying her anger. "I certainly did. How about you, Officer? Enjoy your little break?"

"I did." He stood only inches from her, knowing he should call a truce, but something in him told him that he needed to stay on guard with her.

"You think you're funny, don't you?" she asked, uncomfortable with his closeness.

"I invited you in, Sepia."

"I invited you in, Sepia," she mocked. "You've had a chip on your shoulder from the second you saw me and you've been taking it out on me ever since."

"You ready to go?" He started around the car.

"You're not getting away with it," Sepia said. "I'm going to tell the lieutenant all about your games."

"I'm sure he'll be very upset to hear Princess Davis was left alone for five minutes."

Sepia heard the groan in her throat. "You are a complete—"

The bang echoed against the walls of the building around them.

They both ducked and Sepia's heart caught in her throat as she looked at Paul.

"Get down," he said, grabbing his gun. His adrenaline was running.

"Was that a—"

"Get down and stay down!" Paul opened his car door, jumping inside. He reached out for Sepia and practically dragged her in behind him as he slid into the driver's seat.

Sepia crouched in the car, half of her in the space under the dashboard. "What's happening?"

Paul grabbed his radio. "This is Officer Healy at 782 Augusta. Shots fired in surrounding buildings. I need backup."

Sepia winced at the reality of it. For a second, only a second, she'd thought she heard tires backfiring, but she knew it was a gun and this was all too real when a man on the other end of the radio told Paul to wait for backup.

He looked at her. "Stay there. I'll be back."

"But, wait!" she yelled as he shut the car door. "They said to wait."

It seemed as if forever had gone by, although Sepia knew it was only a few minutes. The tightening in her stomach threatened to suffocate her. She heard nothing happening around her and hadn't heard anything since that one shot. Slowly, she lifted her head to where she could barely see out the window. Looking around, she saw that the street was completely empty. Everyone had scattered.

She sat up, listening to the man come back on the radio calling for Paul.

"Are you there? Officer Healy!"

Sepia reached for the radio and yelled into it. "He went in alone."

"Officer Healy, are you there?"

They couldn't hear her. She looked at the platform, seeing all types of buttons. She didn't know what to do. She was ready to duck back under the dashboard when she suddenly saw movement out of the corner of her eye. Paul!

Sepia looked up, focusing on the figure that ran out of the building next to Sweet Dreams. It wasn't Paul. It was someone else. He was white with wild curly hair, wearing a black T-shirt and sweatpants. He was normal sized, except for a protruding belly.

Sepia gasped as he sped toward her. He was

coming for her! The radio slipped from her hand as she felt the blood rush from her head. Where was Paul? She felt frozen in place as she watched him stop. She was holding her breath as he looked around before he ran into the street, around a small blue car, and jumped into it. She sighed in relief before she realized this wasn't good at all.

He was getting away!

Not thinking at all, Sepia hopped out of the police car. It wasn't safe, but she had to get a license plate and she couldn't see from where she was sitting. She heard the police sirens as she ran into the middle of the street, and felt her breath escape as she noticed the car had no license plate as it drove off.

"What are you doing?"

Sepia turned to see Paul rushing toward her. He grabbed both her arms, when he approached. "Are you all right?"

"Yes." Sepia felt a rush of blood come back. "He . . . he got away," she said, pointing down the street.

"You saw him?" Paul looked down the street. He didn't see anything. He'd heard footsteps when he was in the building, but there was a dying woman calling to him and he had to make a choice.

"Yes." Sepia spoke in breaths like a nervous child. "He was white with—"

"White?" Paul knew that ruled out the Ravens. They were an all-black gang, and unless they were starting a gang affirmative action group, this guy was from something different.

"Hold on."

Paul let her go and headed for the two squad cars approaching. Sepia watched as he instructed them on what had happened and what to do. One officer got on his radio while the other rushed into the building.

"What happened?" she asked when Paul returned to her.

"I told you to stay down. Why did you get out of the car?" He grabbed her by the arm, guiding her back to his squad car.

"I wanted to help you." Sepia jerked her arm away. "I can walk on my own."

"I thought we talked about you trying to get a piece of the action. Don't you remember?"

Sepia stopped. "I was trying to get his license plate."

"Did you get it?"

"Now you're interested in my opinion?" Sepia didn't know which way to turn with this guy.

"Stop asking questions, okay? A murder was committed here!"

Sepia's hand went to her stomach, feeling as if someone had just kicked her there. "Oh, no! I can't believe it."

"Well, believe it. She's dead and he got away." The image of the victim breathing her last breath as he knelt down next to her hit him hard. This job never got easier and there were some things he would never get used to.

"It was a woman?" Sepia leaned against the car. She was touched by the look of anguish in his eyes as he looked past her for a moment. She had never seen someone who had been murdered and he'd probably seen a hundred, but it still ripped at him.

"It wasn't just a woman," Paul said. "It was Dishwana Grimes. You know her, don't you?"

Sepia felt like she was going to be sick. "Yes. Everyone does."

Sepia closed the last mug shot book. She was so tired and angry that she couldn't help more. She'd been there for a few hours, first giving a statement of everything she had witnessed to a detective named Luke Drasutto. A sketch artist spoke to her for a few minutes, but she wasn't able to help much. It was weird to her, but the only thing that gave her any comfort through it all was that Paul kept checking in on her asking if she was okay. The man who seemed to earlier have nothing but disdain for her was being caring and comforting.

A murder puts things in perspective and checks attitudes.

"I'm sorry," Sepia said as Luke passed the last mug shot book to an officer who took it and walked away. He was sitting across from her at his desk, with Paul leaning against the wall behind him. "I didn't see his face very well. I just remember the hair because it was so wild."

"But you're sure he was Caucasian?" Luke asked. "Could he have been Hispanic?"

She shrugged. "He was a very pale white."

Luke looked back at Paul and Paul's eyes lowered. Paul knew they were both thinking the same thing and it wasn't good.

"What?" Sepia asked.

"Nothing." Luke slid his card across the table. "I'm going to be the lead investigator on this case. If you think of anything else, you can call me or Paul here."

She looked at Paul and his smile made her smile. "I wish I could help more."

"You're helping fine, Sepia." Paul could see she was still shaken. He hoped she would remember more when things calmed down.

"I just can't believe . . ." Sepia's words trailed off as her mind wandered.

The last time she had seen Dishwana Grimes was at a black writers' conference in Baltimore. It included a book signing with some of the top African-American authors in the country. The table that Sepia was set to sign books at was placed only two tables from Dishwana's.

The Black Woman's Guide to Getting Hers. All Sepia could think of was how distasteful she and many of the other authors found her and her topic. Her guide to gold digging was based on a woman using men, doing everything possible to get as much money, jewels, and property as she could before moving on to the next man. Men were dogs in her opinion, only interested in sex. Women, in her opinion as well, were only interested in money, and those that didn't agree were lying to themselves. Why should men get what they want and women get left with the short end of the stick?

What had frightened Sepia and so many of the other authors was that Dishwana's book-signing line was just as long as hers and longer than some others. She was a local celebrity, gaining national recognition. She was about to set off on a tour of seminars on how to put her book into action.

Now she was dead and Sepia regretted all of the nasty things she had said about her.

"Let me take you home," Paul said as he approached her. He held his hand out to her.

Even though she was perfectly capable of standing up on her own, Sepia took his hand and his help. "No, really, I'm fine. I can drive myself. My car is in the lot."

"It can stay there."

Sepia looked at him, his dark eyes seeming to

hold a tenderness she wouldn't have thought he was capable of only hours ago. "I'm sorry, Officer . . . Paul."

"For what?"

"For being so difficult this morning. I know this is not a joke, but I pouted and made myself a burden to you. "

"Stop." He touched her arm, overwhelmed by the softness of her skin. "I was the one who was difficult. Guess you got more than you bargained for?"

She smiled as he laughed a bit. He was really very tender. Or maybe she was just tired. "I guess so. I really should get going."

"Are you sure I can't take you?" Paul ignored the little nagging voice behind him that said he wanted to spend just a few more minutes with her. He had too much work to do.

"I'm sure." Besides, Sepia felt a warm rush up her arm from his hand and it made her uncomfortably aware of him. It made her forget for a second that she wanted to get rid of this day. "Thank you, Paul."

"Good night, Sepia."

Paul watched her leave. She had a dignity about her that was not off-putting, but attractive and compelling. You knew she was about something and it was likely something you'd want to be about too.

"Aren't you the gentleman?" Luke asked with a teasing smile.

Paul fell into the chair on the other side of the desk with a boyish smile. "She's an attractive woman."

"Interested?"

"Are you kidding me? She's from Cromwell."

Luke sighed. "They don't have a disease, man. Just because your wife was obsessed with that society stuff doesn't mean they're all bad."

"Have you ever met anyone from Cromwell that you liked?" Paul asked.

Luke had been there when Elaine divorced him. He knew the whole story.

Luke's brows centered. "I can't think of one right now, but I'm sure there are some good people there."

"You can't be good if you think you're better than anyone else."

"I give up." Luke looked intently at Paul. "I need to pick that genius brain of yours."

"I'm thinking what you're thinking, Luke." Paul had been thinking it the second he saw the woman. "Elliott Jackson."

"They knew each other. Ran in some of the same circles."

Paul nodded. "He was shot coming out of a crack house. She was shot inside a massage parlor, which we all know means a whorehouse."

"Both black." Luke was writing as he spoke. "Both well known, and now we know her killer was white."

"You think it's a race thing?" Paul didn't even want to consider that. It would change the pitch of everything.

Luke shook his head. "Too early. We don't have any witnesses to Jackson's murder and he has a ton of people with motive."

"Dishwana wasn't well respected," Paul said, "but I don't know of anyone who hated her enough to want to kill her."

"You're thinking of her professional image. It could be more personal than that. It usually is."

Paul leaned back in the chair, wondering what was going on. Something inside him told him there was a connection and it was nagging him to death.

Three

The Cromwell Golf and Yacht Club was absolutely perfect. The decoration was superbly unique and traditional at the same time. It held all the greenery and polish of a traditional country club, giving one the feel of being at a resort although one was only minutes from home. However, Laurence hadn't stopped there. He worked hard, getting the best architects on the East Coast to make the place modern and sleek without looking cold.

The result was a luxurious retreat that was smart and conservatively imaginative. With two banquet halls, a trendy restaurant, teen dance hall, day care, three racquetball courts, a two-thousand-square-foot lobby, sitting area, bar, and state-of-the-art business center, the inside of the club was only enhanced by the incredible adult pool, children's pool, two large saunas, and world-class eighteen-hole golf course that reached to the edges of the Potomac where Cromwell's finest would keep their yachts and boats.

As Sepia congratulated the perfectly dressed club greeters, who were mostly the children of the members who spent the summer greeting and score-keeping on the greens, she entered the paradise with such conflicted emotions she didn't even recognize herself. There was so much pride in what they had done, and she had been a part of it from the beginning in every way she could. Fund-raising, financing, planning, decorating, everything. So many of her old friends that she saw here tonight had put blood, sweat, and tears into the club and it turned out to be more than they even expected. And the expectations of this crowd were higher than most. The club was already getting calls from every design, society, and golf magazine to do feature articles and put its picture on their covers.

She could see some of the photographers there for the opening gala, their cameras lighting up the best of the East Coast. Sepia could see the fine families of Cromwell that she had known and loved all of her life. She also saw families that joined from other parts of Maryland, some from D.C. and even Virginia, who would gladly travel Interstate 495 to come to the club. There were also some New York and Philadelphia families there. Politicians, lawyers, corporate executives, business owners, leading government officials, professors, doctors, judges, university presidents, philanthropists that were really changing the lives of others crowded the lobby.

Then why did she feel so empty? Why did she feel almost a sense of anger toward these people? There was no reason or right for it, but Sepia had the feeling nonetheless. It was welling in her stomach and it was real. It had been since being at the center of the awful murder two days ago.

She had been able to think of nothing else. Not the book she was writing or tonight's momentous event. She had thought only of Dishwana Grimes, that man she saw running from the building, and Paul. She'd tried so hard to busy herself with whatever duties Laurence would give her and listening to Louise go on and on about what she would wear and who she wanted to impress, but nothing helped.

The last two nights, she had woken in the middle of the night in a sweat with visions of that man. In her dreams, or nightmares as they were, he didn't turn and run to his car. He came toward her, his face blurred but his entire being exuding anger. He pointed a gun at her and she screamed, certain her life was about to end, before waking up.

She read the newspapers filled with stories of Dishwana Grimes's past as a mistress to two very wealthy men, a groupie who slept with athletes, and finally a gold digger teaching her skills to women everywhere. It was as if the world was ignoring that she, despite her faults, had been a human being who was now dead.

Then again, Sepia had to remember with shame how she had ignored Dishwana's humanity that day in Baltimore when the other authors gathered in the author reception room saying the most awful things about her. She hadn't contributed to the insults, but she did nothing to stop the others from talking about their sister. She was their sister, no matter how misguided she was, and she deserved more respect than anyone had shown her. Maybe if she had been shown some respect, she would have been a different person.

Then there was Officer Paul Healy. She kept seeing his angry face as he berated her for her snotty remarks and remembering his compassion when she was in the precinct after the shooting. She surprised even herself at the sense of joy she'd felt

when he called her yesterday to ask if she had remembered anything else. She hated having to say
she didn't but was grateful he called.

He was frustrated, she could tell that much even
over the phone when he asked her what she might
remember, but then the tone of his voice turned
tender when he'd asked her if she was all right. If
Sepia didn't know better, she would have thought
he cared, but how could he? He didn't even know
her, and the few minutes they had spent together
were better forgotten, even though she wasn't ever
going to forget anything about that day.

"Sepia, darling!"

Judge Sierra Reid came toward her with arms
open wide and grabbed her in a tight hug.

"Judge Reid." Sepia tried to catch her breath and
smile at the same time. The woman was at least 250
pounds and could kill you with a hug. "It's so nice
you could come. Where is Dr. Reid?"

"He's here somewhere," she said as if it didn't
matter if he was there at all.

She stepped back looking at Sepia, who was
dressed in a peach Versace gown that was simple
and understated everywhere except the tastefully
flirtatious low neckline. "You look devastating as
usual, Sepia. No date?"

Sepia kept her smile even though the judge's
words bit at her. She had been one of the first to
pull Sepia aside to tell her this "Jason boy" she was
dating was not from any family she knew and she
shouldn't waste her time.

"Not tonight, Judge." Sepia touched her arm
gently. "You enjoy yourself, okay?"

Sepia quickly made her way to the bar, saying
hasty hellos to those who made an attempt to stop
her. She was feeling uncomfortable in her own skin.

If someone asked her about Jason tonight she was going to scream. She pretended to study the selection of wines presented on the bar table, but she could hear the whispering around her.

"She broke off the engagement with him."

"It's about time."

"She came to her senses. He wasn't at all worthy of her."

"He was a lawyer, wasn't he?"

"Of course, but he comes from nothing. He went to a state school, for Pete's sake. Got his law degree from nowhere."

"I'm sure Dr. and Mrs. Davis are happy with this turn of events."

"Oh, I heard they were disappointed in her. She is thirty after all. Distractingly beautiful, but not getting any younger."

"The Chianti please," Sepia said to the bartender, her hands gripping the edges of the bar. She squeezed tighter. Anything to keep her from turning around and telling off whoever that was.

"Where are her parents anyway? I thought they would be here of all places."

"Can you believe it? One of the finest families in Maryland and they choose to go to Antigua instead of this."

"Unbelievable."

"Believe it," Sepia said under her breath.

She wanted desperately for her parents to be here. Especially after what had happened to her a few days ago. Things had been so strained between them since she'd started dating Jason. At first they were against it for the same reasons most of the people in this room were. He was a social climber, but Sepia had been so insistent that he really loved her. Only he hadn't loved her at all. He wanted to use her to climb the social ladder and she ignored it until the last minute. By the time she'd figured it out, it was her parents who told her that it was too late to change her mind. It would embarrass the family too much. When she refused to go ahead with the wedding, their response was to tell her they were on their way to London for a week. After being back a few days, they decided to go to Antigua and told a thoroughly disappointed Laurence they would have to decline the opening gala invitation, but would make it up with their own special bash, a delayed retirement party for the doctor, in October. Laurence accepted their apology and reserved the grand hall. Sepia's mother had written her a letter saying she regretted what happened between her and Jason and hoped she would learn something from the experience.

Sepia took a hard sip of the Chianti. She had to stop thinking about Jason. She had already spent too much of her life on him anyway. Sepia loved her parents and she couldn't go on blaming them or Jason for her own bad choices. She was done with it and men for the time being. All she cared about now was the new book she was writing. She didn't have room in her life for anything else.

Sepia suddenly needed some air. She made her way to the verandah off the lobby, listening to the gossipers go on about Dishwana Grimes as she passed.

"Did you hear about that?"

"They found her in a whorehouse, didn't they?"

"Figures."

"I say good riddance."

"Dishwana. The name alone. I mean, really."

"Sepia's here." Stevie Modette waved her over to her table as soon as she got outside.

She was sitting with Kimberly Smith and her husband, James. Sepia took another sip of her Chianti and headed past the live band to join them.

"How are you all doing tonight? Having a good time, I hope?"

"It's amazing," Kimberly said. "Worth all the time and money. Laurence is amazing."

"He definitely did it up this time," James said.

Laurence had told Sepia yesterday that James just opened his own practice and Kimberly rented the small ballroom for a congratulations party in a few weeks.

"Where is Laurence anyway?" Sepia asked, looking around.

She had gone to school with Stevie her whole life and never liked her. She was one of those holdovers from the old days that still talked about skin tone and hair. She joked it off, always saying she was kidding, but Sepia didn't think she was.

"He's around," Stevie answered. "Louise is of course following him around like a puppy."

"She's not a puppy," Sepia retorted. "And she's not following him. They're together. Everyone knows that."

Stevie looked at her, swallowed hard, then smiled. "I'm just kidding. You know I love Louise. You've helped her along so much."

"What does that mean?" James asked. "She's not a child."

Sepia looked at James and he winked at her. James was cool.

"Louise is an incredible woman," she said. "If anything, I've learned from her."

Stevie cleared her throat and said sweetly, "How nice."

Kimberly leaned forward, looking lovely in a

white Dolce and Gabanna strapless dress. "We were just talking about some of the scallywags here."

"You know," Stevie said, "some of those people who think their money can get them in."

"Well, it did," James said. "They're here, aren't they? If they can afford the fee, they should be able to join."

Kimberly shook her head. "If your parents heard you say that, James."

"I agree with him," Sepia said.

"I don't," Stevie said. "If you let money be the only determining factor, then you'll have athletes and entertainers joining."

"That would be horrible," Kimberly said, shivering. "I couldn't imagine it. Rappers in Cromwell?"

"It would liven things up a bit," James said. "I could stand for a little bass in the drums. This place is great, but we could use a little 50 Cent up in here."

"I think I'm going to be sick," Stevie said.

Sepia smiled. She had had enough. "I see Louise. I'll see you guys later."

"Be sure to come back," Kimberly said.

Sepia nodded although she had no intention of going anywhere near Kimberly and Stevie again tonight. Or forever for that matter. She wasn't too interested in being there at all tonight anymore. Tonight had been what she'd been looking forward to for the longest time, but after the other day it just seemed burdensome. The only thing that kept her there was that Laurence would kill her if she left and she owed him more than that. She would just have to steer clear of . . . well, most everyone.

No wonder Paul had assumed so much of her. If this was her crowd, what else could he have expected?

* * *

"What are you still doing here?"

Paul looked up from his desk to see Luke standing over him looking as tired and unkempt as he felt.

"Hey, Luke." He closed the Grimes file. "I'm just looking at some of your stuff."

"I thought you had my files."

"Sorry," he said. "You've been looking for them? I thought you were gone."

"It's okay." Luke grabbed a chair from another desk and sat down. "I was going to show them to you tomorrow anyway. What are you thinking?"

"They're definitely connected."

"We still have to rule out Jackson's ex, who has no alibi."

"Being at home with her baby is an alibi of sorts."

"No one saw her at all that day."

"I don't think she did it." Paul held up his hand to Luke's protest. "I know. She was suing him for child support, but according to the court records and her, he was going to pay."

"Okay." Luke grabbed the Jackson file, looking through it. "And we have a blue Volkswagen spotted in the neighborhood of the crack house, but that could be a coincidence. I get the feeling that if someone saw a white guy in that neighborhood, maybe they would have remembered it. They would have told on a white guy."

"Well, no one saw him at the Grimes killing except Sepia. She just happened to look up from where she had gone for cover."

Paul thought of Sepia again. He had been thinking about her too much lately. As he tried hard to concentrate on his work, she kept seeping into his thoughts. She had a face that demanded your memory.

"Did you speak to her?" Luke asked.

"Yesterday." Paul shook his head. "Nothing. I think we got all we're going to get out of her."

"Don't say that." Luke smiled. "Then you won't have an excuse to see her again."

"Enough." Paul had to be honest with himself. He would like to see her again even though there was no reason to. He could still smell her perfume. "She's from Cromwell."

"Don't get started on your ex-wife again."

"Just because I had a bad divorce doesn't mean I'm afraid to find the right woman." Far from it. Paul was eager to get married again and start a family. He was a traditional guy at heart. "But I'm not going to go after someone who is my complete opposite. You know who this girl is, don't you?"

"She's a woman," Luke said, reaching for his beeper as it went off. "And you're a man. If you let anything else matter, you're stupid. Do you think I would be with my wife if I had let anything else matter?"

Paul couldn't begin to explain to Luke how more times than not, class was a harder bridge to travel than race. He waited as Luke read the text message on his beeper, his face tightening. Paul knew what that expression meant.

"Another murder?" he asked.

Luke nodded. "Let's go."

Sepia rushed to Louise the second she saw her, so grateful to be near someone she could trust. It was suddenly hitting her that she had known so many of these people for twice as long as she'd known Louise, but she didn't really trust them or want to be near them as much. Louise was leaning against a table that held some beautiful ice sculptures, waiting patiently as Laurence stood a few feet away giving instructions to the catering manager.

"Finally I found you." She sidled up to Louise, who looked agitated. "What's wrong?"

"I was looking for you." Louise leaned over and kissed her on the cheek. She looked almost regal in her very fitting lavender Vera Wang. She had a great figure even though she didn't think so.

"I was doing the same."

"Are you sure you're up to this?" Louise asked. She had been more concerned than Sepia when she'd told her about what happened on the ride-along.

"I'm fine, honey, please." Sepia placed her empty glass on the waiter's plate as he passed.

"Nightmares are not fine."

"They'll go away," Sepia said. "I just wish I could do more to help."

"I can't believe you saw him. You must have been terrified." Louise looked with passion at a passing plate of caviar and crackers. She had been dieting to fit into this dress and was depriving herself that night so she wouldn't bust out of it. "This food is killing me."

"Interesting choice of words."

Louise looked at her seriously. "Really, Sepia. He could have shot you if he'd seen you looking at him."

Sepia felt a shiver go down her spine.

"That cop shouldn't have left you there."

"Don't blame him," Sepia said. "He's a good cop and he did what he could. He told me to stay down. I'm the one that put myself in danger by looking up."

Louise studied her curiously.

"What?" Sepia asked.

"You were saying how much of a jerk this guy was to you and now you're defending him?"

"I'm not . . ." Sepia wasn't sure what she should say. "I told you that he was also kind to me at the precinct and on the phone yesterday."

"He called you?" Louise's eyes widened as Laurence joined the two of them.

"Who called who?" he asked.

Sepia could see the excitement in his eyes. He was on the top of the world tonight. The wonderful evening would all be attributed to him, and this was the stuff Laurence lived for. Finally, he had to feel like he was more than the famous judge's son.

All the scandal that emerged as a result of the judge's death was behind him. His mother dying of a heart attack when it came to the surface that the judge had another family on the side could be put in the past. The sight of some woman from Crawford coming forward wanting some of his money for her little girl whom she claimed, and later the lab test revealed, was the judge's daughter would take a little more time to get rid of. It had been a hard year for him.

"It's a wonderful evening." Sepia leaned forward, giving him a peck on his cheek. "You should be so proud."

"I am," he said, beaming. "But hey, you can take some credit too. You volunteered for just about everything. I couldn't have—"

Louise hushed him with her hands. "I want to hear about this phone call from the cop. He's calling you now?"

"I told you they were going to follow up with me to see if I remembered anything."

"I'm so sorry to hear about that whole thing," Laurence said. "Louise told me what you went through. I'm glad your name didn't get in the papers."

"That was for my protection," Sepia said, "but I'm pretty certain he didn't see me."

"So why was this cop following up?" Louise asked.

"His name is Paul, and he called to see if I remembered anything."

"Did you?" Laurence asked.

Sepia shook her head. "I don't want to talk about it."

"I don't blame you," Laurence said. "There's no reward in getting that real."

Sepia wasn't so sure what he meant by that and she let it go. Laurence always said silly things like that.

"All you need to think about is your upcoming book signing." Laurence looked around. "We're going to set you up in the lobby and set up enough chairs for all of these people because I know they'll be back."

Sepia was flattered, but more realistic than Laurence. "I sincerely doubt these people from New York and Philadelphia will come back all this way to get a signed romance novel."

"Don't put yourself down," Louise said. "I'd come from New York, but of course I love you."

"And so do they," Laurence said. "You're a Davis after all."

Sepia blinked. Why was she noticing little comments like that? She'd never noticed them before. What was changing?

"If you'll both excuse me, I see the mayor." Laurence kissed Louise on the cheek. "I'll be right back, honey."

Louise cursed under her breath as Laurence walked away.

"What's wrong?" Sepia was ready and willing to deal with anyone's drama but her own.

"Why didn't he want to take me to meet the mayor?"

"I don't know." Sepia shrugged, although there was a part of her that thought she did know.

"If I was a Davis he would want to introduce me."

"What did I do?" Sepia asked, laughing. She wanted to make Louise feel better. Laurence was generally a gentleman, so there was no reason for him to have forgotten to invite Louise to meet the mayor unless he didn't want to. "Maybe he just wasn't thinking. He's under a lot of pressure tonight."

"Whatever." She grabbed an hors d'oeuvre off a passing plate. "When is dinner?"

"Take it easy, size seven," Sepia said, pinching at Louise's waist. "This dress is a six, remember?"

"Forget that. I want to hear about this cop."

"Why?"

"Your eyes kind of danced when you mentioned him."

Had they?

Sunday morning was a slow one for Sepia. She had left the party earlier than most last night, but woke up with no energy and knew she was going to miss church, which always made her feel guilty. The inevitable calls she would get from those wondering if she was okay were sure to come. After all, any real Christian had to be deathly ill to miss church.

She slumbered out of bed and made her way, sans robe, to the front door of her Tuscan-style home. After a few weeks in Tuscany, Sepia had redecorated with Tuscan plaster frescos, antique-white finishes with mixtures of green, yellow, and ocha cream. The rustic granite and steel appliances finished the touch.

The down payment on the three-bedroom, which was way too big for her, was an engagement present from her parents. Jason wouldn't live there until they were married, of course. That was unacceptable, but it was to be their first family home, the size that most people would pick as their maybe-one-day dream home.

She didn't care who saw her come out onto her porch in her nightgown just to grab her morning paper. She was tired of having to look made up every second you stepped out the doors in this town. She was tired of a lot.

Half awake, half sleep, Sepia grabbed her cup of coffee, the first of many even though she vowed to give it all up. Caffeine was the devil, Louise said. Easy for her to say. This coffee thing was the equivalent of a drug addiction for Sepia.

She flipped through the papers, wanting to read something that would mean enough to her to make her forget about the nightmare she'd had again last night. At least this one ended differently. Instead of her waking up just before she was shot, an unseen gunshot was heard just before the killer fell to the ground. Behind him stood Paul, who had just saved her life. She ran to him, jumped into his arms and thanked him for saving her as if she were a nimble idiot who didn't know what she would do without this strong man.

The dream was quickly forgotten as soon as Sepia flipped open her paper. No need for coffee to wake up this morning.

"Oh, my God!"

LOCAL MUSICIAN SHOT DEAD IN HOME.

This time the murder hit closer to home. Willis Connor lived in Cromwell. He was a well-known Go-Go musician. Sepia had seen his band play at a few clubs around the city. Since its emergence in the middle 1970s, Go-Go had been D.C.'s most important voice for indigenous African-American expressive culture. It was more than just music. It was an event, encompassing dance, visual arts, and dress as well. It was called the heartbeat of D.C. and it permeated into the Maryland and Virginia suburbs as well. It was the kind of music everyone either loved or hated.

Sepia sighed as she read the next paragraph. Police weren't answering media questions, but sources believed the murder was racially motivated as neighbors reported witnessing a suspicious white male walking by the block several times earlier that evening.

The doorbell rang and Sepia jumped halfway out of her chair. Putting the paper down, she rushed to the door. She hadn't been thinking about the fact that she was in a pretty revealing nightgown with no robe when she opened the door, but the second she saw who had come calling, she was aware of nothing but.

"Officer . . . Um, I mean Paul." Sepia wasn't sure
what to do. Should she close the door and run upstairs to grab a robe or just close her eyes and pretend this wasn't happening? "I . . . I . . ."

Paul felt a rush of heat hit him at the sight of
her in the silk and lace nightgown that went just
above her knees, hinting at creamy thighs. Her short
hair had strands sticking out in awkward places and
her face without makeup made her look innocent
and completely worth devouring.

Now if only he could remember what he'd come
here for.

"Did I wake you up?"

"No, of course not." The last thing she needed
was for him to think she was a lazy woman who
slept until noon. "I've been up for hours, I'm just
enjoying my . . . can you excuse me? I need to go
get my robe."

"Why?" Honestly, he would be incredibly disappointed if she did.

Sepia just stared at him, uncertain what to think
of his words and what to say back. Then he smiled
and she felt her temperature rise a few degrees.
He was teasing her. He knew she was embarrassed
and he was making fun of her.

"Gotcha," he said. "Can I come in?"

She stepped aside, her eyes belying her amusement at his joke even though she wanted to smile.

Paul took a few steps into the foyer of the house,
looking around. The place was very nice and he
was impressed, but he had enough experience in
this kind of thing not to show it. Crawford and
Cromwell had an incestuous relationship, and
crimes in Crawford led to Cromwell more than the

citizens of Cromwell would care to admit. He had been in many homes like Sepia's and nicer.

He turned around to face her as she closed the door. He fought his eyes, but they betrayed him and took in her backside. She had a nice curvy figure and it definitely provoked a reaction from his gut. He had to remind himself he was here about a murder and he was a professional.

Sepia turned around, still feeling naked. Observing his dress, she found him looking less intimidating without his uniform in a plain blue button-down and jeans that fit him better than they had any right to.

"Is this a personal call?"

Paul looked down at himself. "Not really. Well, I'm not on duty today, but I'm working."

"Are you?"

"Last night's murder. You've heard about it. You've been up for hours, right?" He looked her over again.

Sepia held her chin high. "Yes. I was just reading the paper, but you're a cop, not a detective, right?"

"I'm sort of in between. I'm helping Luke out."

"Of course." Sepia looked away, feeling awkward. He had no idea she had dreamt about him last night, but she was still embarrassed by it. She knew she was being silly and really needed to put some clothes on.

"Please have a seat in the living room. I'll be with you in a second."

He nodded and turned for the next room as he heard the patter of her bare feet rushing away on the hardwood floor. Something about that sound made him smile. It made him feel familiar.

Paul couldn't figure out Sepia from her house, something he had come to be able to do with people. The inside of people's houses, the little knick-knacks, told you a lot about them. Sepia's house was filled with expensive and lush items, the best of fabrics, the classiest of tiles, and all that would be expected. It resembled a fine European villa.

There was also a smattering of intimate objects that seemed to hold some meaning but no value. Pictures, ceramics, and trinkets that looked to be from the islands and some from Europe were everywhere and grouped together in a way that meant something to someone.

The wall above the windows that overlooked the front of the house was what caught his attention. There were three paintings in wild colors with graceful strokes, all abstract but symmetric. Each was different, but Paul could tell from the style they had the same artist. It reminded him of . . .

"Do you like those?"

Paul turned around as Sepia entered the room in a thick ocean-blue robe that looked as if it was going to swallow her whole. As she walked toward him, he felt himself warm to the soft way her eyes looked without any makeup to highlight them.

"Yes," he answered, turning away from her. He didn't need to see those eyes. "They kind of remind me of Fargeson."

Sepia was stunned. "Fargeson? You know your art?"

"That obviously surprises you," Paul said.

Sepia cleared her throat. No need to get off on the wrong foot with him again. "No, I . . . I just didn't know a lot of people knew about Fargeson."

After a few seconds too many of silence, Paul decided he didn't want to be the source of the apprehension on her face. "It's okay. A lot of people don't know much about Spanish art. When he was painting, Italy was really the focus."

"Unfortunate," Sepia said, sitting down. He did know art well. This was interesting. "He was under-rated."

"So they are his?" Paul leaned against the large fireplace.

"No, but he is the inspiration." Sepia remembered how much she had ached to discuss art with Jason, but he wasn't at all interested unless it would help him get ahead with someone. "Those are mine."

Paul looked at the paintings again. Wild and graceful. He turned back to Sepia. "They're beautiful. Did you train?"

"One summer in Rome," she said, feeling as if she was boasting. "It was an exchange thing in college."

"Sounds like fun." He looked at the pictures on top of the fireplace. Every picture was of Sepia accepting some award or plaque. There were many. "You've won a lot of awards."

Sepia blushed, wondering why this man made her feel so self-conscious about herself. "I'm sure that appears narcissistic."

He picked up one that particularly stood out to him. One of her with a young man's arms around her. "What is this one?"

"That was for a Junior League fund-raising event." Sepia would remind herself to toss that picture in the garbage the first chance she got. "We raised money for a women's shelter in Crawford."

"The shelters need the help." He put the picture back. "Who's the guy?"

"What guy?" *Change the subject please.*

"He's in a few of the pictures." Paul hated his own curiosity. "Is this your boyfriend?"

"My ex." Sepia sat down on the sofa, picking up

an issue of *Savoy* magazine off the coffee table. She rolled it up tight. "My ex-fiancé actually. Jason."

"Interesting." Paul wondered what would make her end an engagement. Or was it him? Couldn't have been him. He himself didn't care for her type, but for those who liked the princess type, she had to be a big catch. "What did this, Jason, do?"

"Nothing really interesting at all," Sepia said. "I do recall you not wanting to talk about your ex the other day either."

Paul approached her, standing at the other end of the sofa. "Can I sit?"

"I'm so sorry, please sit down, Off . . . Paul."

"I was a little rude to you yesterday."

"A little?"

"You gave as good as you got," he said with a smile.

Sepia liked his smile. It was contagious and made her smile as well. "Mine was in self-defense."

"I'm trying to apologize, if you don't mind."

Sepia shrugged.

"Okay." Paul leaned back. "I'm sorry then."

"So am I," Sepia responded.

"Excuse me?"

"I'm sorry, okay?" Sepia rolled her eyes. "I mean, I already apologized when I was in your car, so really I don't owe you one now."

"You're a piece of work." He couldn't deny he liked her little rip of stubbornness. "Too much for Jason, I presume."

"None of your damn business!" Sepia couldn't believe he was being so intrusive.

Paul bit his lip to keep from laughing at the way her face tightened when she was angry. With herself made up, she was a distractingly beautiful woman. Without, she was something close to teasingly perfect.

"My ex-wife owns an art gallery," he said.

Sepia's interest was piqued. What kind of woman would marry this guy? Hot and cold. "Have I heard of her?"

"The Edison Gallery here in Cromwell."

"Of course." Sepia couldn't put a face to any of her visits there. It had been a while and she never really paid much attention to who was helping her. "I've been there. Is she from Cromwell?"

"No." Paul laughed at the irony.

"What's so funny?"

"Nothing." Paul shook his head. What the heck? "She's from Crawford like me, but she's in Cromwell now. With her new husband. What she's always wanted."

"What do you mean?" Sepia could see a flicker of anger in his eyes that quickly faded away.

"Just that she's always wanted to be here and now she is."

"I know what you're feeling."

Paul was surprised to hear her say that. "I don't think you do, Sepia."

"Jason wasn't from Cromwell either. He was from New York and he moved here after he got a big job in D.C." Sepia couldn't believe she was telling this to a man who was practically a stranger and probably didn't care at all. "All he wanted was to belong. It's why he wanted to marry me."

"I don't believe that," Paul said, fighting the urge for compassion. "I can't imagine—"

"What, that someone would use someone to get into society?" It was Sepia's turn to laugh. "It's the oldest trick in the book."

"You don't think he loved you?" Paul asked, wondering himself if Elaine ever loved him.

Sepia thought about it for a moment. She had

to face this fact eventually. "I think he loved what we could be, but not me."

"I think Elaine loved what she could be without me."

Their eyes connected as his voice trailed off, its regretful tone pulling at something inside Sepia. Sitting across from him, she saw something that she hadn't seen in a man in a long time. Genuine emotion, raw and uncovered. It appealed to her too much.

"Why are you here, Paul?"

Her abrupt turn startled him. Actually, Paul hadn't thought of his real reason for being here since the second he saw her at the door. "I was worried about you."

"You were?" she asked just above a whisper.

"Luke was too."

"Oh." Sepia flicked the pages of the magazine in her hands. "I'm fine. It's been a few days and—"

"I mean about what was in today's paper." Paul realized she might not know. "You said you were reading the paper, right?"

"Oh, yes. I read about the murder." Sepia shook her head. "Awful. I can't believe this is happening."

"We're really sorry about the leak," Paul said.

"What leak?"

"You didn't read the whole article?"

"You rang my doorbell before I could finish." Sepia felt a tightening in her chest. "What leak?"

"The article cites a police source that said there was a witness to the murder of Dishwana Grimes."

Sepia gasped. "What? I didn't witness any murder!"

"They got it wrong," Paul said. "Or maybe they got it right and wrote it wrong because it would sell better. Either way, we're very sorry. You haven't told anyone, have you?"

"Just my best friend, Louise." Sepia slid closer to him on the sofa, completely unaware of her actions. "Am I in danger?"

"It doesn't say anything about you or give your name. It doesn't even say that you're a woman." Paul could see the apprehensive expression and he wanted nothing more than to make that go away. "Honestly, you aren't in danger."

"If this was a police leak, then that cop knows who I am."

"I'm pretty sure he won't tell that. You see, some cops give leaks because the papers will pay them, but they never give it all up. Don't worry."

Sepia wasn't so quick to buy that. "It's too late for that. I really don't want to be involved in some serial murder case."

Paul's antennae went up. "What makes you think this is a serial murder case?"

Sepia tilted her head. "Come on, Paul. You can't expect anyone to believe that these are three random crimes."

"This last murder has some differences that are worth noting."

"Like what?"

Paul raised his finger to her. "I'm not going to fall for that. I'm not telling you anything."

"I don't need you to," she said, even though she was extremely curious. "He was killed in his home as opposed to some ill-reputed place downtown. He was in Cromwell instead of Crawford."

"Not bad."

"I'm trying to think like a cop," Sepia said. "For my book."

"Yes, the book."

"Seriously though, Paul, there are more similarities than differences."

"You don't know that."

"All three are public figures in the local area with some national acclaim. All three are . . ."

Paul saw her eyes light up with concern. He knew where she was going. "Black."

"Do you think this is racial?" Sepia didn't even want to think that. The murders were bad enough, but if racism was added to it . . . not good.

"There are going to be people who make it racial no matter what," Paul said, "but Crawford and Cromwell are both seventy percent black. The chance of any murdered person not being black is rare."

"But the murderer was white," Sepia said. "At least I'm sure he was."

Paul looked away, thinking the same thing.

"What is it?" Sepia asked.

"A couple of Willis Connor's neighbors said they saw a white man somewhat fitting your description. Luke is getting them to a sketch artist now."

"I hope they can do better than I did."

"If so, we'll need to call on you to help identify him again."

Sepia nodded. "I'll help in every way that I can."

She meant it. As unpleasant as all this was, people were dying and she had to do whatever she could to stop it.

Without thinking, Paul reached out and placed his hand on her arm. He looked into her uncertain eyes. "You've already helped, Sepia. Without you, we wouldn't have anything to go on. All of our other leads have dropped. This guy might be our guy."

Sepia smiled at him, appreciating his tenderness. What was she feeling right now? Whatever it was, she wasn't scared.

Paul felt a pull at the pit of his stomach as he looked into her eyes. She was a woman unused to this type of problem. Danger.

Speaking of . . . Paul removed his hand and stood up.

"I have to get going now."

"Do you?" Sepia stood up, wanting to slap herself for sounding so needy. "Of course you do. Let me show you out."

Paul stood in the open doorway ignoring the desire he had to stay. He turned back to Sepia, who sighed heavily as she looked across the street. When he looked back, he saw an elderly woman across the street picking her newspaper up from the ground. The woman never took her eyes off of him and Sepia as she leaned over, got her paper, and stood upright. She gave them one last lingering look before turning and walking away.

"Sorry," Paul said, turning to Sepia.

Sepia shrugged. "We'll be the talk of the town by tomorrow."

"I sincerely doubt she knows me," Paul said.

"She'll find out." Sepia knew that Mrs. Allison Parker was one of the biggest gossips in Cromwell. "She'll know all about you by dinnertime tonight."

"Good-bye, Sepia." Paul nodded one last time before heading for his car.

A phrase popped into Sepia's mind. *I hate to see you leave, but I love to watch you go.* A smile crept at the edges of her lips as she took in the view. Not bad. Not bad at all.

Four

"David!"

Paul ran as fast as he could to catch up to him. When he'd driven in to the station, a glimpse of his partner leaving caught his eye. He could have sworn that David saw him as well, but he kept on walking instead of coming into the garage like usual. When he reached him, Paul had to grab his arm to get him to turn around.

"David, what's the matter with you?"

David turned around, his eyes bloodshot red, his face unshaven for days. "I didn't hear you, man."

"How could you not hear me?" Paul asked. "I was screaming at the top of my lungs."

"I was thinking, man." David looked around.

"Where are you going?" He didn't look good at all.

"I'm off duty. I'm done."

"But your car is in the garage, isn't it?"

David shook his head. "I don't . . . I really got to go, Paul. Catch you later."

"Wait a second." Paul grabbed him again, but

this time David jerked away almost violently, something Paul hadn't ever experienced with him. "What's the matter with you?"

"I said nothing!"

"Why don't you want to talk to me?"

"I've been working all day," he said. "I'm tired."

Paul sniffed the air. Could it be? "David, have you been drinking?"

"Hell no." David backed up a few steps. "I've been working, I told you."

"I smell liquor," Paul said, knowing how many cops took a quick swig during the day. Not David though. "Where is your car, David?"

"I don't have it anymore," he said. "It got re-poed."

Paul couldn't believe this. "Is it that bad? Look, man, if you need some money, I can help you."

"You can't help me with anything, man," David said, his somber tone matching his vacant eyes. "Not anymore."

Paul was speechless as David walked away. He reached for his vibrating beeper, wondering what he could do to help David without hurting the man's pride. He wasn't going to let his brother go down like that. He had a family to provide for. Paul had savings, as good as any cop could have. Maybe Patsy would talk to him, but he'd have to call her later.

The lieutenant wanted him in his office ASAP.

Paul was pacing the lieutenant's office trying to control his anger. The second he walked in, already concerned about David, the sight of Internal Affairs waiting for him put him completely on edge. Then, Lieutenant Pitt sat back, saying nothing as the two guys from IA told Paul they suspected David of being a leak to the Ravens gang. Paul wanted to strangle them for even suggesting it, and the fact that Lieutenant Pitt didn't back him up made him even angrier.

"No way!" Paul turned to the two men who looked like identical twins in their beige suites, glasses, and slicked-back hair. No expression or emotion on their faces, that was what they were famous for. "I'm not going to listen to you talk about him like this. He's my partner."

"Paul." Lieutenant Pitt used an even tone, unusual for him. "Take it easy. You have to listen to their proof."

"I don't want to hear it."

"We've traced some phone calls," said the man who introduced himself as Mathers. "You should know."

"I know what I need to know," Paul said. "He wouldn't do this. He's been having some rough times, so that makes you automatically suspicious."

"We don't place baseless blame on—"

"You do it all the time," Paul said. "I've seen you destroy reputations of cops only to come out and find that they aren't guilty of anything. You say, oh, well, we did our job, and walk away, but the cop never really recovers. David is already going through enough. You can't—"

Lieutenant Pitt stood up. "How do you think that thug got away from you last week? David should have gotten him and you know it."

The flicker of truth in his words only angered Paul more. "So what are you saying? The Ravens are paying him to tip them off on us?"

"Yes," Mathers said.

"Well, I got you there," Paul said. "Nobody's paying David anything. He's dead broke. He doesn't have a cent. His car just got repossessed."

"He's been spending it all on gambling." Mathers offered him a folder. "Look at it. We've been trailing him. He's been spending thousands."

Paul just looked at the man, who eventually put the folder back at his side. "So, what do you want me to do? Wear a wire? Give him up?"

"Talk to him," Pitt said. "Let him know that you want to help him and that it's not too late."

"Is that it?" Paul asked, staring stone-faced.

"You're dismissed," Pitt said.

When he got outside the office, Paul almost ran into Luke, who was coming his way. Paul looked at him, and the look on Luke's face was as if he was saying he was sorry without words.

"You knew?" Paul asked.

Luke nodded. "How you doing?"

Paul shook his head. "I can't talk about it now. This is crazy. Why didn't you tell me they were thinking this?"

"I thought you knew. You're his partner."

"I told them they're crazy. They are."

"One thing you're gonna have to learn if you want to become a good detective," Luke said, "is that sometimes you have to shut up and listen instead of talk."

Paul tried not to let his uneasiness show. He didn't mind Luke seeing it, but he didn't want any of the other officers catching on. That is, if they didn't already know about it. Rumors moved fast in the station.

"I talked to Sepia this morning like you asked," he said, wanting to change the subject.

"Like I asked?" Luke smiled. "I remember it being your idea."

"Yeah, well, she's worried."

"Better to be informed and worried than not know."

Paul looked at him, wondering if Luke was telling him everything. "She's not in any danger, is she?"

Luke didn't answer. He patted Paul on the shoulder and walked away, leaving Paul wondering how he was going to solve all of this.

"Sepia. Sepia!"

Sepia snapped out of her trance to see Louise staring at her strangely. "What?"

"What's going on with you?" Louise asked.

They were having dinner together at Louise's request. Initially Louise had wanted to vent about Laurence and how he was still spending too much time at the club instead of with her. When Sepia showed up at the Italian Café, Laurence was there and Louise only shrugged her shoulders in explanation.

"Nothing." Sepia pushed her plate away. "I'm gonna get this wrapped up. I'm not hungry."

"Are you ready for your book signing?" Laurence asked. Unlike Sepia, he had a voracious appetite and was starting on Louise's plate after finishing off his own.

"No country club talk." Louise slapped him on the arm. "You promised. Nothing about the club tonight. I swear you're going to give yourself an ulcer."

"I just want things to be perfect," Laurence said. "And with all these damn murders, it's putting a damper on everything."

"You say it like they're just an inconvenience," Sepia said.

"That's how he talks about them," Louise said. "Like it doesn't matter that they were killed. He just wished it was somewhere else."

"Can you blame me?" Laurence asked. "Since this last guy in Cromwell got it, no one wants to go out. It's hurting our bottom line."

"They've all paid their dues, haven't they?" Louise asked.

"I'm talking about the money they spend lunching and drinking."

"Is everyone really scared?" Sepia asked, having been able to think of nothing but the murders all day.

Louise nodded. "You know everyone is saying it's a racial thing."

"That's ridiculous," Laurence said, taking a sip of wine. "It's crime plain and simple. I'll bet this last guy was into something just like the other two."

"He wasn't," Louise said. "He was a respectable musician."

"With that jungle music," Laurence said. "Doesn't it make you think of the old days when we weren't allowed in clubs as patrons, but only as performers dancing around like idiots?"

"He's dead," Louise said. "Have some respect."

"I am. That's what the music is called outside of D.C."

Sepia didn't want to make waves, but she didn't appreciate Laurence's disrespect for his own culture. "Actually, it has a proud history. It originated in Africa and Egyptians called it the king's music. It's considered a way of reaching our ancestors. And it was the white slave traders that called it jungle music."

"I'm sorry." Laurence acquiesced reluctantly. "Can we dispense with the history lesson?"

Sepia shrugged as Louise winked at her.

"I have to admit," Laurence went on, "I was looking around when we were on our way to dinner. What about you?"

"I am on edge about it." Sepia thought of Paul and when she would see him again. "But Paul is working on it and he's a great cop."

"Paul again?" Louise scooted her chair closer to Sepia. "What is really going on with you two?"

Sepia couldn't fight the smile that spread across her lips. "He came by this morning to see if I was okay."

"Why wouldn't you be?" Laurence asked.

"It's a long story," Sepia said, "but we talked about a lot."

"What did he tell you?" Laurence asked, leaning forward. "What should we be looking out for?"

"We didn't really talk about the case."

"What did you talk about?" Louise asked.

Sepia wanted to hold the conversation to herself for now, but she would tell Louise when they were alone. "Just stuff. He did say that I shouldn't be afraid."

"We're not like them after all," Laurence said. Louise and Sepia looked at him with disdain and he raised his hands in the air. "Don't kill me for saying what you're both thinking."

"I wasn't thinking that at all," Sepia said.

"Weren't you?" Louise asked her. "I mean I was, kind of. I hate to be such a snob about it, but I didn't like Elliott Jackson or Dishwana Grimes."

"What about Will Connor?" Sepia asked.

"I didn't have a problem with him," Louise said.

"I hear he was a good family man. He wasn't found in a whorehouse or crack house."

"Maybe he's just a coincidence," Laurence said. "Maybe we're tying him in and he's just an abstract murder. Maybe they all are."

"Someone saw a man fitting the description of what I saw on Connor's block," Sepia said, realizing as soon as she spoke that she had said too much.

"Really?" Louise shivered, looking at Laurence. "Laurence, I want to go home. I'm scared."

Louise leaned into Laurence, but he didn't comfort her or put his arm around her, and Sepia could see the disappointment in Louise's eyes. Laurence wasn't the touchy-feely type like Louise wanted. Sepia hoped she could understand that and be okay.

"I'll take you home," Laurence said, reaching for his wallet. "Sepia, why don't I take you home too?"

"Yes," Louise said. "Good idea. We need to stick together."

Sepia shook her head. "I'm fine really. I don't want to give in to this fear."

"Then we'll follow you home," Laurence said. "Louise won't be able to sleep unless we see you walk into your house."

Sepia looked at Louise, who was nodding with pleading eyes. "Okay. Let's go."

Outside the restaurant, Sepia made her way through the parking lot to her car. The lot was across the street. Laurence and Louise were at the steps of the restaurant, waiting for the valet to bring his car around. Sepia had to admit, she was feeling a little nervous. Louise tended to overreact to anything, but the dark and empty lot she was walking in didn't help any.

She wondered if she was letting fear explain away all of the other feelings she was experiencing. For a mature woman of thirty, Sepia knew she wasn't as good at detecting her own true feelings as she should be. Jason used to tease her about it, telling her that she had lived such a charmed life that her intuition was irretrievably damaged. She waved his words away at the time, but he turned out to be the greatest form of proof that his own words were true. She had lived a life where there was an expectation that the people around her, including her boyfriend, were a step above others and she could trust them for what they were. A life where everything worked out. Where everything was there and waiting for her. There was always something to fall back on, and all she saw around her was success and prosperity. No one feared job loss, paying the bills, not getting into school, or danger.

Sepia had assumed that all those people who complained about life did so just because they weren't taking ownership of it. She had taken ownership of her life and was getting everything she wanted out of it. Until Jason. She had wanted to get married and had loved Jason, so she ignored his social climbing plans and scheming. She believed him when he said he was just thinking of her when he urged her to go to society events she didn't want to or was too tired for. He told her he was just trying to make her look good when he hobnobbed all night and begged her for contacts into the right men's groups. It was all a lie. He wanted status and was going to use her to get it, and when she dumped him he told her so in about the cruelest words she had ever heard.

She relived Jason's words over and over again since she had tossed him out of her life. The truth was, she had been falling out of love with Jason well before she faced the realization of what she tried to believe wasn't true. The pain she felt about him was waning in its power to hurt her. She had never been one to let mere words tell her who she was.

That was until she met Paul for the ride-along almost a week ago. Something about his insults slapped her in the face the same way Jason had. She couldn't even understand why she cared. Once this case was solved, she would never see Paul again. They would never run in the same circles or come across each other, so what did his treatment of her, good or bad, matter?

Sepia looked back at Laurence and Louise. Louise waved to her just as the car drove up. Sepia waved back. Everything was fine.

She pressed the button on her remote key, opening her car door. Just as she reached her hand out, she heard a scratch on the pavement and looked to her left. Her heart leaped into her throat as a hand grabbed at her right arm and pushed her entire body forward. She slammed into the car, letting out a scream as the pain of the impact shuddered through her.

"You're next, bitch!"

"Please!" Sepia felt something jab into her right side. She couldn't even think. "Take my purse. Take my car. Anything you want."

"What I want is your life."

"Hey!"

The scream from across the lot startled them both. Sepia could feel the man behind her change his position to see who it was. Whatever it was he had at her side, and Sepia knew it was a gun, moved. She didn't waste one second.

Her free arm went swinging backward and con-

nected with his jaw. She heard him curse and fall
backward. Sepia turned and ran as fast as she
could. She'd only gotten a few feet away before she
slammed into Laurence.

"He tried to . . ." She looked back, seeing only
the back of the man who had pushed her weaving
around cars. He was wearing a black T-shirt, showing very visible white arms. That hair. That wild,
black curly hair. "It's . . ."

Louise arrived, looking in a panic. "Oh, my
God, Sepia. Are you all right? What happened?"

"I'm going to go after him," Laurence said, letting Sepia go to Louise.

"No." Sepia grabbed his arm as he started into
the dark lot. "It's him, Laurence. He's the killer.
Please don't put yourself in danger."

"Him?" Laurence looked back at her. "The guy
you saw?"

Sepia nodded. Others were gathering around
them. She held on tight to Louise, thinking of
Paul. She wanted Paul right now.

"Please don't," Louise said. "He would kill you,
Laurence."

Laurence looked back as if he wanted to go anyway. With a sigh, he calmed and turned back to
Sepia. "I'll call the police."

"Call Officer Paul Healy," Sepia told him. "I
want Paul."

Paul felt something rip through him when he
opened the door to the interview room and saw
Sepia sitting in the wooden chair. She was terrified,
shaking and looking like a lost child. He rushed to
her, feeling a sense of protectiveness for her that
he wasn't familiar with.

"Sepia, I'm sorry. I'm so sorry."

Sepia looked up and saw him coming toward her. As he came to her side, she fell into his arms. She didn't care that it was a totally inappropriate gesture and she didn't care who saw them. All that mattered was that she felt something close to normal for the first time since this had happened to her.

"Where were you?" she asked through choked sobs.

"I was on the other side of Crawford," he said. "But when Luke called me I came as fast as I could. I know you hate me, but I could never . . ."

She looked up at him, searching his face for an explanation. "Why would I hate you?"

"I told you not to worry." Paul tried to control his anger. It was raging through him, but he knew it wouldn't help Sepia or anyone else. "Someone leaked who you were, and it got to him. Someone in the department. I can't believe it."

"I thought he was going to kill me."

Paul took her face in his hands, gently holding it only inches from his. He wanted to kiss her so badly. Not in a sexual way, but to comfort her and show her that he was feeling her pain. "I can't believe I took it so lightly. It's not how I work, honestly."

"I don't blame you," Sepia said softly as she felt herself drawn to him. Her tears stopped as she felt the heat on her cheeks from his hands and sensed her face moving closer to his. She was helpless to stop it. She wanted to kiss him.

"Ms. Davis."

Paul jumped a few feet back, realizing what Luke must think as he stood in the doorway to the room. He would assume what he'd seen meant something, and Paul couldn't deny it. If Luke hadn't come in, he would have kissed Sepia and probably made a bad situation worse.

"Are you feeling better?" Luke asked as he sat next to her.

Sepia nodded. "Officer Healy has been a great help."

Luke gave Paul a stern stare. "I can see that. Is there anything else you can tell me about what happened?"

She shook her head, looking at Paul, who looked ashamed. Had she felt that magnetism alone? "No, I can't think of anything."

"Are you sure you didn't tell anyone that you'd seen this guy before the article came out?"

"Only Louise. I told you."

Luke nodded, looking at Paul. "You talked to her?"

"She swears she told no one but her mother over the phone two days ago," Paul said. "They were having their regular weekly chat."

"Where is her mother?"

"She's in San Francisco," Sepia said. "And she's eighty years old."

Luke's hand formed in a fist. "Then it's got to be inside."

As Luke looked at him, Paul could see what he was thinking. "Not David. No way."

"I didn't say that." Luke stood up.

"Who is David?" Sepia asked.

"He's my partner," Paul said. "And he has nothing to do with this."

"Except through you," Luke said.

"I haven't even had a chance to talk to David about anything, let alone this case."

"I know," Luke said. "But there's something dirty inside and it almost got this young woman killed."

"What now?" Sepia asked.

"You need protection," Luke said. "I've talked to the chief of police. He's very concerned about you. He wants to make sure you're given high-level security."

Sepia looked at Paul, wondering what he thought of her. She was sure that the chief of police didn't say that about every crime victim. Paul didn't seem to care and that made her feel better.

"You mean a bodyguard?" she asked Luke. "To go everywhere with me?"

Luke shook his head. "I mean a safe house. This guy is serious business and he knows who you are and where you go. It's giving him too many chances. We want to take his chances away."

"But if someone here is tipping him off," she said, "won't he know where I am anyway?"

"Not if you go to this place." Luke looked at Paul.

Paul nodded. He knew what Luke was talking about. He was talking about his own cabin. Five years ago, they kept a Raven informant there after suspicions arose in the department that someone was tipping the Ravens off as to where he was. It had only been known by Luke, his partner at the time, named Deke, and Paul, who watched over him. Asked time and time again, no one told where they'd kept the man. They hadn't even told the chief of police.

"Perfect," Paul said. And it wasn't more than an hour from Cromwell.

"What's perfect?" Sepia asked.

"Where Paul will be taking you," Luke said.

"Me?" Paul hadn't known about that part.

"I think it's only right," Luke said. "Don't you?"

"Yes," Sepia said. "Paul, you'll take me, won't you?"

Paul didn't know what to do. He wanted to take care of her, but he didn't want to be away from the action where he could probably save more lives. It seemed like a hard decision, but when he looked at her large dark eyes so uncertain and anxious, it became much easier.

"I'll take you there," he said, smiling. "And I'll watch over you."

The smile on Sepia's face pleased him so much that Paul was certain he had just made the wrong decision.

"You ready?" Luke asked as he and Paul stood at the back door of the precinct.

It was all very secretive as they moved fast. An unmarked car was ready and waiting in the back. A female officer was taking Sepia to the bathroom to get cleaned up and Paul was taking her right to Scully, the small town where Luke's cabin was hidden behind a forest of trees, surrounding a small private lake.

"I'm ready," Paul said. "This is deep. I'm still reeling from it."

"Something's wrong with this Willis Connor," Luke said. "He's not like the other two in a lot of ways, but I know he's linked."

"He is," Paul said. "Just with a different slant. Something kept the killer from following his M.O., but it's still the same killer."

"He didn't have any enemies as far as I can tell."

"He had one," Paul said. "Or he wouldn't be dead."

Luke let out an exasperated sigh. "There is absolutely no way for that guy to know who Sepia was and find her in time to follow her to that restaurant."

"We're sure it's him?" Paul asked.

"She's sure," Luke said. "And he told her she was next. It's him."

Paul nodded. "How did he get in? He has to be connected to somebody that would get the interest of a cop."

"There are a lot of holes there," Luke said, "and I've got to fill them fast or someone else is going to die."

"Did you mean it when you said . . ." Paul didn't want to finish it.

"David?" Luke lit his cigarette. "I'm sorry, but I'm going to have to look into him. We have caught about six Raven members since he went on desk duty and was out of the loop."

Paul felt a heavy heart. "He's drinking and gambling all of his money away and it might be dirty money."

"Have you been able to talk to him?"

"No. I went by his house today, but he didn't even come home last night. Patsy is at her end with him. She's a wreck and it's affecting her pregnancy and the kids. He won't answer his cell or his beeper."

"You've got to get through to him, Paul."

"I'm on my way to oblivion now. How can I reach him?"

Luke contemplated. "I think there is one other person we can trust."

"You trust someone?" Paul knew that since his partner Deke's death a few years ago, Luke hadn't worked with anyone else. He didn't trust very many people.

"He's a kid I'm taking under my wing. He's so much like you it's scary. I call him White Paul."

Paul smiled. "How fast can you get him?"

"I can get him tonight. He's eager to help out. You just get her up there and situated and I'll have him relieve you as soon as possible. You can get back here and—"

"Talk to David. Thanks, Luke."

Paul knew he was running out of time with David, and as much as he wanted to be there for Sepia, David needed him as well.

"I'll have—" Luke stopped as they both heard the back door open.

Paul stepped aside for Sepia, joined by Donna Pillant, the department's only female cop. He looked at Sepia with a reassuring smile as she stepped out into the dark.

"It's going to be okay," he said.

"What about Louise and Laurence?"

"They've been sent home," Luke said. "I've let them know you're being taken care of."

Sepia couldn't imagine Louise going that easily. "Okay."

"Let's go." Paul opened the door to the tan Chevy.

Sepia knew she should have been scared to death, but something in Paul's eyes told her she was in the safest place she could be as long as she stuck to him.

When they drove down the dark, gravely road toward the wood cabin, Sepia felt herself exhale. It had been a tense ride. Paul had been kind to try to talk to her about art on the drive up, but the reality of her situation and what had happened to her settled into Sepia and she couldn't even speak for a long time. Paul was understanding and when he'd put his hand gently on her thigh, she knew the intent was to comfort. And it was a comfort, at first. After a moment, it began to feel like more than that and Sepia found herself becoming aware of this man in a way that didn't seem rational considering what she'd just been through.

She looked at Paul in the dark of night as they drove into a part of Maryland where she hadn't even known homes existed. She looked at him as he drove in silence, his profile strong and determined. She wondered about chance and how this man had come into her life by such a mistake, but had suddenly become her protector of sorts. She wondered who he really was inside and who he shared his life with.

Paul pulled up to the cabin, warming to its familiar rustic design. It was a fifteen-hundred-square-foot red pine cabin with all the basics for Luke and his wife. They had had no children, so there was only one bedroom. It hadn't even had a television until Paul made him get one when they were hiding the other witness there years ago. Paul wondered if it was still there. He needed the distraction.

On the drive up, he had put his hand on her thigh to comfort her, but only felt a rush of heat take him at the touch. He knew it was completely inappropriate and he didn't like himself very much for it, but he was reluctant to remove his hand because he wanted Sepia to know he was there. It had been torture, feeling her eyes on him, knowing that if he looked at her he might reveal something unintended and unknown to himself.

"Here it is," Paul said, as he opened the door for

her. He watched her as she stood in the doorway, looking around.

"It's dusty," Sepia said, not knowing at all why that was all she could think of.

"He hasn't been here for about six months." Paul flipped the light switch. The lights flickered for a minute before coming on.

"Who is he?"

"Luke," he answered. "This is Luke's family cabin."

Sepia wondered how safe this was if the leak was coming from the station. "What do I do now?"

"You don't have to do anything," Paul said. "The bedroom is at the end of the hallway. I know you're tired."

"I'm exhausted." Sepia sat down on the red-and-brown-plaid sofa. It felt hard to her. "But I don't think I can sleep. I'm still . . . wired."

"I hope we have some better news in the morning." Paul sat next to her, but not too close. She looked so vulnerable in a way that drew him to her, but he didn't want to do anything stupid. "The statement from your friend Laurence was helpful. He saw the guy a bit too."

"Oh, my God." Sepia opened the purse she was grasping tightly, searching around for her cell phone. "I've got to call Louise. She'll be dying."

"You can't," Paul said. "She was told—"

"She expects me to call her." Sepia saw that her cell phone was not in service in this area and would not offer roam. "Where is the phone here?"

"Sepia, you're not listening to me. You can't call her and she was told she can't call you. It's for your own safety."

"Louise isn't any danger to me."

"It's not about that."

"What is it about then?"

"Your situation isn't easy to explain. Until we know where the weaknesses are, everyone is a danger to you."

"Not Louise." Sepia stood up, searching around the cabin for a phone. Where was it? "Louise is my best friend. You don't know how much she means to me."

Paul stood up, knowing what this was really about. She was having the breakdown that always came hours after. He'd seen a lot of people in her condition.

"Sepia, please sit down."

"I will *not* sit down!" She threw her purse on the floor and went into the open kitchen. No phone. "There has to be one here."

"No." Paul spoke in the most calming voice he could muster.

"I want a phone!" Sepia felt as if she were having an out-of-body experience. She was watching herself lose it.

Paul reached her as she was opening cabinet doors frantically. "Sepia, calm down. I do understand."

"You don't!" Sepia pulled away from him, but he grabbed her tighter, pulling her to him. "She's my best friend and she'll die if she doesn't know I'm okay."

"I understand," he said softly, looking into her eyes.

"She was the only one who knew I was making the right decision when I ended things with Jason and she stayed up with me when I was crying every night."

"I understand."

Sepia felt the hot tears streaming down her face

as she tried to break free from Paul. Why did he keep saying the same thing?

He wouldn't let her go and she felt that crazy voice inside her begin to calm. She looked at him, searching for something to let her know that this wasn't as bad as she thought it was.

"Paul, I . . . I . . ." She stopped struggling and her entire body sighed. "I thought I was going to die."

"I understand," he said again, feeling the over-whelming emotion that she was emitting. It was working, she was calming down. But he wasn't. He wasn't calm at all. He was heating up and her close-ness was the reason.

Sepia felt her body becoming aware of his strength and hold. She felt a pull in her belly and a hot fire rip through her as she looked up at him.

When her lips came to his, Sepia felt a relief from her pain and a burst of pleasure rip through her. The press of his lips radiated through her en-tire body and she felt a hunger that she could only describe as animal. Her hand went up to his head, pulling him closer if that was possible.

It was like a volcano erupting inside him as Paul kissed her back. Her lips were so soft and demand-ing at the same time. He returned with a demand of his own as he separated her lips and his tongue peeked inside. As his arms wrapped around her waist, pulling her body closer to him, everything in-side Paul wanted to kiss away her pain and soothe every inch of her. His body told him what his mind wasn't willing to ignore, and that was that he really wanted this woman. Only, his mind wasn't com-pletely obliterated yet. Close, but not yet. And what was left of it was screaming at him to fight the pas-sion that threatened to consume him, because it was all wrong. It felt better than right, but it was all wrong.

Paul used all the strength he could to part his lips from hers and push away. He felt as if a part of him had been ripped away and he didn't know where he could find the strength to stay away from her. He backed up a few steps, hoping the distance would bring him back to his senses.

"We can't," he said, stepping back some more. "I can't."

"We can," Sepia said. She wanted him now more than she could remember wanting anyone. "Paul, I need—"

"I know what you think you want," he said, "but that's not what you really want. You just want something and this isn't the right something."

With renewed humiliation, Sepia looked away. She had never used sex to cover for something else before, but she had never been in this situation before either. She'd felt completely alone one second, but in his arms she felt safe and she needed that more than anything. Making love to him would have soothed her desperation.

She was certain she had really wanted him, but how could she be certain of anything tonight?

"Go to bed, Sepia."

Sepia looked up to see Paul's back to her as he walked into the living room. She watched him, unable to move from where she stood as he turned on the tiny black-and-white television and laid himself out on the sofa.

She waited. Waited for him to look at her, to even acknowledge she existed, but he didn't. Minutes passed, seeming more like hours, before Sepia finally found the strength to walk and then hurried down the hallway to the bedroom.

She fell onto the bed, crying for the first time that night. She felt stupid and angry because she had been rejected. Whether it was right or wrong, she wanted Paul and she was offering herself to him. She felt tossed aside.

Sepia cried herself to sleep, still hoping until the last minute that he would come to her room.

Five

Sepia could open her eyes, but nothing else was moving. She couldn't remember when she had finally gone to sleep last night, but she obviously had slept well because as her head turned left, the clock on the nightstand read eleven in the morning.

Her eyes surveyed the room that she hadn't even noticed in her haze last night. Although it was simple and rustic, it gave off a nice, warm feeling that made Sepia believe there was love in its decoration. It reminded her of summers at Highland Beach in Annapolis. Those days were so happy and carefree. She longed for them to come back.

After a few moments, she sat up and paid for it. Her head was throbbing, making her moan in pain. There was nothing like a headache after a night of crying like a baby. She needed an aspirin and looked around the bed for her purse before remembering she had left it in the living room.

She didn't want to go out there and face Paul after having made such a fool of herself last night.

She was certain he would give her a pass, considering she had been through a near death experience, but she felt stupid nonetheless. Thank God she hadn't said anything after he rejected her. It wouldn't have changed his mind and the further humiliation would have made it impossible to even look at him again.

At least this way, she could maintain a certain sense of dignity and, God help her, she would accept some pity for once in her life. She had to first thank him for watching over her and apologize for putting him in such a situation. He had been right. If they had made love last night, she would have regretted it. Wouldn't she? Of course, she told herself over and over again. She would have regretted it and felt used, which was why Paul wouldn't let her go through with it. She was certain he had wanted her from the way he kissed her, but he was a good guy and wouldn't let his libido interfere with his vow to serve and protect.

"Paul?" Sepia searched the cabin as she entered the living room.

The living room was the center of the cabin, where you could see the dining room and kitchen, but as Sepia looked around she couldn't see what she came looking for. Trying to fight the panic rising inside her, she came up with a ton of reasons why he wasn't there.

"Paul?" She peeked into the bathroom. It was empty. *Stay calm. He's just outside getting some fresh air.*

As Sepia rushed toward the front door, she thought she heard hard footsteps. She froze in place, hoping she was just crazy, but she wasn't. The footsteps were coming from the other side of the door and a chill ran through her.

Something was wrong.

"Paul?" His name came as a whisper from her lips as the knob turned and the door opened.

Before she could see a face, she saw an arm. A white arm with a hand carrying a black duffel bag. Her mouth opened to scream, but nothing came out as the figure came full before her. In a police uniform.

"Who are you?" she asked.

"Morning, Ms. Davis." The young blond-haired, blue-eyed officer smiled as he closed the door behind him. "You had a good sleep?"

"Who are you?" she asked again.

"I'm Officer Dunleavy." He approached her, holding out his hand. When Sepia didn't take it, he pulled it back. "Detective Drasutto sent me."

"Luke?"

He nodded. "I was just getting some snacks from my car."

He held up the duffel bag and Sepia felt herself breathe for the first time since she had heard his footsteps. "Where is Paul?"

"He's gone, ma'am." He unloaded the bag onto the kitchen counter. Candy, chips, and other goodies spread across the table.

"What do you mean gone?" Sepia couldn't imagine he would leave her. Leave her and not say anything? "When?"

"Last night. Well, kind of this morning. He left around three A.M. He had to wait until I got here."

Sepia wandered restlessly around the room. She had really wanted to see him to apologize about . . . It suddenly occurred to her that she may have driven him away.

"Did he say why he wanted to leave?"

"He didn't," Dunleavy said.

"He didn't say anything?"

"I mean he didn't want to leave, but he didn't have much choice. Detective Drasutto called him in." He looked at her, confused for a second, and then smiled. "Of course you don't know. You just woke up."

Sepia felt her stomach tighten. She knew what was coming and hoped she was wrong.

"There was another shooting last night." Dunleavy stuffed half a Snickers bar into his mouth. "It's on the television. Some rich lawyer guy."

A bit of nausea swept over Sepia as she turned the television on and slid the folding chair that was against the wall in front of it. Only one channel worked, if you could call it that, and she waited on pins and needles for the commercial to end.

Dunleavy joined her, standing beside her chair as he crunched on a bag of chips. "He said that you would be moody when you woke up."

"Paul said that?" Sepia shrugged. "I'm fine."

"You're lucky," he said. "Looks like the other guy got it just a few hours after he went after you."

When the commercials ended, the scene was chaos. A camera was on a crowd of people protesting outside the Crawford Police Department screaming all sorts of things that Sepia couldn't decipher but knew weren't good.

"You are looking live outside the Crawford Police Department," the young reporter said. "The citizens of the city are protesting the department, complaining that the Crawford police aren't paying as much attention to the murder of its citizens as the Cromwell Police Department is to its own. This comes after news of a fourth shooting that seems likely to be related to the others even though police aren't saying so."

A picture of an elderly man came on the screen and Sepia knew who he was before his name flashed underneath. She'd known the man her entire life.

"The latest victim," the reporter continued, "is Richard Sanders, prominent attorney and head of the prestigious Sanders Law firm. The lifetime Cromwell citizen was found shot in the chest in his home late last night by his daughter, who was coming home for a surprise visit from overseas. His wife, Shelby Sanders, was sleeping in the upstairs bedroom of the massive home and was not harmed. Sanders is currently in critical condition at the hospital."

Her shock subsiding somewhat, Sepia's doubts began immediately.

"He's not right," she said.

"What?" Dunleavy was laid out on the sofa now, flipping through a magazine.

"Richard Sanders," she answered. "I know him. He's a leader in the community. He has a spotless reputation."

"Trust me, lady, nobody is spotless."

"I know, but he's not like Elliott Jackson or Dishwana Grimes."

"Yeah, he's alive."

"I mean his profile. His reputation."

"What about the other victim?"

"That's where I'm stumped. He is more like Willis Connor in the sense that he isn't as hated as the others, but unlike any of them, Richard Sanders comes from all the right stuff."

"What's the right stuff?"

Sepia knew Dunleavy wouldn't understand. Richard Sanders was from a long line of black blueblood lawyers. The Sanderses were powerful on the

East coast. He went to the best private schools, the top colleges, and belonged to all the right clubs.

"When is Paul coming back?" she asked.

"He said he'd be back as soon as he could."

"Well, how soon is that?" she asked impatiently.

"He's Mr. Detective now, so who knows?"

"He's not a detective, he's a cop."

"Yeah, but he's about to make detective and he acts like one now." He tossed the magazine aside. "Don't get me wrong, I like the guy. He's an awesome cop and he should have made detective already. He just can't do the butt kissing that's needed. Maybe this case will do it for him."

Sepia saw her purse lying on the kitchen counter. She was thinking of something that she had heard about Sanders but couldn't remember. Laurence would.

"Do you mind if I get some fresh air?" she asked, grabbing her purse.

The cop's eyes narrowed at her. "You don't need to take your purse, ma'am. I'm not going to—"

"No." She laughed, smiling flirtatiously. "I just want to get some aspirin out of here. Is it okay?"

"Sure, but stay at the cabin."

As he took her seat in front of the television, Sepia reached inside her purse and grabbed her cell phone instead of the bottle of aspirin.

When she got outside, she was hit first by the breath of fresh mountain air. She looked around, seeing this place for the first time. The house was immersed in the beautiful woods, with a path leading to the tranquil lake where a small boat was docked. She could barely make out another house on the other side of the lake, deeply hidden in the woods as well. It was incredibly romantic and Sepia

wished she had been here under other circum-
stances.

She kept her eyes on her phone as she walked to
her left, to her right. She looked up at the sky and
thought maybe she could get reception closer to
the water, where the trees weren't blocking the sky.
As she rushed to the water, Sepia kept looking back,
wondering when Officer Dunleavy would figure
out that she had been gone too long.

Her phone beeped its beacon just as she reached
the dock. Sepia didn't hesitate to call Laurence's
phone at the club. She was frustrated with getting
voice mail, because she didn't know Laurence's
home phone number by heart. She did know the
second best thing.

"Sepia?" Louise came through scratchy and
strained. "Is that you?"

"Yes, hon." Something was so comforting in hearing her best friend's voice even though she had
just spoken to her the day before. "I'm so sorry to
leave you without saying anything last night."

"It's okay. The officer made it clear that we had
to leave you alone and not try to contact you for
your own safety. Laurence and I were so worried.
He wanted to contact your parents, but he didn't
know how."

"It's better he doesn't, but thanks for trying."
Sepia didn't need them getting involved. They would
only worry and ruin their vacation trying to get
back. At least she hoped they would. "I saw the
news. I'm so sorry, Louise."

"About Richard?" There was a heavy sigh and a
pause. "I know. I can't believe it. I couldn't go in to
work today. I just can't . . . What is happening here?"

"I don't know, honey, but is Laurence there?"

"You're calling here for him?"

"I can't find him at work. Is he there? I know you two have been staying over at each other's places more, haven't you?"

"Yes, we have." Louise hesitated. "I was cautious to say anything because I know you don't like the idea of living with someone before getting married, but we've been going back and forth and I think . . . I hope it moves to . . ."

"Louise, honestly, girl, I'm happy for you. I really need to talk to Laurence."

"He's not here. I'm glad he's gone anyway. He was being such a jerk. I mean, my boss is dead and he's not even comforting me."

"What's he so upset about?"

"Guess. Richard Sanders was one of the premiere members of the club. He's just mad that he's going to lose a name he could sell."

"I'm sure it's more than that."

"And he was going on about those people protesting on the news, calling them all kinds of names. Loudmouths, ignorant, and some I'd rather not repeat."

"They're just angry. They feel slighted." Sepia couldn't remember when Crawford citizens didn't feel slighted on any issue in comparison to Cromwell. Things were uneven and it wasn't fair. "Do you know when he'll—"

Sepia yelled and fell back a few steps as the phone was ripped out of her hand. She turned to face Paul, his brows centered in anger, his jaw tight and locked. He turned her phone off and threw it in the lake. When he turned back to her, the angry growl on his face, matched with his crisp uniform, was intimidating.

"What are you doing?" she asked, running to the edge of the dock. "That's my phone."

"I told you!" Paul grabbed her by the arm and began leading her toward the cabin. "What were you doing?"

"I was just calling Louise." Sepia jerked away. "I can walk on my own."

"Get in that damn cabin!" He was fuming and wasn't trying to hide it.

Here he was doing everything he could to help David and work this latest shooting with Luke as quickly as possible so he could get back here to her and make sure she was okay, and she was doing everything to get herself killed.

"Don't give me orders!" She kept walking still. She talked a good talk, but the look on his face as he stormed after her let Sepia know this man meant business and she needed to listen this time.

"I told you!"

"I know," she said. "I'm sorry. It's just that this latest murder had me thinking of something."

"Cell phones can be traced too, Sepia."

"Are you listening to me?"

"Why should I listen to you?" he asked. "You haven't listened to a word I said."

"I'm sorry, okay?" She honestly felt bad, but he didn't have to throw the phone away. It was very expensive. "I was only on with her for a minute, two at most."

"That's all it takes."

"Do you really think this person has the technology to—"

"He had the technology to get into a house with the best security system available last night."

Sepia thought again of Richard and realized

that it was trivial to argue. "You're right, okay. I just wanted to tell you that something is wrong with Richard Sanders's shooting and I know you think so too."

Paul stopped as they reached the steps to the cabin. "I'm not telling you the secrets of this case."

"The only thing Richard Sanders has done that could be considered even partly controversial was vote Republican."

"How do you know how he votes?"

"I know a lot about him. My family has known his forever."

Paul was intrigued. "Go on."

Sepia smiled, happy he wasn't angry at her for the moment at least. "He's loved by Cromwell, and Crawford respects him for all his family has done for that city."

"Like Connor?"

"Sort of. Connor wasn't as liked in Cromwell."

"Why not?"

"It's hard to explain, but Cromwell isn't crazy about entertainers."

"Cromwell isn't crazy about a lot of things. Except money. And they don't seem to be crazy about Crawford unless it's some charity."

"That's not completely accurate and you know it. Cromwell is full of good citizens who contribute and use their money and standing to help others."

Paul didn't want to get a chip on his shoulder about Cromwell now. He didn't need anything blocking his ability to help Luke.

"The reason I know about his political persuasion is not because of my family ties," Sepia said. "It's because of the club."

"The Cromwell club?" he asked. "He's a member?"

"Charter. It wouldn't have opened without him. Laurence worships the guy. He begged Sanders to be a member and Sanders agreed, but we still had to go through the background check before admitting him."

"Background check? It's a country club. Don't you just pay the dues and get in?"

"Not private clubs."

"Did you pull up something dirty?"

Sepia wondered how best to play this. "I need a promise from you."

"No promises, Sepia."

"Fine." She started up the steps. "I'll just go hang out with Dunleavy. I like him better than you anyway."

"All right." Paul shook his head as she returned to him. She had a grin on her face that told him she knew she had him. "We need all the help we can get. People are dying, so this better not be a game."

"After last night?" she asked. "This was never a game for me. This is my life and I'm involved now. I want to go with you."

"Come with me where?"

"To the club. I have information that might tell you who had a motive to want Richard Sanders dead so you guys don't go on a wild-goose chase. You can get back to focusing on finding the guy who tried to kill me."

"You're safe here, Sepia."

Sepia stepped closer to him. "I'm safe with you, Paul."

Paul let the wave of heat rush through him. He definitely wanted this woman. Why did he want to inflict this pain on himself? Even if he wasn't charged with protecting her, they were a class apart and he would only be in the same situation he had been with Elaine. Hurt and alone.

"Do you promise to do everything I tell you?"

"Completely." Sepia felt a tingling sensation run through her as he looked down at her with determination. She usually liked to be in charge, but could see herself giving over to him. Fighting him would probably be a waste of time anyway.

"Besides," she said, "security at the club is heightened because of what's been going on."

"Okay." Paul wondered if he was using his better judgment. It was subject to question in the face of this beautiful woman. "I'll go get Dunleavy."

"Paul." Sepia winced as she heard herself call his name. She didn't want to ask him this and hoped he would get inside before she gave in to the urge, but no dice. She had to do it. She had to know.

"Yeah?" he asked, turning around.

"I was upset this morning when I found out you'd left."

Paul cleared his throat. "I had to go in because of the shooting. It's in Cromwell, but Luke is lead invest—"

"I know you had to go, Paul, but why didn't you tell me you were leaving? It would have taken a second and would have been nice."

Paul's expression stilled and grew serious. "The truth?"

"Yes."

Had she repulsed him so much by coming on to him that he couldn't face her? That's what she was worried about.

"The truth is, I wanted to tell you. I just couldn't risk it."

"Risk what?"

"Risk going into your bedroom. I don't think I would ever have left."

Sepia was speechless as he turned and went inside. What a hit-and-run that man was. A warm glow framed her face as she smiled to herself. She hadn't been mistaken when she'd felt his passion for her. Even if that was all it was, it was comforting to know it was real.

"This is something," Paul said as they entered the club.

The Cromwell Golf and Yacht Club was a lot closer to the cabin than he had expected and was comfortable with. It took them only forty minutes to reach it, and if the wealthy black residents of Cromwell were the killer's targets, Sepia was a little too close to take any chances.

"It is, isn't it?" Sepia took a deep breath as they entered. "It smells so new and looks so perfect."

"So does everyone in it." He looked around at the members in the lobby who walked past them.

Beautiful black folks for miles all dressed up in their tennis and golf outfits, living a life of leisure on a weekday morning when slugs like him had to work for a living. Oh, well, he thought as he looked at Sepia. His work wasn't all that bad today.

"Can I help you?" A large man dressed in a business suit met them as they took a few more steps into the large lobby area.

"Who are you?" Sepia asked, uncomfortable not recognizing a face.

She and Laurence shared duties in hiring for the club, using a staffing agency that specialized in the hospitality field. She had hired all of the "inside" employees and she had never seen this man's face before. Today wasn't the day for suprises.

"I'm security, ma'am. Who are you?"

"I'm Sepia Davis. I work here."

As the man checked the clipboard in his hand, Sepia turned to Paul.

"What good are you if your uniform can't get me into my own club?"

"It could be a costume," Paul said with a shrug before leaning in closer to whisper, "Or a God complex. People with clipboards have been known to become suddenly possessed by it."

Sepia's hand went to her mouth as she tried to stifle her laugh.

"You're not on this list as an employee," the man said abruptly. "Are you a member?"

"Yes, I am." Sepia took her ID out and handed it to him. "But I've been working here since before it opened and I need to get back to the offices."

He nodded to confirm her name as a member and handed her ID back to her. "We have heightened security now, ma'am. I'll have to go ask. You can wait in the lobby."

"Thank you," Paul said as he led Sepia farther into the lobby.

"It's a little early for a drink," she said as they sat down on a plush sofa. "Why don't I just order us some pop?"

"I'll go to the bar." Paul began to stand.

"No, sit down." She waved him back to his seat. "There are people here to do that for you. They'll come to us."

"I can get my own drink." Paul shifted on the sofa. It was softer than his own bed and, he was certain, more expensive than anything he owned.

"For the fees this club charges, you wouldn't want to do anything whether you could or not."

As she noticed someone walking toward them, Sepia realized she was in the same clothes she had on from last night and probably looked a mess. She hadn't been concerned about that before now, seeing Elita Smith and Jane Tramone come toward her. Both old-guard friends of her mother who were bound to have something to say about her less than perfect appearance.

"Sepia, dear," Jane said with concerned eyes. "Are you all right?"

"I'm fine, Jane." She smiled, smoothing out her hair. "You look well."

"We just came from the spa," Elita said, throwing Paul a quick disapproving look. "It just opened today. You should go. You look very tired."

"I think she looks fine," Paul said.

Sepia looked at him and they traded smiles.

"I beg your pardon," Jane said.

Sepia could tell from the way she was standing and the tone of her voice that Jane had no idea that Paul was with her.

"Jane—" she started.

"What are you doing here, young man?" she asked, a hand on her hip. "I'm certain the head of security would not be happy to know you're lounging in the lobby like a member and flirting with the ladies here."

Paul rolled his eyes.

"How rude," Elita said. "I'm going to find Laurence."

"No, Elita," Sepia pleaded. "He's with me. He's supposed to be here. This is Paul—"

"No matter who he is," Jane said, "why are you being flanked by a policeman?"

"It's a long story." Sepia was feeling an incredible amount of embarrassment as she could only imagine what Paul was thinking. "Paul is here as my guest."

Jane huffed. "Well, there is a dress code. Work clothes don't apply."

"Oh, really?" Paul asked.

"Paul." Sepia glared at him. He would only make it worse. She could tell he wanted to unnerve the women, which they deserved. Still, the best choice was to get rid of them.

"Thank you, ladies, for stopping by," she said. "I hope you enjoy yourselves."

"We'll be here tonight as well," Jane said. "I've already purchased my book."

Sepia looked at Paul, who raised an eyebrow in curiosity. "I forgot, yeah. My book signing is tonight."

"We're so looking forward to it," Elita said. "It's so grand to see how you've gotten yourself along after getting rid of that . . . What was his name?"

"Jason," Jane said, rolling her eyes. "That Jason."

It was getting interesting now, Paul thought as he leaned back. He wanted to hear more about this Jason.

Elita's face scrunched into a pitying expression for Sepia. "Dear, he was so beneath you anyway."

Sepia wanted to fall into the floor. "Elita, I—"

"I mean there is nothing worse than a social climber," Jane added. "I knew it all along. So did so many of us. You should stick to your own kind, Sepia. Men who are born to good families with good names that would never embarrass you or make you call off an engagement."

Sepia knew of many good men from good families who embarrassed the women in their lives in many ways.

"Yes," Elita said. "These men come out of nowhere and think their education and pocketbooks make them husband material. Maybe for some . . . regular woman, but not for you."

Sepia stole a glance at Paul, who was staring at the women as if he were watching a Broadway show. It wasn't far from it.

"Ms. Davis!"

Sepia had never been so happy to hear her name as she turned to the security guard, who was waving at her.

"Oh, I'm so sorry, but we have to be going." Sepia nodded to Paul, who was already standing.

"So nice to meet you, ladies," he said with such extreme sarcasm.

Being ladies of good breeding, they had to say likewise, but Paul could tell that they hated every second of it and were happy to get away from him.

"I'm sorry," Sepia said as they headed for the executive offices.

"For what?"

"You know what. Don't make me go into it. Some of these people are . . . well, you know."

"Snobs? No surprise there."

Sepia felt defensive at his tone. "What does that mean? You know we aren't all snobs."

"I didn't say you were."

"You should know that Jane Tramone and her husband have funded the children's art class at the Crawford Community Center for five years."

"But they wouldn't dare associate with any of those children's parents, would they?"

"Not true," Sepia said, although she knew it was. So many people contributed to organizations and causes that help poor people who they would oth-

erwise never want to be around. "I was at the opening, when they cut the tape at . . ."

"What?" Paul asked, seeing her hesitation.

"Never mind." Sepia didn't even want to say it.
She knew being at the ribbon-cutting ceremony
meant nothing real. Her life had been a series of
ribbon-cutting ceremonies. "You can go ahead."

"Go ahead and what?"

Sepia stopped outside the door to Laurence's
office. "Make fun of us all. We're all rich snobs
who don't know anything about the real world and
don't show respect to anyone who isn't one of us."

"I don't think that about you."

Sepia couldn't explain her physical reaction to
the way he was looking at her. As if he were pho-
tographing her with his eyes. Not in a lewd way at
all. She felt like art. She felt desired.

"Not anymore at least," Paul said, smiling.

She hit him on the arm, unable to think of anything else to do in order to break the tension. Her
mother had told her it was always a good quality in
a man when he took it upon himself to end a dis-
agreement. The worst thing a woman could do was
to bring it back up after he had made the hum-
bling gesture.

After knocking twice, Sepia ignored Paul's warning and opened the door herself. It wasn't locked.

"I work with him," she said. "I come in here all
the time."

They entered the office, designed with neat, ef-
ficient modular furniture in stainless steel and pinewood. The silver shelving stood against the wall,
opposite stark-white filing cabinets. As he looked
around, Paul's first impression was that whoever
worked here, this guy had an anal retentive nature. It was neater than he had ever seen any of-

fice. He wasn't even comparing it to the station. He'd been in plenty of business offices, and this one looked like a model, made to be looked at, not touched.

"The files are in here." Sepia led him to the back of the office where six-foot-high file cabinets were kept. Sepia opened the cabinet that read MEMBER-SHIP. "This is it."

"What is it?" Paul asked. "You can tell me now. You're safely here."

"This cabinet has all the membership applications." Sepia skimmed through the files, selecting the one she wanted. "This here is the master list."

Paul followed her to the desk where she sat down and opened the file. He leaned over her, overly aware of how close he was to her. "Master list."

Sepia nodded, trying hard to ignore the exciting chill that came from him being so close. She wasn't feeling particularly sexy after a night in rustic land, but all she could think of was when he'd kissed her last night and the rush of heat that swarmed over her when he had grabbed her earlier by the lake. Why she would respond to a grab in such a way was a mystery to her, but there was something sexual and tender in the aggression, and her physical reaction to it intrigued her.

Sepia slid the sheets over the desk. "These white pages indicate all members confirmed, the yellow is for all the members we are currently soliciting to join or reviewing their applications, and the pink sheet are those we have declined membership to."

"Are the victims on here?"

"Richard Sanders is." Sepia pointed to one of the white pages titled PREMIER MEMBERS. "These premier members are the families that the club solicited as the best families in the area. The club couldn't exist without them. This is what made me think of Richard Sanders. He's on this list."

Paul scanned the list of about twenty families, not recognizing any of the names except one. "Your family is on there."

"Yes," she answered with a lowered voice.

Paul looked down at her, sensing the tone of the voice, and it bothered him. "You don't have to be embarrassed by that, Sepia."

"I'm not. I'm proud actually, but I know that to some people it's just a snobby thing and they make me feel bad about that."

"I wouldn't do that."

Sepia looked up at him and the honesty in his dark eyes moved her. She was in trouble. "Thank you."

Stop it! Paul yelled to himself, knowing that he couldn't go down this path. Luke would be very disappointed that he was flirting with a witness and victim during an investigation. "So what did you want to show me?"

Sepia blinked, trying desperately to remember what she had been saying before falling under the quick spell of Paul's eyes. "Yes, uh, well, my parents are out of town, which is a good thing. I hope this is solved before they get back. I'd be too worried about them."

"Let's see what we can do," Paul said, trying to focus on the papers in front of him and not the sweet-smelling woman next to him.

"This list is what made me think of Richard Sanders," Sepia said, "because unlike the other victims, besides still being alive, he has a very different background."

"If the murderer is just killing those blacks he

feels are prominent now, what would it matter what background they came from?"

"It might not." Sepia noted the file number next to Richard Sander's name. "But I was thinking of what else might make someone want to kill Richard."

Paul stepped aside as she stood up. "He's perfect, right? You said so yourself."

Sepia pulled Richard's file. She opened it and quickly found what she was looking for, handing the sheet of paper to Paul. "There is a standard background check we do on members before we admit them."

"It's a country club, not a government agency. What do you need to know?"

"You'd be surprised how many fine people have a crime or very well hidden skeleton in their past." Sepia watched as he read the paper. "Laurence was determined to make sure we wouldn't admit someone to the club who would later embarrass us or give the club a bad name."

"Richard Sanders was having an affair with a young woman in Crawford." Paul noticed the words that were doubly underlined. "A young, white woman."

"Laurence was upset about that," Sepia said. "His father died a year ago and it was found out that he had another family in Crawford and it brought up some bad feelings."

"But he admitted him anyway?"

"He got over it quick. Laurence felt that the pros of Richard Sanders outweighed the one con, and it was the only thing. Laurence knew that it could come out and be ugly, but he was willing to risk it. A society club in Cromwell isn't worth its salt without the Sanderses."

"This doesn't do a lot for me."

"I just thought you should know," Sepia said. "That woman was married, by the way. What if her husband found out? What if the man that tried to kill me is her husband?"

"We'll definitely look into this, but it doesn't make sense."

"He could have killed the other three as a distraction from his real victim, so we would think Richard Sanders was part of a racist plot and not murdered for something very personal."

"He made sure those other three were dead. Shot in the head. Sanders was shot in the chest and he certainly didn't stick around to make sure he was dead."

"Is it the same gun?"

"I can't talk to you about that, Sepia." Paul wanted badly to tell her Luke was pretty sure it wasn't the same gun.

Sepia understood his resistance, but it was killing her to know. "Something is weird about Richard Sanders and I think it's a different crime."

"So do I," Paul said, returning to the lists on the desk. "What about the others?"

"None of them were members."

"Did they apply?"

"They could have." Sepia returned to the desk, flipping through the pink pages. "Oh, my God, Paul. Willis Connor is on here. He's being considered."

"Is that a surprise?" he asked, taking the pink sheet of paper.

Sepia nodded. "He's new to Cromwell and it looks like most of the committee didn't want him on, but there were a few that felt he should be considered because he had done a lot of charity events and bought some musical instruments for Crawford High."

"That's good, isn't it?"

"I'm not on the committee, but I would think so."

Paul's cop antennae went up. "Who is on the committee?"

"A bunch of Cromwell socialites. Older women with nothing else to do but define who belongs and who doesn't."

"Like those two ladies we met in the lobby?"

"They're both on. Laurence is the chair, but really he makes the final decision."

"What was his decision?"

"It only has by numbers who voted against and for, but I'm sure Laurence voted against him. He didn't like that guy." Sepia searched the sheet of paper for the member number and quickly retrieved it from the cabinets. "Maybe I'm wrong."

"About what?"

"It looks like Laurence was considering him based on some of the committee members' insistence that he be added for his charitable acts." Sepia was surprised to read that. Maybe Laurence wasn't as snobby as he seemed. "This is clearly his handwriting. He was going to see what he could do."

"Look, Sepia." Paul handed her the yellow pages. "Elliott Jackson and Dishwana Grimes were declined. Unanimously."

"I don't doubt it, but what does it mean?"

"There's nothing consistent," Paul said, his mind racing, "but that's fine. The killer isn't using this list. He's using his own perception of who these people are or aren't. But at least we have a list of the most well known blacks in the Crawford-Cromwell area."

Sepia watched Paul gathering the papers together and placing them back in the file. "We have to ask Laurence if we want to take this list."

Paul didn't want to have to go through that. "Can't we have your permission?"

"I don't think so." Sepia remembered Laurence saying that the confidentiality of the records could be kept if only he had access to them.

"Maybe we can just copy it with your permission."

"I'm not on the membership committee. Each of those folders says confidential. Paul, let's just find Laurence."

Paul sighed. She was right. Luke had told him to always go by the book so it didn't come back to bite you. Even when it didn't seem like it was necessary.

"Is he here?"

They found Laurence standing outside the main dining hall giving orders to the catering manager. When he looked up and saw Sepia, a look of surprise was followed by a smile.

Paul didn't get a smile.

Laurence dismissed the manager as soon as they approached. "Sepia, what are you doing here? I thought you were under protection."

"I am." Sepia nodded at Paul. "He's my protection. You remember Officer Healy, don't you?"

"Of course." Laurence glanced disapprovingly at Paul. "We like our officers to wear plainclothes. The uniform makes it seem like we're expecting trouble."

An Important Message From The ARABESQUE Publisher

10 ANNIVERSARY
1994-2004

Dear Arabesque Reader,

Arabesque is celebrating 10 years of award-winning African-American romance. This year look for our specially marked 10th Anniversary titles.

Plus, we are offering *Special Collection Editions* and a *Summer Reading Series*—all part of our 10th Anniversary celebration.

Why not be a part of the celebration and let us send you four more specially selected books FREE! These exceptional romances will be sent right to your front door!

Please enjoy them with our compliments, and thank you for continuing to enjoy Arabesque.... the soul of romance bringing you ten years of love, passion and extraordinary romance.

Linda Gill
PUBLISHER, ARABESQUE ROMANCE NOVELS

P.S. Don't forget to nominate someone special in the Arabesque Man Contest! For more details visit us at www.BET.com

SPECIAL OFFER!
4 BOOKS FREE!

ARABESQUE
BET BOOKS

A SPECIAL "THANK YOU" FROM ARABESQUE JUST FOR YOU!

Send this card back and you'll receive 4 FREE Arabesque Novels—a $25.96 value—absolutely FREE!

The introductory 4 Arabesque Romance books are yours FREE (plus $1.99 shipping & handling). If you wish to continue to receive 4 books every month, do nothing. Each month, we will send you 4 New Arabesque Romance Novels for your free examination. If you wish to keep them, pay just $18* (plus, $1.99 shipping & handling). If you decide not to continue, you owe nothing!

- Send no money now.
- Never an obligation.
- Books delivered to your door!

We hope that after receiving your FREE books you'll want to remain an Arabesque subscriber, but the choice is yours! So why not take advantage of this Arabesque offer, with no risk of any kind. You'll be glad you did!

In fact, we're so sure you will love your Arabesque novels, that we will send you an Arabesque Tote Bag FREE with your first paid shipment.

* Prices subject to change

THE "THANK YOU" GIFT INCLUDES:

- 4 books absolutely FREE (plus $1.99 for shipping and handling).
- A FREE newsletter, *Arabesque Romance News*, filled with author interviews, book previews, special offers, and more!
- No risks or obligations. You're free to cancel whenever you wish with no questions asked.

INTRODUCTORY OFFER CERTIFICATE

Yes! Please send me 4 FREE Arabesque novels (plus $1.99 for shipping & handling). I am under no obligation to purchase any books, as explained on the back of this card. Send my free tote bag after my first regular paid shipment.

NAME _____

ADDRESS _____ APT. _____

CITY _____ STATE _____ ZIP _____

TELEPHONE ( ) _____

E-MAIL _____

SIGNATURE _____

Offer limited to one per household and not valid to current subscribers. All orders subject to approval. Terms, offer, & price subject to change. Tote bags available while supplies last.

Thank You!

AN074A

ARABESQUE

Accepting the four introductory books for FREE (plus $1.99 to offset the cost of shipping & handling) places you under no obligation to buy anything. You may keep the books and return the shipping statement marked "cancelled". If you do not cancel, about a month later we will send 4 additional Arabesque novels, and you will be billed the preferred subscriber's price of just $4.50 per title. That's $18.00* for all 4 books for a savings of almost 40% off the cover price (Plus $1.99 for shipping and handling). You may cancel at any time, but if you choose to continue, every month we'll send you 4 more books, which you may either purchase at the preferred discount price. . . or return to us and cancel your subscription.

THE ARABESQUE ROMANCE BOOK CLUB
P.O. BOX 5214
CLIFTON NJ 07015-5214

PLACE
STAMP
HERE

"Good thing I don't work here," Paul said.

This guy didn't like him, he could tell that. Actually, Paul realized that this guy didn't think of him either way. Elaine would have liked Laurence.

"Is Louise okay?" Sepia asked.

"She's just worried about you. You should call her."

"I will when I get a chance." Sepia reached out to Laurence, touching his arm with her free hand. "She worries about me so much. Please be there for her, Laurence."

Laurence looked at her, confused. "I am."

Something rubbed Paul the wrong way seeing Sepia touch Laurence. He wasn't jealous. It was clear the gesture was innocent, but it made him wonder how well she knew this guy and if she had a past with him. He was curious about her love life even though he shouldn't be.

"If you're fine," Laurence said as Sepia removed her hand, "then you'll be at the book signing tonight. I didn't cancel it, because I was hoping you'd make it."

"I want to," Sepia said, turning to Paul with pleading eyes.

Paul nodded. "I guess we can, but we'll need extra security."

"The guy wouldn't dare come here," Laurence said. "She can ID him. I think I could as well. There are very few white members in this club and no one is getting in who isn't on our list or specially invited. He wouldn't dare."

"Sounds good," Paul said.

Sepia showed Laurence the file she had taken from the office. "I need to talk to you about this."

Laurence looked at the file, and then Paul. He

was clearly suspicious and his concern didn't seem to wane as Sepia told him what she and Paul had been doing, why, and that they wanted the list.

"You can't possibly think those murders had anything to do with the club?" he asked.

"No," Paul said, "but it's a list we can work from. And we'll want the files of the previous victims."

"What would you use them for?" he asked.

"I can't tell you that," Paul said.

Laurence sighed, looking at Sepia. "Sepia, isn't it dangerous for you to be involved in this more than you already are?"

"I really can't be," she answered. "Can he take the file?"

Laurence paused, looking at the file as if it would give him the advice he needed. "I want to help you. I mean, Richard Sanders is a close friend of mine and I don't want to see anyone else murdered."

"I can't promise this list will stop anything," Paul said, "but it will help us to start with."

"I'm just concerned about their privacy," Laurence said. "These are Cromwell's finest families, you know."

"He knows who our members are," Sepia said, not wanting him to go on one of his "finer people" tirades. "Paul won't expose anything to anyone except the detective on the case."

Paul nodded as Sepia looked at him for confirmation. "It will be confidential."

"That's what you always say," Laurence said. "Somehow things get out. Most of these people don't even know what we've found out about them. We have their incomes and everything in those files."

"Laurence," Sepia said, "people are dying."

Laurence nodded. "I know and that's what really matters. I want to help you, but I have to protect myself and this club from a lawsuit."

"What do you mean?" Sepia asked.

"He means I have to get a warrant," Paul said.

"The files will be here waiting for you," Laurence said, "but I have to do it. If anything got out and it was found out that I just let you come in and take them, they'll sue me and the club will go down."

"I understand," Paul said. He did. As much as they tried to maintain confidentiality in investigations, sometimes these things got out. Usually at trial and it could get ugly. "I'll call the detective now."

"You can use the phones in the lobby," Laurence said.

"Thanks, Laurence." Sepia could see he wasn't at all comfortable with this, but she knew he wanted to help. "I'll go put the file back in your office. I'll meet you in the lobby, Paul."

Paul nodded to Sepia and watched as she walked away. She walked with such dignity and clarity and its magic was that it was so careless for her. So natural.

"She is beautiful, isn't she?" Laurence asked.

Paul turned to see the man staring at him with distrust. "You said the phone was in the lobby, right?"

Laurence nodded. "Your presence here is just professional?"

Paul nodded, not that he had to explain to this man. "I'm here to protect Ms. Davis."

Laurence looked him over, his hands folded

across his chest. "She's a good friend of mine and a fine, fine woman. She doesn't deserve this horrible thing that's happened to her."

"Would you like to tell me something, sir?" Paul asked. He didn't have time to waste with words.

"She's vulnerable right now," Laurence said, his face cold and tight. "A better man would know not to take advantage of that. I hope you're that better man."

"I'm gonna go make that call now," Paul said, backing away. "You have a nice day."

When Sepia returned to the lobby, Paul was surprised to see her dressed in a tennis outfit, a nautical blue and white tank and skirt set. She looked playful and cute. She also looked like a girl with a lot of money and free time. He wondered what he was thinking when he'd considered himself with her. Looking at her now, looking like the perfect debutante, he knew better than to think he could ever relate to her.

"You've changed," he said, managing a smile for her despite what he was suddenly feeling.

"I kept this outfit in my office just in case." Sepia could sense a change in him and it wasn't a good one. She was certain that all this time in the club was making him think less of her, and it bothered her deeply. "Are you okay?"

"I'm fine," he lied. "You mean you expect a tennis match to break out at any moment?"

"It does here," she said. "I know it sounds frivolous to you, but—"

"I didn't say that," Paul interjected.

Sepia looked at him, unable to tell what he'd meant by it, but a little afraid to ask him to clarify.

She believed it was a compliment and wanted to keep it that way.

"I'm sorry we couldn't get the files."

"I just talked to Luke. He's working on the warrant. I want to take you back to the cabin. Dunleavy is there."

"You won't be staying?"

"I'll be back to take you to your book signing."

"That's all fine and good, Officer, but what's really important here isn't being taken care of."

Paul looked at her, not certain if she was joking or if she was seeing through him right now. "I beg your pardon?"

"What am I going to wear tonight?" she asked. "We have to stop by my place so I can get some clothes."

"Of course," he said, smiling. "Where are my priorities?"

Laughter between them lightened the moment, but only a bit as Sepia felt like something had definitely changed. Something inside her had at least. She was caring for Paul and that wasn't a good thing considering how different their worlds were and how much that seemed to mean to him. And maybe to her as well.

Six

Dressed in the appropriate suit jacket and slacks, Paul didn't look any different from the other attendees at Sepia's book signing, but he knew better. As he looked around the room, he saw people for whom any outing was a chance to show the most expensive designer goods and talk about the latest financial or real estate conquest.

The hardest problem these people faced in any given day was finding good repairmen to fix whatever was wrong with their boats, which was exactly what the two men standing next to Paul were discussing. They had looked his way, almost mistaking him for one of them at first, but understanding upon further inspection that he was not at all one of them and turning away.

Paul didn't care. He had bigger worries on his mind. There had been tension between him and Sepia all day. At the police station, she pressed him for more information on the case, and his refusal made her angry. Having to wait an hour for him to update Luke on the case at the station didn't help

the situation either. She didn't say anything, but
Paul could see she was upset and it bothered him.
Not really because she was upset, but because of
how much he cared how she felt about him either
way. He had dealt with beautiful women in the
course of his work before, and would admit there
had been some attraction, but nothing like this.
He had never felt anything resembling nonphysi-
cal attraction and he had never crossed the line
and kissed any of them.

When they went to her house, Paul was grateful
to have Dunleavy join them, because he didn't
want to be alone with her. He was too tempted by her
and he wanted to kiss her again so bad it was becoming painful. Sepia, on the other hand, seemed
very annoyed by Dunleavy's presence and was determined to blame Paul for it by sending him
angry glances.

What bothered him now had nothing to do with
her angry look. What had him worried was the way
he felt after seeing her in the suit she wore for the
signing. Although Paul had changed at the station,
Sepia brought her clothes to the club. He waited
outside the women's locker room for what seemed
like forever until he saw her. When she finally
emerged, Paul knew he could have waited there
for days and it wouldn't have been too long.

She was wearing a porcelain white nylon pant-
suit with a notched collar that made her look dis-
tinguished and fresh. The fully lined outfit was
accented with nothing but a thin black leather belt
to match her shoes. It was a clean, understated look
that Paul found classy and humble at the same time.
He realized that this woman would look perfect no
matter what she wore because her self-confidence
came through in everything.

Paul was unsettled by the physical effect that seeing her had on him. She was obviously an incredible-looking woman. What struck him was the way she smiled at his visible approval. It made him feel like she had dressed for him and he was jealous of all the other people he would have to share her attention with tonight.

"Nice?" she had asked.

"Nice," he had answered, barely able to get the one word out and not trusting himself to say any more.

As he led her to the main lobby area, which was set up for the signing, all eyes turned to see her, the room full of beautiful people of various shades of brown clapped like she was a star, and Paul realized that she really was. For a second, he felt a sense of pride that he would when others admired his woman. Only she wasn't and he had to remember that before he got into some real trouble.

It wasn't easy. She really was a star.

It was in the way she worked the room and made everyone feel so happy they had come. She had all the grace and poise of royalty, but never laid it on too thick or too sweet. It was in the way she spoke to the crowd about her inspiration, her ideas, and her attachment to the characters she wrote with true passion and eloquence. Paul had to admit he wasn't a fan of romance novels. He rarely read fiction at all, but the way Sepia talked about her books, she made them sound like the great American novel that everyone hoped one day to write. She made him want to read every one of her books just at the chance that any of them might give him a glimpse into her mind and her heart.

He couldn't take his eyes off of her, even though he should have been focused on the crowd. He was at least happy to see that no one fitting the killer's description was at the signing so far. His earlier conversation with Luke nagged at him. All the other suspects in the previous murders either had a perfect alibi, were out of town, or had no way of being connected to the murder. None of the descriptions of the suspected killer were any help with the criminal database or the mug shots they were showing everyone. No prints were found at either the Cromwell or Sanders houses that didn't already belong there. Richard Sanders, the only surviving victim, was still in a coma that doctors weren't giving him a good chance of coming out of.

Paul was worried about the next victim if they didn't catch this guy, and most of all he was worried about Sepia. He barely knew the woman, but he knew he couldn't stand it if anything happened to her. Especially on his watch.

"Now some of you may be too old for this," Sepia whispered into the microphone. The crowd laughed, knowing what was coming. "So I hope you'll cover your ears. I just read an emotional scene, so I have to balance it with the good stuff."

A couple of whistles came from the crowd as Sepia cleared her throat.

> *"Tim's lips were on hers in that moment, the hunger deep and needing. Connor felt her entire body tremble from the passion swelling inside her. Their lips connected as if molded to fit each other. He pulled away from her gently, his breath quick and loud. 'Tell me right now if you want this, because if I touch you again I don't think I'll be able to stop.'*
>
> *"She grabbed hold of his face, her hands shaking in anticipation. She pulled him to her, taking con-*

trol of his lips with an aggressiveness she had never shown before. She clung to him as his arms engulfed her body. The kiss became hard and demanding, neither of them able to get enough.

"Connor heated up to a boiling point as Tim began sliding her white satin blouse upward. She lifted her arms, allowing him to take it completely off. She felt herself flush, a warm glow flowing through her. It wasn't embarrassment, for she was proud of her body and knew her breasts were soft and firm. She could hardly remember the time she had bared them to a man. She was about to again, but it felt as if it were for the first time.

"She would hold nothing back, ready as ever to give all of herself in a way she never had. Her whole being seemed to be filled with waiting. It had been so long since a man had touched her in this way. Too long. Even then, it didn't arouse her the way it was now.

"His hands were steady, his eyes concentrated on her lacy bra as he removed it. The look of desire as he took in the firmly rounded breasts excited Connor. When he took one breast gently in his hands, Connor knew if she had been standing, she would have fallen to the ground. She felt her entire body quiver as he gently lowered his head, softly touching her brown nipple with his lips. The gentleness was unbearable. A fire was ignited with every touch of his lips. She felt as if her body had been aching for this sensation for a lifetime.

"He lifted his head and she could see his eyes blazing with passion as he pressed his lips against hers again. He lifted her body as if she were light as a feather and laid her across the bed. Desire was fierce on his face. He called out her name before

lowering himself on top of her, supporting himself with his strong arms. Connor let out a moan as she felt the heat and hardness of his body on hers.

"As he possessively licked her neck with his rough tongue, impatience was tearing her apart as she wanted the rest of their clothes off immediately and he obliged by undoing her jeans. She began quickly doing the same for him. His hips were hard and muscular and his thighs were firm."

When she closed the book, Sepia looked to her side where Paul was standing staring at her. Their eyes connected and she felt as if he'd known that the entire time she read that passage, she was not imagining the characters she had written about in the book. She was imagining herself and Paul exploring every inch of each other's bodies, and felt as if she were about to explode from the heat. As the crowd erupted in applause, Sepia wondered if they could see that her brow was moist and her nipples were taut, just at the idea of Paul's tongue touching them.

Paul smiled at her, wondering what in God's name he was going to do to stop himself from wanting this woman. He didn't think he could do anything but get as far away from her as possible. That wasn't an option tonight, so he would have to pray.

Reaching for her glass of water, Sepia took a sip to quench her throat and cool herself down. Instead of a sip, she drank the whole glass and the crowd laughed and applauded, believing it to be a part of the reading, but it was all too real. Sepia put the glass down, took a deep breath, and looked into the crowd. Time to get back to work.

"I'll take questions now."

* * *

"They aren't boring you to death, are they?"

Paul turned around as Sepia approached him. She was holding a glass of wine in her hand, and the smile on her face was like a night star.

"I thought I'd lost you," Paul said.

"I was pulled away. I'm sorry. I hope I'm not being too difficult to watch over."

"I've talked to all the security guards here tonight. We're tag-teaming your surveillance. I want you to be able to walk wherever you want to and not have to drag me with you."

Sepia wondered what he would think if she told him that she walked away from him because being close to him made her temperature go up about twenty degrees and she would have a problem explaining why she was sweating in the air-conditioned lobby.

"I really do appreciate you accommodating this event for me." As she leaned toward him, Sepia knew she was being flirtatious, but she hadn't felt this way in a long time and couldn't help herself. "I've been a bit of a princess, I know."

"I thought you were great." What about her made Paul feel like a high school boy asking a girl out to the movies? He'd been face-to-face with murderers, but this woman made him nervous. "You really had them going for a while there."

"That's what it's all about," she said, handing her glass to the waiter who passed by. "People read my books to escape their day-to-day life. In their fantasies, the man is handsome and the woman is just short of perfect. They're both so overwhelmed with passion that the world could fall apart while they were making love and they wouldn't notice."

"Why does that have to be a fantasy?" he asked.

Sepia's interest was piqued. "You saying you've felt that way before for real?"

"Not yet." He smiled wide. "But when I find the right woman, I know it will happen. I'll make it so she forgets her own name."

Sepia swallowed. "Presumptuous of you, isn't it?"

"I'm not perfect at anything," Paul said, "but I am great at a few things. That's one of them."

"Bragging isn't your style," she said, although she was enjoying it way too much.

Paul smiled. "I'm just playing with you, Sepia. See, you're not the only one that can shock a crowd."

She socked him playfully in the arm and he didn't budge. He was strong and masculine, yet looked stylish and sophisticated when he wanted to. She was liking him more and more every minute. A man in her life was the last thing she needed, but something made Sepia want to throw caution to the wind.

"So tell me, who's been holding your interest in my absence?" she asked.

"No one," Paul said. "I've been standing here alone. None of these people seem to want to talk to someone they don't already know."

"I'm sorry." Sepia knew it could get like this.

Sometimes, if you didn't belong, you might as well be invisible. She had seen several women send Paul approving glances, but they wouldn't dare go up and talk to him without knowing who he was and whose family he was a part of. Sepia knew if she wrapped her arm around his, he would suddenly become interesting.

"Do you want to talk to any of them?" she asked.

Paul didn't know how to respond, but Sepia

seemed to understand from his expression and he knew then that he'd hurt her feelings.

"You don't," Sepia said, looking away so he couldn't tell how it affected her.

"I want to meet the ones you like." he said.

"Why?"

"Because if you like them, I know they're good people."

Sepia smiled at his attempt to compliment her, but his true feelings were clear. He didn't like these people and he had every right not to. They weren't being the least bit hospitable to him.

Everyone's attention turned to the stage as Laurence asked them to come closer. With a proud smile, he held up his hand for silence.

"I just wanted to say how pleased I am to see all of you here tonight." He paused for some applause. "If it wasn't for you, the finest people in Cromwell, the Center for Adult Literacy in D.C. would not be able to receive this check for the one hundred and twenty thousand dollars we've raised here tonight."

More applause rang out, with Paul joining in this time. He found it amazing. There couldn't have been more than a hundred people there that night. He'd been to fund-raisers for the police association with five hundred and they'd gotten less than twenty-five grand out of it.

"You see, Paul?" Sepia said, speaking over the applause. "They aren't all bad. These people give hundreds of thousands to charity every year."

Paul wasn't sure if there was a hint of sass in her tone until he saw her walk away without looking back at him. He had insulted her, and although he tried to save it, the damage was done. She couldn't begin to understand the reasons behind his feelings about Cromwell's finest and how they had all changed his life.

"I want to add," Laurence said into the microphone, "that our brother Richard Sanders couldn't be here tonight. Yes, I know we're all upset about this. Richard is at the hospital with his wonderful wife, Shelby, at his side. We should all pray for them both and hope that whoever this horrible person doing all of this is, he is brought to justice soon."

Paul looked around the room and saw the emotion in many of the attendees' eyes. He wanted to feel for them because they were concerned about a friend, but he wondered how teary eyed they would be if Laurence had mentioned Elliott Jackson, Dishwana Grimes, or Willis Connor. In fact, Paul realized that Laurence hadn't mentioned them at all and he didn't intend to. Those people hadn't existed to this crowd well before they were actually gone.

Sepia and Louise found each other at the same time. They had only a few minutes to hug and talk before the reading and the subsequent book signing, and Sepia was glad to see her again even though she didn't seem to be in a good mood.

"Sepia, where have you been?"

"Everywhere," she answered. "It's been wonderful, hasn't it? Are you having fun?"

Louise shrugged and Sepia suddenly felt selfish. Something was wrong and she was focusing on herself.

"What is it, Louise?"

"You've been with that cop, haven't you?" she

asked, her tone sounding like that of a disapproving mother.

Sepia nodded. "He's guarding me."

"Laurence said he was looking at you like anything but a guard."

"When?" Sepia felt a little cartwheel in her belly.

"When you were here earlier today. And thanks, by the way, for not telling me."

"Sorry, it was a hectic afternoon. How exactly did Laurence tell you he was looking at me?"

"Just that he was. He didn't go into detail." Louise leaned slightly to the left, lowering her head a bit. She sighed heavily. "I'm surprised he even bothered to tell me that."

"You guys aren't getting along well, are you?" Sepia supposed that Laurence hadn't taken her advice about Louise today.

"I think he's seeing someone." Louise looked around the room as if searching for the woman in question.

"That isn't his style," Sepia said. "You know what happened with his father and how it killed his mother when she found out. He wouldn't cheat."

"He won't talk to me anymore. It's like since we've been staying together, I see him less than before."

"You know how men are, Louise. When the relationship reaches the next stage of commitment, they tend to draw away. It just means they're scared. You have to back off and let him adjust to this."

"I feel like maybe I rushed him into us staying at each other's places. I thought it would be okay, because I wasn't suggesting we live together."

"He agreed, didn't he? Laurence doesn't do anything he doesn't want to."

Louise couldn't seem to be satisfied, and Sepia couldn't stand to see her heartbroken.

"He's been so busy with this club. It's the first month. I'm sure things will calm down soon." Sepia wasn't so sure she believed this and she loved Louise too much to keep it from her much longer even if it did hurt her.

"Could be," Louise said, trying to reason. "But he's on the phone all the time and has to run out constantly. I ask him to talk about it, but he brushes me off. Honestly, telling me about seeing you today was the most he's talked to me in a while."

Sepia brushed Louise's hair with her fingers gently. "Poor baby. I'll talk to him, okay?"

Louise's eyes lit up. "You will? Promise?"

"Of course." Sepia was just happy to see her smile.

"Don't let on that I know you're doing it though."

"Of course not. Look, he's just not the real emotional type, Louise. You have to understand that sometimes he's not going to be what you need unless you let him know."

"I don't expect one of the characters from your books," she said, "but I expect him to care. I want to marry him and belong here."

"You belong anywhere you want to be," Sepia said. "With or without Laurence."

"Do you really think I would be here if you weren't my friend and Laurence wasn't my boyfriend?"

Sepia didn't really have an answer for that. She was pretty sure what the answer was, but didn't want to say it. She cared too much for her.

"So how was Paul looking at me exactly?" she asked.

Louise smiled suspiciously. "Like a man looks at

a woman, I guess. I would think you'd be offended, but you don't look at all offended."

Sepia spoke somberly. "It doesn't matter. The fact is that no matter what faults these people have, this is where I come from, and if he can't respect that, he'll never respect me."

"You could do so much better anyway," Louise said.

Sepia smiled, but deep inside she was doing anything but smiling. The truth was the more she got to know Paul, the more she believed that she could do a lot worse. Any woman could do a lot worse than Paul Healy.

Paul watched Sepia with Louise from a distance. He was feeling fine about the security, but upset with himself for angering Sepia. She was easily offended when it came to her social set, but he had to be honest. He wanted this case to be solved more than anything, but he knew what that meant for him and Sepia and it wasn't what he wanted even though he knew it should be.

His eyes followed Sepia as she and Louise made their way outside onto the verandah. He waited until they were far out before stepping outside himself. He nodded to one of the security guards closer to Sepia, and the guard nodded back before turning to follow Sepia. Paul relaxed a bit. Maybe he could take a little break and get a bite to eat.

He made his way to one of the various buffet tables set up with duck skewers, prosciutto, caviar, and foie gras. He was used to a gathering of black folks with a much different menu, the kind that made a man have to lie down for a long time after he ate. Still, this stuff looked good too and Paul was hungry. As he started for the plates, he was stopped in his tracks when he saw who was standing right at the edge of the buffet table.

Elaine. Not just Elaine, but Elaine and her new husband, Trent Ryden. Paul felt anxiety rip through him. He hadn't seen her in over two years, when she'd made a point of stopping by his apartment to show off her fat engagement ring and tell him about how successful her pediatrician fiancé was. She had seemed disappointed when he showed no jealousy or anger. She actually asked him why he was holding back. The truth was he had let her go a long time ago and she didn't want to hear that. She wanted to hear him say he regretted letting her go and admit that he should have tried harder to give her what she wanted. He didn't say any of that. He just said, "Congratulations, I hope you'll be happy," and felt bad when she cried and ran back to her new Lexus.

He never understood these things about Elaine, but when he met her he was young and he loved her. She wanted to get married and he sort of did. Paul could look back and see so many signs that it wasn't right, but he wanted to make something of his life, and Elaine seemed to have faith in his potential. Only their goals were complete opposites and, in the end, it became a wide-awake nightmare of a marriage until she finally left him.

Now looking at her, Paul couldn't ignore her beauty. She was thirty-four years old and looked refined and delicate. She fit in with the country club crowd so well and Paul knew she had spent years changing herself so she would. When he'd met her, she had a girl-next-door look about her. Now she was a glamorous woman who looked worldly and expensive. Her cocoa-brown skin was shiny. Her long black hair held tight, classic curls around her face. The black designer dress hung perfectly on her petite figure.

Paul felt guilty for looking at her and not wanting her anymore. He felt as if their marriage at least deserved that he would feel something whenever he saw her, but he didn't. The end had been ugly and the time apart had been healing. He could only hope she was happy, even though it didn't look like she was.

She was arguing with Trent, a stodgy, proper, previously divorced man in his early forties. Not arguing in the way she used to argue with Paul, shouting at the top of her lungs. They were arguing in the high society way. Their lips were barely moving and no raised voices could be heard, but her posture and the look on her well-made-up face told Paul everything he needed to know. She was mad about something and Trent didn't seem to be too far away from her with his eyes almost slits as he spoke to her. With a forceful move, he slammed an empty wineglass on the table and turned and walked away. Paul looked at Elaine, seeing shock cloud her face. Elaine got very angry when someone walked away from her.

Only she wasn't getting angry, and as Paul saw a tear begin to trail down her cheek, he knew he couldn't stand by and observe anymore.

"Are you okay?"

Elaine did a double take and her eyes widened. She almost stepped back as she took a moment to make sure it was Paul she was actually seeing.

"Paul?"

"Hi, Elaine."

"What in the hell are you doing here?"

Paul wondered if she had meant to be as rude as she sounded, but it didn't matter much to him. "Nice to see you too."

She smirked. "You can't possibly be a guest here. How did you get in? Did you come because of me?"

"Don't get ahead of yourself, Elaine. I'm not here for you. I'm here for the book signing."

This time she laughed out loud, flipping her hair back. "Yeah, right. You don't even read."

"Actually I read a lot, Elaine. If you had been paying attention while we were married you would know that."

Elaine scowled, looking at him with threatening eyes. "You never read romance. I can vouch for that at least."

Paul smiled at her, showing no sign of wear due to her nasty attitude. "Are you suggesting I wasn't romantic? I would disagree, but what does it matter? It's the past and you seem extremely happy now, so you couldn't care less."

The injured look on her face caught Paul off guard and he felt bad.

"I'm sorry," he said. "That wasn't nice. I could see you two were fighting."

"It was nothing," she said hastily. "Trent is so passionate about some things, it gets frustrating. He's not a big romance fan either, but he knows that when the Davis family is involved, you show up."

"Does he know Sepia?"

"He knows her father." Elaine searched the room. "I haven't met her myself, but I plan on making introductions tonight. I can't seem to find her at all."

"I can introduce you to her."

Elaine's brows centered. "Like you know her, right?"

"I came here with her tonight, so I probably could say I know her." Paul watched with amusement as Elaine tried to search him to see if he was kidding or not. "I'm guarding her, Elaine. That's why I'm here."

"Oh." Elaine sighed as if monumentally relieved to hear this. "Because of that awful mess in the parking lot across from the Italian Café. Are you moonlighting?"

"No, I'm doing this as a favor to the chief of police."

Elaine gave that mildly approving smile she was so famous for. "Isn't that impressive? Well, I know you'll do a good job. You're a good cop."

"Thanks." He honestly appreciated that.

"I'm glad they have you on the case. We couldn't lose a woman like Sepia Davis." Her eyes seemed to dance just at the mention of the woman's name. "Unlike some of those others."

Paul frowned, wishing he wasn't sure what she'd meant by that, but he was, and it hurt his feelings to know a woman he'd once cared for thought like that. "It was nice seeing you again, Elaine."

He turned to walk away, but she called his name in that voice that he knew meant she was vulnerable. It usually preceded an apology. Reluctantly, Paul turned back to her.

"You asked me if I was okay," she said.

Paul nodded. "You said it was nothing, right?"

She looked at him, her eyes glossing over a bit. "I did love you, Paul. I know you don't think I did."

"Elaine, there is no need for that." The last thing he needed was to dredge up those conversations, fights, or whatever they were.

Elaine continued as if she'd never heard him. "I know I told you I hated you more than I told you I loved you, but I was so angry."

"I know." Paul braced himself as her hand came to his arm. She was rubbing his arm, looking at him with distant eyes. Her always distant eyes made him wonder if anything was genuine. "Elaine, please."

"I am happy now," she said. "That's what you said you wanted for me."

Paul placed his hand over hers, squeezing it as he smiled at her. "Yes, that's what I wanted."

"Hello."

As soon as Paul saw it was Sepia joining them, he removed Elaine's hand from his arm. She had a look of polite curiosity as she glanced from Paul to Elaine.

"Sepia!" Elaine pulled herself together quickly. "It's so nice to meet you. You were wonderful tonight."

"Thank you." Sepia leaned forward to shake the woman's hand, but the woman unexpectedly grabbed her and hugged her as if they were friends. "You are?"

Paul began. "This is—"

"I'm Elaine Ryden." Elaine acted as if Paul weren't even there anymore. "You might know my husband, Dr. Trent Ryden."

"Oh, yes," Sepia said. "Nice of you to come."

Sepia found herself compelled to come over the second she saw Paul talking to this very attractive woman. She could be honest with herself and admit it was a little bit of jealousy, but she'd rather believe it was just curiosity as to whom Paul had deemed worthy of his conversation. That is, until she touched his arm and Sepia's feet picked up the pace. The look in her eyes as the woman looked at Paul told her this was not their first meeting, and Sepia couldn't mind her own business like she knew she should.

"I wouldn't have missed this for anything," Elaine

said, her words laced with saccharine. "I've read all of your books. I told my husband he should read them too. You know it's so nice to read about positive black love. Everything else is so trashy and dirty."

Elaine was still talking, but Sepia had turned to Paul and felt full of wonder as to why he was looking everywhere but at Elaine Ryden. He was upset and uncomfortable and Sepia couldn't stand not knowing why.

"And how do you know Paul here?" she asked.

Paul's head whipped around as he caught Sepia's eyes. Her smile wasn't hiding anything. She was being possessive and he couldn't deny that he liked it. However, with Elaine's penchant for attitude, this situation could go bad any moment, so it would be best to end it quickly.

"Actually," he said, "we were—"

Elaine cleared her throat. "I want to introduce you to my husband. He's inside."

Not even bothering to wait for a response, Elaine turned and headed inside. Her hand was waving to Sepia to follow her, but she didn't look back. She assumed Sepia was following, but she wasn't. The second Elaine turned, Paul grabbed Sepia by the arm and pulled her the opposite way. She allowed him this, not bothering to say a word as he led her far from everyone.

She looked at him as he leaned against the waist-high stone fence that guarded the verandah from the edges of the golf course. He was looking out at nothing and she was touched by the length to which she cared about what he was feeling right now. She watched his strong, proud face until he sighed and looked at her. He stared into her eyes and she saw a burden inside him that she wanted to lighten.

"You are incredibly beautiful," he said, unable to keep it inside. "In the moonlight, you shine."

Sepia almost caught her breath. His words slid over her like a warm blanket and made her tingle. It wasn't just the words. It was the way he looked at her. There was no pretense, no guard up. He was completely open right now.

"Thank you." Her words came out as more of a whisper.

"Did I hurt you?" he asked.

Sepia just now realized that she was rubbing her arm where he had grabbed her to lead her out here. "You do have quite a grip on you."

"I'm sorry." He reached for her, rubbing the spot as she let her hand go. "I'm used to dealing with perps and you have to have a strong hand."

Inside, Sepia felt like the calm before a summer storm ready to leash out. "I didn't mind."

Paul looked at her, feeling the quickening of his pulse in response to the softness of her skin. He didn't want to ever stop rubbing. As a matter of fact, he wanted to rub her everywhere and he knew that was why he had to stop. When he removed his hand it was like fighting gravity, taking force on his part.

"It's much better now, thanks." Sepia felt her body reacting to his touch, and for once she wasn't confused or concerned by it. She was turned on and she wanted to enjoy it, but as he pulled away she didn't protest.

"She's my wife," he said matter-of-factly.

"What?" Sepia wasn't sure what she'd heard. "Elaine? That woman is your wife?"

"My ex-wife." He nodded, turning back to the greens. He looked over the expanse of the course, hoping its distraction would keep him from getting emotional. Something about Sepia made him want to let go.

"I could tell you knew her," Sepia said, thinking all sorts of things at the moment. "The way she looked at you."

"Don't confuse anything she does with real feeling, Sepia."

"You want to talk about it?" She leaned against the fence, wanting to move closer to him but deciding it best not to.

"You don't want to hear this," he said, looking down.

"I do. So much etiquette and well-wishes tonight. I want to hear something real."

After a short pause, Paul spoke again. "We were married for four years. From the beginning, I knew she wanted more than a cop's salary could give her, but I'm a forward-thinking guy. I wasn't intimidated by the money her gallery was bringing her. I was glad it was making up for what I wasn't making yet."

"Most guys couldn't stand it if their wife made more money than them."

"I just wanted her to be happy," Paul said. "I loved her and I felt like I was a good husband. Only, money wasn't the real issue with Elaine. She wanted to be somebody."

Sepia knew all too well what he meant.

"I didn't want anything to do with Cromwell," Paul said. "I was proud of where I came from, and as much as I liked nice things I didn't have a need to be accepted by people I knew would never really accept me. I have friends and I had Elaine. At least I thought I did."

"That's why you divorced?" Sepia wanted so badly to reach out and touch him, but she didn't trust her own feelings right now.

"That led to so many other problems. It was the underlying factor that made everything else such a big deal. In the end, I wasn't enough for her so she left. I let her go."

"I'd never seen her before, but when she told me who her husband was, I thought it sounded familiar."

"She says he knows your father."

"Daddy is sponsoring him to get into this elite men's club that he wants to join. It's very hard to get in. He's a pediatrician, right?"

Paul nodded.

"I overheard Daddy saying that he wasn't happy in his marriage. He didn't say why, but I think they're having problems."

Paul thought about what she said for a moment. She was trying to be helpful. "I know I'm supposed to be happy to hear that, but I'm not. Honestly, I don't love Elaine anymore, but I loved her once and I want her to be happy. I hope they work it out."

Sepia couldn't hide the emotion that rushed through her. She felt tears welling in her eyes. He really meant what he said. "That's why I like you so much, Paul. You're not happy she's having problems and that says so much about you. The quality of your character. It's just so . . ."

He was soaking in every word. It meant too much, what she thought of him. "What?"

"Different, I guess." Sepia sighed. "I'm so used to people who give you love and kisses to your face, but the second something falls apart they just relish the opportunity to talk about you behind your back."

"You seem to be the queen of the court tonight at least."

"Of course, but look at them." She pointed to the crowds of guests several feet away from them. "They aren't paying attention to us, because they don't see us. Right now, they're talking about how much of a shame it is I got caught up with that boy, Jason. How they all knew he was no good. Poor Sepia just has no luck, they say, as a little smile forms at the edges of their lips."

Paul smiled. "It sounds like you're writing a book."

"Reality is more painful than fiction," she said. "Because what will happen is I'll walk back that way and the second they see me, they'll fawn all over me and tell me how great they think I am. It's all so empty."

"Not all of them." He looked at her. "You said there are some good apples."

Sepia thought of Louise and Laurence and others she knew to be genuine. "That's right. There's good and bad in every bunch."

"That's the lesson, I guess. You take your chances. Sometimes you end up with good ones, sometimes bad ones, but you never give up searching for the right people to surround your life with."

She looked at him, taking pleasure in his optimism and encouraging smile. "Amen, brother."

"Jason was a fool." Paul turned back, leaning over the fence.

Sepia smiled inside, leaning toward him. "So was Elaine."

"I wish I had done better," Paul said, shaking his head. "A failed marriage is a painful thing."

Everything he said made her want him more. "The fact that you believe that tells me that when you get the right woman, you'll do it right."

She laid her hand gently on his back and she

rubbed it with all the intentions of being comforting. She knew she was getting herself into danger, but she wanted to show him in more than words that she understood him. "You'll find her, you know."

Paul didn't respond. He didn't even trust himself to speak with the feelings her touch was raising within him.

"You're a good man, Paul." She removed her hand, too distracted by the pull in her belly. "Last I checked there's still a market for that."

He laughed, turning his head slightly to look at her eye to eye. "You think so? I doubt it would be good enough for any of the women here tonight."

"Don't be too sure of that, Officer."

The intensity he felt as he looked into her eyes floored Paul. He knew he was attracted to this woman, but what he was feeling now was so much more than that. A smoldering flame ignited between them as he pulled her to him. His lips descended down on hers with a tenderness he fought to maintain because his desire for her was so strong.

Sepia's skin tingled all over as his lips claimed hers. She felt herself melt into his body as she reached out to pull him closer. She wanted to taste every bit of him with this kiss and pressed harder. Tenderness wasn't enough. She wanted more.

A delicious sensation swept through Paul as their lips parted and their tongues explored each other. His hands traveled up her arms, gently cradling her neck as he savored every bit of her. He had never known such a painful sweetness as the taste of her lips.

Sepia felt her mind begin to leave her, the world escape her, and she knew that she only had one last chance. As her body's pleasure tried to drown out the rest of the world, she held on to the one truth and it was that Paul had just seen his ex-wife and now he was kissing her. It nagged at Sepia enough to make her push away, uncertain of the pain that could come if she let the pleasure continue.

"I don't want to . . ." She had to catch her breath to continue. "I'm not a snob, Paul. I don't think like all of those people."

"I know." He reached for her, wanting nothing but her lips on his and his hands on her body again.

Sepia stepped back, trying so hard to look into his eyes without throwing herself at him. "But I'm not a replacement for your ex-wife either."

Paul stopped, struck by her words. "I didn't think that, Sepia. You know this has been building between us for a while now."

"I know." Sepia felt uneasy about admitting it, but after that kiss, there was no way she could deny it. "But like the last time I couldn't honestly say it wasn't about my fear. Can you honestly say now this isn't about seeing Elaine?"

"It's about seeing you and standing here talking to you." He saw the doubt in her eyes and didn't want to push it. "But I will admit that I'm feeling a lot of things tonight, Sepia."

"Me too." She was seeing him in a different light now. He wasn't a cop. He wasn't her protector or guard. He was a man and she was a woman who wanted him. "This is just so unexpected and I don't know what to think right now."

Paul didn't see the need to think at all right now. He knew what he wanted, but it wasn't that simple and that was the problem. Nothing was simple between them. He looked over at the crowd, seeing Louise walking toward them waving her hand to get their attention. It all reminded him of what made this anything but simple. As much as the world disappeared when he touched her, it would be there waiting for them when their lips separated, and he had to consider that their worlds were completely different.

"I understand," he said, forcing a smile so she would feel better. "I've got a job to do tonight anyway."

"You're doing great," Sepia said, happy that he understood. The last thing she wanted was for him to feel rejected, but she was too scared of the feelings that kiss stirred inside her. "I've got a job tonight too."

Paul watched her as she headed toward Louise, who promptly led her back to the adoring crowds. He had to smile even though he was anything but happy. The irony of this woman coming into his life, representing everything he thought he hated, resented for that matter. Now here he was, wanting her more than he could ever remember wanting anyone and not sure what in the world to do about it.

To say that night at the safe house was extremely tense would be an understatement. From the bedroom, Sepia could feel the heat coming from the living room where Paul was sleeping. Although he had kept his distance from her for the rest of the evening, Sepia had been aware of his presence every second. His eyes on her were searing through her clothes, her skin, and she felt herself begin to sweat at the thought of his lips on hers. She was in trouble in more ways than one, but she knew her life being in danger had to take priority here. If she got involved with Paul now, couldn't things get confused or sloppy? What then?

Paul got up and began pacing the living room floor, wondering if he was better off sleeping in his car. He was too tempted to walk down the hall and into her room. He wouldn't be able to turn back then. He had wanted her more and more as the night went on, unable to take his eyes off of her. He was jealous of everyone as they touched her, kissed her cheek, and received her smiles and conversation. During the ride home, he was preoccupied with making sure he wasn't followed, but once he was certain of it, he was only aware of Sepia and the light way with which she spoke of the evening. She'd had a couple of glasses of wine and the staid, proper woman in her was more relaxed, making her all the more enticing. All the more dangerous, considering he knew he should be thinking of nothing but her safety. There was a sadistic serial murderer out there somewhere and he was after Sepia. Paul would never be able to live with himself if he let his distraction for her take him off guard and something happened. Nothing was worth that.

Seven

Having gotten barely any sleep, Paul was ticked off that his cell phone went off just as he began to doze a bit. It was light outside, so he knew it was morning, but he wanted every bit of sleep he could get. He checked the LED display before answering.

"What's up, Luke?"

"Not you from what you sound like."

Paul sat up on the sofa. "Any news?"

"We haven't gotten him yet, but we're doing better."

"What do you have?"

"We have a new witness who remembers the blue VW near the first murder, so that just ties him to everything. The chief finally got that group of protestors to back off. I mean, jeez, they got to give us a day or two. Their feeling is, there aren't a lot of white folks in Crawford, so if one is going around murdering people, why can't we round them all up like we seem to be able to do so easily when it's the other way around?"

"We don't do that."

"I know, but you know what they meant. What's important is that they aren't going to protest today, so we can get our work done without hearing that yelling. I'm on my way to follow up on some pawnshops."

"Why?" Paul remembered Luke telling him that nothing was stolen from either the Connor or Sanders house.

"Just wishful thinking. Sanders's wife is a basket case, so it's possible something is missing she can't remember. The daughter doesn't think so."

"What about the list from the country club?"

"Got it. That guy. Uh . . ."

"Laurence?"

"Yeah, Laurence. He was nice. We showed him the warrant and he helped us out right away. I wish they all went like that."

Laurence, nice? Paul wondered what that was about. He remembered that Laurence liked Sanders a lot and maybe he was being honest when he said he wanted to help. Paul could only figure that the rude way he was treated was because Laurence thought it was two different things to be polite to the working class and to date them.

"I don't think we'll get anything," Luke said. "But you do, don't you?"

"Me? Not really. I just thought it would help. If the murderer strikes again, it will probably be someone from that list. The more information we have on the previous victims, maybe we can find a pattern that tells us who might be next."

"Good thinking, Healy. Between this and the deal guarding the princess, you're covering your back real well."

"She's not a princess, Luke. She's actually a very

nice woman." There was a long silence on the phone and Paul knew what was coming. "Don't start with me, Luke."

"She's a very nice woman? Isn't that a gentleman's code for I want to get with her?"

Paul laughed. "That would be unprofessional, wouldn't it?"

"You got to do something while you're out there."

"What I really want to do is help solve this thing so we can all get back to our regular lives."

"We all do, buddy. Look, I want you to know that what you're doing is great. You're helping me out a lot and the chief mentioned you and all that. You just remember that you're doing what it takes to make it to the next step and that's something to be proud of."

Something was wrong. Paul knew whenever Luke waxed poetic like this, he was holding back on something. Softening the blow. "What's going on, Luke?"

Another pause. "It's David."

Paul tightened up. "Just tell me he's okay."

"He's not hurt, if that's what you mean."

"Good. What is it then?"

"He's in jail, Paul."

"What in the—"

"Not what you think. None of those . . . suspicions have come down on him yet."

"They're just suspicions anyway," Paul said. "So what happened?"

"It was Patsy." Another, longer pause. It was gonna get worse. "He hit her."

Paul dropped the phone. He reached for it again, certain he had heard wrong. "You're kidding, right?"

"No. Well, he didn't really hit her. He shoved her, but she's pregnant, so what's the difference, right?"

There was no difference. It wasn't possible that David would do that to Patsy, pregnant or not. "Go on."

"Well, they apparently got into a big fight about money and he lost it. She called the cops and Donny and Bill came over and calmed him down. They didn't want to bring him in, but she was so upset they all thought it would be best."

Cops were like that. Paul knew it wasn't always right, but they wanted to give each other the benefit of the doubt. Only in situations like this, you had to follow the law. If David really hit Patsy, which Paul was having a hard time believing, then he was where he belonged.

"This is my fault," Paul said.

"How do you figure? He's a grown man."

"I'm his partner and I've been running off to country clubs and book signings while his life is falling apart." Paul wondered if David had even tried to reach him in the past couple of days. "He blew up at me the last time we talked and I should have reached out to him."

"You're not Superman, Paul."

"But it looks like now I'm all he has."

"We'll see what Patsy wants to do. She hasn't pressed charges yet."

"I have to see him," Paul said.

"I sent Dunleavy over about a half hour ago, so he'll be there soon."

Paul looked down the hallway toward Sepia's bedroom. He didn't want to leave her. He remembered how upset she was before. She would have to understand this time. He was too angry to even talk to her right now. He cursed himself for having all these balls in the air. This was why things were falling apart.

"I'll be ready when he gets here."

* * *

Sepia hadn't slept well at all last night. Part of her wondered if Paul would come to her, some of her wishing that. When he infiltrated her dreams, it was passionate and warm, but the dreams would inevitably turn to terror. The problem was, every time she dreamt of Paul, that man would soon come. The man who had tried to kill her before and had likely killed at least three other people. The switch from desire to bloodcurdling fear woke her several times in the night and now she had exhausted any chance of getting any more sleep.

She sat on the edge of her bed for a long time, wondering what she would say to Paul when she walked out there. Would she pretend last night never happened? Or for that matter, the other night he had kissed her? The intimacies were starting to pile up. Would she ask him to talk about it? Would he be angry and reject her because she turned away from him last night? All of these questions were sweeping through her emotions and Sepia had sworn to herself not to let this into her life so soon again. She wanted to take time off since Jason and get back to herself, but she was finding that this was not something you could schedule according to your comfort.

Still, she couldn't let it consume her. Her life was in danger, after all, and if Paul needed to keep his mind clear in order to protect her, then she would leave him alone. For now.

When she opened her bedroom door, the smell of bacon and eggs streamed up her nose and brought a smile to her face. He cooked breakfast too? This guy was getting better and better every minute.

"Paul, I . . ." When she entered the kitchen,

Sepia stopped in her tracks at the familiar face she met. "Dunleavy, what are you doing here?"

"Cooking some grub!" He smiled, waving his spatula in the air. "I had to get over here real early, so I didn't have time to eat. I'm starving. How 'bout you?"

Sepia was searching the rest of the cabin. "Just tell me that Paul is outside."

He turned to her, unsure of what to say. "Will you blame me if he isn't?"

"No, I'll blame him," she said. "But I might throw something, so you've been warned."

"Well, he's not here." Dunleavy ducked for a moment, but came back up.

Sepia was fuming. But wait. . . . "Was there another murder last night?"

"No, thank God." Dunleavy turned back to his food. "This was a personal thing, I think."

"What do you mean?" Sepia rushed back to him. It was one thing for his job to take him away, but what personal business would make him leave her?

"Not sure," he said. "It's about some woman, I know that much."

Sepia's mouth opened, but nothing came out for a few seconds. "A woman?"

He shrugged, his back still to her. "Yeah. Luke said it was about some woman. I don't remember her name. Something about marriage problems. I asked who she was and he said don't worry, it was personal, but that Paul needed to get back and see her."

Sepia felt as if she had been knocked over. She had to grab the edge of the kitchen counter just to keep upright. What had she been thinking? Paul had never mentioned whether or not there was a woman in his life. She had assumed not. After all, they had opened up to each other, and if there was a current girlfriend . . .

Sepia felt the green monster nipping at her when she thought of Elaine. Of course. That had to be it. Marital problems. Had Elaine called in the middle of the night? Sepia was sure that their encounter at the club had to have some effect on Paul. She remembered the look on Elaine's face when she had approached them in the middle of their conversation. Elaine still had feelings for him, that was obvious.

Sepia was fuming as she played scenarios out in her mind. A phone call in the middle of the night. *I was thinking of you. Seeing you again made me think. I'm so unhappy, Paul. Can you come over? I need to talk to you. We loved each other once.*

That was why he left without talking to her. He was feeling guilty after kissing her, protesting her suggestion that it was because he wanted to kiss Elaine, and then going to Elaine after all. Was he holding her now? Was he in her bed?

"Stop it!"

Dunleavy turned around, a little confused and slightly scared in reaction to her yelling. "Me? Stop it? I'm just cooking—"

"Not you," Sepia corrected. "Me. I have to stop it. Stop this. All of this."

"What are you doing?"

"Never mind." She turned and rushed down the hallway.

Falling onto the bed, Sepia dug her nails into her palms to keep from crying. She was not going to cry over this. Over that man. She barely knew him and it was just too soon to care that much. She couldn't let jealousy get the best of her. It was an emotion that could cause nothing but pain and harm and she had too much to worry about to let it matter.

She wanted to call Louise and whine to her. That would get it out of her system and she could let this thing with Paul die. But she wouldn't. She knew that Louise was going through her own romantic problems. The last thing she needed was to hear Sepia cry about a romance that really didn't even exist. What she needed was for Sepia to be a friend and do what she had promised she would. She needed to talk to Laurence about communicating more and doing what he could to sway her concerns about their future. Maybe that would make her feel better. If her own love life wasn't worth anything, she could focus her energy on helping someone else's work. That's what friends were for, right?

The only thing left was figuring out how she was going to get out of the safe house and to the club. She had to figure it out, because Sepia knew if she stayed here waiting for Paul to come back, if he ever did for that matter, she would go crazy.

Paul slammed the door to his apartment, staring David down as he slumped onto the sofa. After bailing David out of jail, he offered to let him stay at his place while he worked things out with Patsy. Paul had tried to reach her as well, but she wasn't talking to him or anyone. She was especially not talking to David, and Paul tried to impress upon him the importance of the situation. David didn't want to hear much of anything. He was brooding and complained the entire time, only speaking up once to thank Paul for the use of his place.

Paul paced the floor in his living room. He had

all the requisites for a bachelor pad that was comfortable, but not stylish. His place was small, but it was also in one of the nicest neighborhoods in Crawford. He had been one of the first tenants in the garden-style apartments. The landlord was excited. It was his intention to let everyone know that a cop lived there, so any riffraff would steer clear. He even offered Paul a cut on the rent if he parked his police car out front every night. Paul had refused the cut of course, but promised to park it there on the nights he had it.

The size of the apartment didn't matter much. When Paul wasn't working, which was hardly ever, he was usually at David's house or Luke's. They had families, after all, and he wasn't going to have one any time soon.

"You're gonna talk to me," Paul said as he sat on the chair across from his sofa. He stared intensely at David, who looked like a moody teenager in the principal's office.

David shifted in the seat, avoiding eye contact with Paul. He sighed, lowering his head into his hands. Paul was waiting patiently when he saw David's shoulders heave and heard a whimper. He was crying. Paul had been so angry with him after finding out that Patsy's accusations were true, and he was ready to flip his lid now.

"You're crying?" Paul asked. "Patsy's the one who was abused and you're crying?"

David looked up, his eyes red, tears coming down his face. "I know that."

"You know what?"

"I know I've ruined my life."

"You're still talking about yourself, David."

"Cut me some slack, Paul. I've been in jail all night."

"I'm not going to cut you anything. You hit her, David. How could you do something like that?"

David threw his hands in the air. "I don't know! I mean it, man. I don't know why I would do that. I love Patsy more than myself and I've never, ever done that before. I tried to apologize."

"Saying I'm sorry isn't going to cut it," Paul said. "What are you going to do to fix this?"

"I'm gonna talk to her." David nodded quickly as if this would solve all of his problems. "She'll understand me. She always understands."

"This is different, David, and you know it." Paul was losing his patience. "This is the moment for you."

David looked at him as if he didn't understand.

"Your life," Paul said. "This is the moment where you decide you're going to go one way or the other."

"I know that."

"So cut the self-pity and hopeful explanations and come out with it. Come out with everything."

"I love her."

"I'm talking about what led to all of this," Paul said. "You know what I mean. That's the beginning and that's where you have to go to start to make this right."

David looked at Paul and their eyes locked for what seemed like a long time. Paul could see that David was on the edge of the character of the man he would be from this day forward. He had regretfully not been there for David the way he should have been, but he was here now and he would not blink. He would stare David in the eye and not let him cop out this time for anything.

David blinked, turning away with a sigh.

"It started with the gambling," he said, leaning

back as if settling in for a long story. "Betting on every game I could. College and pros. Even some high school hoops."

"I thought it was recreational," Paul said.

"In front of you it was. In reality, I'm an addict. I thought I had it under control. Whenever things got tight, I would move money where I needed to in order to cover it up. But when Patsy told me she was pregnant again, I knew I couldn't hide this anymore. I couldn't pay Spike anymore, but I couldn't stop gambling."

Paul knew that "Spike" was one of the leaders of the Ravens gang, which handled most of the illegal gambling around Crawford. Paul had had a personal hatred for the man since he and Luke failed to tie him to the murder of a fireman who was going to go public about his debts to him.

"Did he threaten you?" Paul asked. "Threaten the family?"

"He gave me a choice," David said. "I could let him know what we knew about them and give him the heads-up when we were closing in."

Paul lowered his head. He knew, but held on to hope it was all a lie, a series of coincidences and misunderstandings that David could clearly explain. "That night when we—"

"I let him go," David said. "He ran right past me and I faked it."

Paul didn't look up for a while, even though he knew that David was staring at him, waiting for him to tell him that he didn't hate him. When Paul did look up, he said nothing, but there wasn't any hint of hatred in his eyes. He was his partner and his friend, and as angry as he was with him right now, Paul wouldn't turn his back on David.

"After I was put on desk duty," David continued, "I couldn't help out and Spike told me I had to pay. So, I . . ."

David looked away again and a whimper escaped him. Paul waited until he pulled himself together.

"I stole money from Patsy's parents."

Paul let out a sigh that said it all. He couldn't hide his disappointment and anger. This was worse than he could imagine. He felt for Patsy even more now.

"When did Patsy find out?" he asked.

"Her mother told her that they got the returned check before I was able to get the money together to pay them back."

"Where did you think you were going to get the money to do that?" The look on David's face answered the question. Gambling.

"Patsy went crazy on me when she found out. She said her father was going to press charges against me and I just lost it. I tried to tell her it was for her and the family, but she started throwing things at me. I tried to restrain her, but she wouldn't stop. So, I . . ."

"She could have lost the baby," Paul said.

"I would never have hit her hard enough for that," David pleaded.

"Exactly how hard is enough?" Paul asked. "You don't know what you could have done. You and the pressure of the situation you've brought on yourself could have combined to cost you everything. You'll have a hard enough time fixing this as it is if she gives you that chance."

David slumped over again. "If she doesn't forgive me, I'll kill myself."

"Stop it," Paul said. "You're feeling sorry for yourself again. How much?"

David looked up, confused. "What?"

"How much did you take from her parents?"

"Um, uh, five grand."

"Five grand?" Paul whistled. "I'll get it out of my savings and pay them back."

"No way," David said.

"You're in enough trouble, David. The last thing you need now is for them to press charges against you. You're a cop. The press will go crazy."

"I still owe Spike fifteen hundred bucks."

"Spike can go to hell. When you tell Pitt what you've done, you're gonna offer up everything on Spike. It better be enough to make it worth it. You'll get a deal for him. You're a cop with a good record and he's one of the leaders of the worst gang in Crawford. They don't want to bring a cop down."

"You want me to turn myself in?"

Paul looked at David as if he were a two-year-old. "Let's focus on what you're going to say."

"I'll go to jail, Paul." David was up now, pacing the room. "You know what happens to cops in jail."

Paul shot up, grabbing David by the collar and jerking him forward. "Stop thinking about yourself and let's figure out what we're going to tell Pitt."

"I'm not just thinking of myself," David said. "You'll never make detective if this comes out. You didn't do anything, but you're my partner and you know it always rubs off."

Paul didn't want to think that mattered, but it did, and David was right. Paul sat back down, thinking of what they could do. David had to confess, there was no debating that. It might hurt Paul and that couldn't be avoided, but there had to be ways of minimizing the damage for both of them. He had seen it before.

"I can figure something out," Paul said. "Right now you focus on Patsy and what you can do to earn her forgiveness and trust back. I'll pay her parents back. I don't know them that well, but I'll make sure they understand it's not helping anyone to make this situation worse."

"Luke gave me the number to a counselor for . . ." David shook his head as if not believing the words coming out of this mouth. "Spousal abuse. I can set up an appointment."

Paul nodded. "Patsy might appreciate the gesture, but don't expect her to tell you. Don't expect anything from her, okay?"

"I won't," he answered. "What about you and your promotion coming up in a few months?"

"I know someone who is connected to the chief in a way that might work in our favor."

"Really?" David asked.

Paul nodded. He couldn't believe he was thinking of this, but this whole situation was too volatile to leave to chance.

"I can't begin to thank you, man." David reached out for Paul and hugged him tight. "You're saving my life."

"Only you can do that," Paul said. "But I'm happy to do what I can. I'm sorry I haven't been around lately. I could have done something sooner and last night might not ever have happened."

"You've been working hard," David said, patting his back. "It's all official, I know that. It's not like you've been running around having a good time or chasing after some girl."

Paul felt guilt creep over him as he reached for his ringing cell phone.

"What's up, Luke?" he asked.

"What's going on with your girl, Paul?"

Paul didn't really know how to respond to that. "You talking about Sepia?"

"Is there any other woman in your life?"

"I don't know what to tell you," Paul said.

"Where is she?"

"She's at the safe house." Paul felt the hairs on the back of his neck stand up.

"No one is at the safe house, Paul. I've called twice."

"Have you tried Dunleavy's cell?"

"Yes, but it's coming back not in service right now. He's not in a cop car, so I can't radio him. Do I need to go out there?"

"I'll take care of it." Paul hung up the phone before he could say good-bye. Luke would understand.

"What's going on?" David asked as he watched Paul rustle through the small center drawer of the pinewood console table standing by the door.

"I've got to go." Paul tossed David a spare key to his place. "It's an emergency."

"I'll be fine," David said. "I've got a lot of thinking to do."

"I'd say so." Paul was halfway out the door.

"What's wrong?" David asked after him.

"I hope to God it's nothing."

Paul had never said truer words. He was slamming the door with one hand while dialing his cell with the other. He needed directory to find Sepia's cell phone number quick, but suddenly remembered that he'd thrown her phone in the lake. Cursing himself, Paul wasn't sure he could take it if anything happened to her after he'd left her behind.

Sepia slid into the booth next to Laurence in the lounge area of the club lobby. She followed Laurence's eyes to Dunleavy, who was sitting several feet away at the bar staring at them.

"Why is he here?" Laurence asked.

"I didn't have any choice," Sepia said. "He's my protection. You have no idea the convincing I had to do to get him to agree to bring me here."

"I'm sure it was easy for you," he said with a wink. "He's not near enough of a man to stand up to your beauty and brains."

Sepia smiled, accepted the mimosa the waitress handed her. "And, oh, yeah, he's drinking for free."

"Isn't he on duty?"

"Yes, but I said all the Pepsis are on the club."

"Money well wasted," Laurence said sarcastically. "I honestly wish he wasn't in his uniform. He sticks out enough because he's . . ."

"White?" Sepia asked. "You can say it. He is white and it's not a big deal. We have some white members."

"None that look like him," Laurence said, shifting a bit. "I'm just saying the uniform makes him even more conspicuous."

"Everyone knows there's heightened security around here." Sepia didn't understand why Laurence seemed so on edge about it. "Because of what's happening."

"It cost a lot of money," he said. "And it's not worth it anymore."

"Laurence, people are being killed."

"Not lately," he said. "It seems like it's over."

"I don't think anyone is willing to risk that. I'm not, considering this maniac just tried to kill me a few nights ago."

Laurence softened, seeming to realize what he was saying. "I'm sorry, Sepia. I haven't forgotten what happened to you. What almost happened to you."

Sepia took a sip. "I can't even bear to think of what would have happened if you hadn't showed up. You scared him off, Laurence."

Laurence smiled. "I don't know about scaring him off. I just messed up his plan. I don't know what would have happened had he stayed. I wasn't going to let him hurt you. Scumbag."

Sepia reached across the table, squeezing his hand and smiling her appreciation. "You saved my life."

"How are you doing?"

"As best as can be expected," she said. "Thanks to Officer Healy."

Laurence made a smacking sound with his lips. "Oh, him."

"Yes, him." Sepia nudged him. "Stop being such a snob. He's a great guy."

"I didn't say he wasn't, but . . . ."

"Not good enough for me, right?"

"I saw you with him at the book signing, Sepia. You were way too close. You're tempted to do the same thing you did with Jason."

"This is nothing like Jason."

"Another man that isn't good enough for you is something like Jason."

"You don't know Paul."

"And you'll waste another year of your life trying to make something work that can't possibly." Laurence shooed away the waitress who came to check on him. "She would make a good woman for that cop. Not you."

"That's cruel, Laurence." Sepia hoped the waitress hadn't heard. "Paul is nothing like Jason. It didn't work with Jason because he was using me to achieve social status."

"That can't be bought," Laurence said.

"Paul doesn't care at all about this stuff," she said, floating her hand around to indicate their regal surroundings. "If he's going to be with me, it will be just for me."

"Of course for him," Laurence said, zeroing in on Sepia. "But look me in the eyes and tell me that he'd be happy with your world. Here."

"This place isn't my life," Sepia said, growing more and more uncomfortable with the turn of this conversation. "It's just my country club."

"It's more than a club," Laurence said.

"Not to me, it isn't." Sepia wasn't sure she would have believed that a few weeks ago, but she did now. "None of this matters anyway. We're not a couple."

"So you go around kissing men just for the heck of it?"

Sepia pressed her lips together, choosing to keep her words. She shouldn't have assumed that she hadn't been seen kissing Paul last night just because, for her, the rest of the world disappeared the second his lips touched hers.

"He's not mine," she said, wondering if those lips were kissing Elaine right now. "That's all I can say."

"All I say I say because I care about you and I want what's best for you."

"I want what's best for me too, Laurence." Sepia

sighed. "Society standing and cotillions don't mean happiness."

"Would you rather have the policemen's ball be the highlight of your year?" Laurence asked. "And Red Lobster be the finest restaurant you dine at?"

"If I had true love, I'd rather have a night at the movies and McDonald's than anything else."

Laurence seemed to notice the determination in Sepia's eyes and he leaned back. He was done with his sermon.

"I didn't come here to talk about me," Sepia said. "I came to talk about you and Louise."

"Is she complaining again?" he huffed. "She's so needy, Sepia. I really can't take it. I'm very busy now."

"I know you are and I've explained that to her."

"Did she tell you to come lecture me?"

"No." Sepia crossed her fingers underneath the desk. "I could tell from last night how upset she was."

"She's always upset," he said, exasperated. "She should be more grateful."

"What?" Sepia was sure he meant that another way. "Grateful?"

"I'm very busy, Sepia. Every moment I spend with her is giving up something else."

"That's the least of what's expected in a relationship," she said. "The right focus would be for you to see that every moment you spend doing something else is giving up time with her. And she loves you. You have to know that it hurts when you love someone and they seem to want to be everywhere but home."

"Her house is not my home." Laurence looked away.

"You know what I mean." Sepia was sensing something bad here and she hated that she was the one to bring it out. "You do love her, don't you?"

Laurence seemed to be searching her eyes to determine what the penalty might be if he didn't answer her like she wanted him to.

"Did she tell you I was cheating on her?"

Sepia shook her head. "No, but are you?"

"I wouldn't tell you if I was," he said, "but I'm not. I barely have time for her. The last thing I need is another woman whining for my attention."

"I sure hope it's more than not having free time that is keeping you faithful."

Laurence smiled at her. "Plus the fact that you would slit my throat."

Sepia smiled back. "I would of course. But afterward, I would try to help you work it out."

"How kind of you."

Sepia waited awhile, wondering if he would pick it back up again. He wasn't going to. "I asked you if you loved her. You can tell me either way."

Laurence bit at his lower lip a bit like an indecisive teenaged boy. "When I met Louise, I assumed she was from a good family. She was with you, after all, and she behaved so perfectly."

"She's not a dog, Laurence." Sepia felt her heart sink. If Laurence loved Louise he would have said yes by now. "And she does come from a good family."

"You know what I mean."

"It didn't seem to matter to you when you found out she wasn't."

He shrugged. "You spoke highly of her. Richard Sanders spoke highly of her. Have you heard anything about Richard?"

Sepia shook her head.

"She was beautiful and aggressive," Laurence continued. "She was eager to please and understanding. After my mother's death, it was what I needed. Someone who was completely focused on me."

Laurence had been deeply depressed over his parents' deaths, and Sepia had known Louise, who had experienced the death of her own mother to cancer only a few years ago, could be a comfort of some sort to him. He seemed to open back up again through her and through the club.

"Things have been difficult lately," he said. "She's always pressuring me to commit more. She constantly wants to spend more and more time with me. She came out of nowhere with this urge for us to spend entire weekends at each other's place."

"It's not that unusual to spend the weekend together. You have been going out for almost eight months. You are not *dating* anymore."

"Yes, but really, how much longer can this go on?"

"What do you mean?" Sepia asked. "If it's love, it can go on forever."

"I can't marry her, Sepia. You can't possibly think it could go there."

Sepia felt a pain in her gut for Louise and she wanted to slap Laurence, but she held back. "How can you say that? You know she wants to get married."

"When I get married, I'm going to marry someone like you. A well-educated woman from a good family with a name that means something. Money and prestige. All of that."

He spoke so matter-of-factly as if he'd expected Sepia to know all of this. Know and agree.

"I don't know what to say, Laurence." Sepia searched his face for some regret, but he clearly had no problem with anything he was saying. "It doesn't have to be that way. Louise fits in here. People love her. She worships you and would make an incredible wife. She would support you and lift you up. She would be with you through thick and thin. Money and prestige can't promise you that. Only love can."

Laurence let out a bitter laugh that startled Sepia. He looked at her as if she were stupid.

"You can't mean that?" he asked.

"I certainly do." Sepia's tone was warning.

"You have a good heart, Sepia, but in the real world, love is the least of what matters."

"What's real is the world you two can make together."

"You think that because you like this cop and you want to believe that as long as he holds you under the covers at night and keeps you warm, you'll wake up to rainbows and kittens every morning."

"Not exact—"

"You'll weather every storm," he continued. "That's bull. My mother did everything for my father, but where did he go? To that low-class, piece-of-trash black whore who—"

Sepia hadn't meant to slap him, but she did and the act stunned both of them. He looked at her, seeming unable to speak for the longest time.

"I'm sorry," he finally said. "That was wrong."

"I know you're angry about that," Sepia said. "And you have every right to be, Laurence. But you can't say things like that. You sounded like a racist."

"That's not what I meant."

Sepia took a deep breath to compose herself. "Besides, that has nothing to do with you and Louise."

"I'm just making the point that love is not all

that matters. My mother loved my father, but it didn't keep him from killing her into humiliation."

"Neither did the fact that they came from money and prestige." Sepia didn't want to detour from the main point. "Still, with Louise, you—"

"You saw that . . . woman, didn't you?" Laurence's voice was choking. "Of course you did. It was on every paper on the East Coast."

"That's the past, Laurence."

"Oh, it's very present for me. I remember the first time I saw her. She looked like . . . It was so damn humiliating."

Sepia didn't know what to do. She wanted to comfort Laurence because she could see the pain racking through him, but she was angry at him for refusing to give Louise a chance.

"You're going to break her heart," she said. "And I don't know what that's going to do to our relationship."

Laurence looked at her as if dazed by her words. As if he never even contemplated the consequences of breaking Louise's heart, and it occurred to Sepia that he never loved her, and even worse, he assumed that Sepia had never expected him to. It was like a knife to her gut to think this was what was expected of her by someone who knew her so well. From a stranger in society circles maybe, but how could someone who knew her think she would go along with that?

How could Paul ever love someone like that?

"Ms. Davis."

Sepia drank the last of her mimosa, wishing it was a scotch as she looked up at Dunleavy. "Yes?"

"Um." Dunleavy looked awkwardly at Laurence,

who seemed to be letting anger take him over. His urgent tone said he sensed an eruption coming. "We need to leave."

"Why?" Sepia really didn't need an excuse. She wanted to get as far away from the club as possible.

"It's Officer Healy."

This got her attention. "Has he called you?"

"He just called here. I guess he got the note we left."

Sepia knew that meant he was back at the cabin. She had initially thought of feeling a certain sense of satisfaction that he would be angry to find her not there when he returned for once. Only now there was no satisfaction to be found in anything. Sepia felt empty inside and wanted to see Paul no matter whom he had just been with.

"Ma'am," Dunleavy said. "He yelled so loud, I thought he was going to reach through the phone and choke me. He said if we aren't back at the safe house five minutes ago, he's coming to get us. I don't know about you, but I would rather avoid that situation."

"So would I." Sepia slid out of the booth. "Can I have a minute?"

Dunleavy nodded, stepping only a few feet away. He was making it clear he wasn't interested in allowing her any more conversation.

Sepia turned to Laurence, who was looking at her with a pained face. "I'm sorry, Sepia. I didn't mean to be so ugly."

"I know you didn't," she said, hoping he meant it.

"It's just that I'm under a lot of stress right now and being pushed brings up all the horrible things that I guess I haven't really dealt with."

Sepia placed her hand on his shoulder. "It's okay. I understand. I have to go."

"To the safe house," he said, nodding. "I know. Please stay safe, Sepia. I don't want anything to happen to you."

"Don't worry about me, Laurence. Think about Louise and search your heart to see if you can't try to love her."

"I will," he said, standing up.

Dunleavy cleared his throat and Sepia nodded to him that she was ready to go face Paul's wrath. She could only hope that after he was done yelling at her, he could find it in his heart to hold her. If only for a second or two.

Eight

"Oh, boy." There was obvious dread in Dunleavy's voice as they drove up to the cabin.

Paul was standing on the top step and the rage in his stance was radiating for miles. Sepia felt it before she could even see his face, but when she did look him in the eye, she wasn't so sure she wanted to get out of the car.

Dunleavy parked the car and gripped the steering wheel with both hands while he took a deep breath. Sepia looked at him as he stared at the wheel.

"I drove here as fast as I could," he said.

Sepia nodded. "I thought we were going to die a couple of times there."

"I'm a good driver." He was saying this as if it would mean something to Paul right now even though they both knew nothing would. "You're here and you're safe."

"What can he do to you, really?" Sepia asked, hoping that Dunleavy would get out before her.

Dunleavy just looked at her as if to say, *You know better than to ask that.*

Sepia sighed. "Look, this was my fault. I'll take care of it."

"I was responsible for watching you."

"And you did." She opened the car door. "I'm safe, so he can't complain. I'll let him know that I made you take me to the club."

"It won't make a difference." Dunleavy cautiously got out of the car.

Paul didn't say a word, but he could hear his own breathing and his chest was heaving as they approached. He stared into Dunleavy's eyes, not caring at all that he was scaring the kid to death. He wanted to.

Sepia swallowed hard before speaking. "Paul, I have—"

"Get inside," he said, not looking at her. He only had eyes for Dunleavy right now.

Startled, Sepia stared at Paul, waiting for him to look at her, but he didn't. "Paul, please don't—"

This time he looked at her and the look on his face made her stop in the middle of her sentence.

"Get inside now," he repeated, feeling nothing but anger right now.

Sepia did what she was told and rushed inside, hoping for the best for Dunleavy. She wasn't optimistic for him or herself. She listened against the door as Paul ripped Dunleavy a new one, not letting the young man get a word in until he was so flustered that he couldn't speak when Paul asked him to. Sepia was tempted several times to go out there and defend Dunleavy, but the truth was she was scared.

When silence came, Sepia jumped away from the door expecting Paul to burst through. Instead, there was nothing until she heard a car drive away. Running to the window, she looked out in time to see Dunleavy rip off so fast, his back tires lifted dirt several feet into the air.

Sepia jumped a few feet herself as Paul opened the front door. He didn't look around for her. He looked directly at her as if he'd known exactly where she would be.

"It wasn't . . . hi . . . his fault," she said, tripping over her own words.

"It was his fault," Paul said. He had taken some time to calm down before coming inside, but he was still as angry as hell. "He was supposed to keep you safe."

"I was safe," Sepia said. "He was with me the whole time. Nothing happened."

"He was supposed to keep you safe here!" Paul slammed the door shut.

He took a couple of steps toward her, but Sepia backed up. He stopped. She was scared and that didn't upset him. He wanted her to be. If scaring her was the only way he could get it into her stubborn head, then so be it, but he didn't want her to think he would actually harm her.

"Where did he go?" she asked.

"Why do you care?" Paul hated that he still found her so beautiful no matter what emotion he was feeling toward her.

"You scared him to death," she said. "He's already a dangerous driver."

"He's going back to the station and I don't care if he wraps that car around a tree."

"Paul!"

Paul knew that was awful to say, but he wasn't concerned about being polite. "Do you understand what this situation is?"

"Do I understand?" Sepia asked. "Are you kidding me? I'm the one who was attacked."

"He's still out there, Sepia! He's still out there and you don't seem to care."

"I was with Dunleavy!"

Paul grabbed a white square candle that had been burned so long it no longer had a wick. He threw it across the room on the wall opposite Sepia, but she still jumped.

"He's a rookie, Sepia. He knows how to protect at a safe house, but he doesn't know how to protect in the field. Not good enough."

"Well, I'm fine now," Sepia said. "So, please calm down."

Sepia walked away from him, the entire scene getting a little too intense for her.

"I will *not* calm down." He followed her into the living room, standing over her as she sat on the sofa. "You're a selfish brat and you think you can have anything you want."

"What?" Sepia shot up, ready for a fight. "How dare you?"

"You wanted to be around the beautiful people," Paul said. "You couldn't stay away from that damn club. Why? Because it makes you feel special to receive all their admiration and compliments? Or maybe this cabin is just a little too middle class for you?"

"You don't know what you're talking about." Sepia felt her hands clenched in fists. "What do I have to do to let you know I'm not that kind of person?"

"How about listen to the rules for once?" he said. "They do apply to people like you as well, you know."

"I'll admit that it probably wasn't the best idea

to go there, but I went there for something important. Not to indulge in a debutante ego."

"It can't have been more important than being safe," Paul said. "You should have been here."

"I should have been here?" Sepia couldn't hold it in any longer. "What about you? Again, you leave me in the middle of the night without any word. And don't give me that line about not being able to control yourself if you came into my bedroom. I know you went to another woman."

Paul stepped back, eyes wide. "What? What are you—"

"I'm not a fool," Sepia said, even though she felt like one for thinking this man could make her feel better. "Dunleavy told me where you went. I knew when you kissed me last night, you were kissing her."

"You're out of your mind," Paul said. "When I kissed you last night, I wasn't thinking about any other woman."

"At least not until she called you. What did you do, help her through a hard night after a fight with her husband?"

"Are you talking about Elaine?" Paul asked.

Sepia pushed against his chest, but Paul didn't budge. "You know who I'm talking about, Paul. If being here was so important, then why weren't you here? Apparently your libido takes precedence over my safety."

Paul grabbed her by the arm and pulled her to him. A gasp escaped her lips as she looked up at him.

"Nothing comes before your safety." The words came through husky and angry as he let her go.

Sepia stood dazed, floating in the mixture of passion, anger, and fear his sudden action created inside her. Not to mention the regret that he let her go.

"Then why did you leave me for her?" she asked, unable to hide the hurt she was feeling.

Paul tried to control himself. He wanted to grab her, kiss her, and make love to her right there. He had hoped his anger would wash his feelings away, but he suddenly realized nothing would.

"I didn't leave you for Elaine," he said.

"Then who?" Sepia didn't want to think there was another woman. Elaine was bad enough, but a new woman who was unattached and available to him seemed even worse.

"It's none of your business why I left." Paul turned to walk away, hoping to get some distance between them that could cool him down.

Sepia grabbed him by the arm with the intention of turning him around, but she didn't have the strength.

"What?" he asked, wishing she would just go away. If she touched him again, he wasn't sure he had the strength necessary to deny himself.

"Do you have any idea how much it hurt me?" she asked. "To wake up and not see you, again? First I thought someone else had died, but then I found out you were just a little too horny to stick around."

Paul saw the pleading in her eyes and realized that she really cared. She thought he was with another woman and it hurt her. What was he going to do now that he could see she cared about him?

"I wasn't with another woman," he said, hearing a tender tone in his voice that he hadn't expected. "I left because my partner and his wife got involved in a domestic dispute and he needed me."

Sepia opened her mouth, but nothing came out.

She couldn't think of words to say. She was so happy
to hear he hadn't been with another woman, but
the reason he really left was so awful. And from the
look on his face as he said it, Sepia knew it was ripping him apart.

"Is . . . Are they okay?"

"Physically, yes," he answered. "In reality, no,
they aren't and I don't think they'll recover. There's
a lot more to it that I don't—"

Sepia reached for him, her hand coming to his
chest. "You don't have to talk about it if you don't
want to. I can tell it hurts you."

Her hand was melting his skin. Paul looked at
her, not knowing he could be in pain, be so angry,
and at the same time want someone more than
he'd ever wanted anyone in his life.

"I'm so sorry," Sepia said, knowing an apology
wasn't enough, but all she had. "I was such a fool. I
just thought . . . I let my emotions get the best of
me."

"It seems like we're both doing a lot of that."
Paul placed his hand over hers on his chest, loving
the softness of her. "It's clouding everything. When
I'm near you I feel like I'm losing control. When I'm
away . . . I can't stand it."

Sepia was speechless. Hearing him say what she
was feeling right now seemed unreal. She was over-
come with emotion. When he pulled her to him,
she gasped, hearing a whimper escape her. Her
body tingled all over and her stomach sent cur-
rents of electricity throughout.

With gentle authority, his lips came to hers.
Waves of sensual desire swept over him. His hands
pressed into her back, pulling her to him, his body
begging for her to give him what he needed.

Sepia felt her knees weakening as she was enticed by the wildest urges her body had ever experienced. His lips devoured hers and she surrendered to the trembling of her body and the desire that swept over her. She was shivering all over as her hands grabbed at him, pulled at him for more.

He guided her body to the floor, unable to wait to move anywhere else. He was aching inside for her and he had to have her here and now. Her lips separated from his, and she buried her face in his neck and seared his throat with fiery hot kisses that made him feel so good his entire body throbbed and he let out a hungry moan.

The sounds he made sent the blood surging through Sepia's veins. Her desire to touch his warm flesh took her over as she began to rip at his clothes. With a forceful domination that she had never known she had, she undressed him and pushed him to the floor. As she looked down at him, the savage desire she saw in his eyes gave her an excitement that scared her.

He was devastated by the appeal of her seductive smile. Everything inside him was aroused as he reached up to remove her clothes. When she moved his hands away, he realized that she wanted to do that, so he lay back, watching with a sense of worship as her naked body sent jolts of lust through him. She had had her fun. Now it was his turn.

Sepia let out a scream as Paul grabbed her by her arms and flipped her over. She was on the floor now and when he came down on her, his lips went straight to her neck. His tongue was like a match all over her body as he lowered himself to her breasts. As he explored every inch of her with his mouth, his hands slow and torturous, Sepia's body wriggled in ecstasy. She was completely naked now and as he spread her legs open, a sense of hysteria fell over her.

She braced herself for the touch of his mouth as he gently licked the inside of her thigh and moved up higher and higher. She was groaning out loud now, the agonizing lust threatening to explode at the mastery of his mouth, his hands.

He taunted her, bringing her to several peaks before teasingly backing away. It enraged her, only increasing her pleasure. She was left alone for only a moment as he went for protection. When he returned, she smiled with anticipation as the look on his face told her that he was done with the games. He was visibly ready, he had been for some time, and when he knelt down to her again, Sepia opened her legs, reaching for him.

He looked into her eyes as he entered her, the pleasure ripping him apart as her eyes closed, her head went back, and she bit her lip. The moan that escaped her made him lose his mind. He moved, loving the feel of her warmth as she tightly engulfed him inside her. He was carried away by her body as their eyes locked. Their breathing, their rythym came into unison. He was groaning out of control as she began to scream, only sending his body into a sexual rage that drenched his soul.

When she exploded underneath him, Sepia dug her nails into his back. She felt as if she were falling off a skyscraper and into oblivion, and it was so good she thought she would die if it ended. It didn't end. It came to her again as he yelled out her name and closed his eyes. His pleasure was her aphrodisiac.

When he returned to earth, Paul looked down at Sepia. The sweat was glistening all over her body and he couldn't hold back the desire that threatened to never give him a moment's peace again with this woman.

"Are you ready to get serious?" he asked her with a mischievous smile.

Sepia's body melted and a current of desire ripped from where he was inside her to her head. "So this was just for starters?"

"I told you I know what I'm good at."

Sepia closed her eyes as he lowered his body and his mouth came down to hers. She bit his lower lip, wanting him to feel some of the lustful pain she was feeling. He felt it, no doubt. And he showed her again.

Sweating and exhausted, Paul and Sepia practically crawled to the bedroom, where they made love for the third time. This time had been like the first, hungry and needing. Sepia had never been so consumed with want for someone. She hadn't known a man could make her feel like this. It was as if every time before this hadn't even happened. Her emotions were so in tune with her body's needs and wants that she almost felt as if it were a dream, because reality couldn't really be this good.

Paul wrapped his arm around Sepia as she leaned against his chest. He had never felt so content, so complete in his life. It was actually a little scary, knowing that this woman had him under her thumb. She really did. He couldn't imagine anything he wouldn't do that she asked of him.

"You comfortable?" he asked as he pulled the covers over them. They felt cool against their hot bodies.

Sepia just moaned her response. No need to even ask that.

"If I have to go to the bathroom," he said, "you won't accuse me of leaving you for another woman, will you?"

She looked up at the smirk on his face, smacking her hand against his chest. "Don't make fun of me. I apologized for being jealous."

"Of nothing."

"I thought it was something," she said. "But none of that matters anymore. Not after the way you just made me feel."

Paul's ego soared to the sky. "I like to do my job well."

Sepia squeezed his left nipple, waiting until he yelled out in pain to let go. "Don't get a big head, Officer."

"Interesting choice of words," he said, reaching under the covers. "And how would you like it if I did that to you?"

Sepia screamed, sliding away from him. She wrapped the covers around herself. "Don't you dare. It'll hurt."

"Like it didn't hurt me?" He was exhausted, but wanted to make love to her again. "Well, to be honest, I think I kind of liked it."

"I know you cops are into the rough stuff." Sepia laughed until her own words reminded her of the source of the entire misunderstanding. "Look, Paul. I'm sorry I gave you a hard time. I know you're upset over your partner and you were right to go."

"Thanks," Paul said, feeling guilty for having forgotten about David for the past couple of hours.

"I hope everything works out," she said.

Paul looked down at her, remembering what he

had promised David. How could he forget? Here David was waiting to be arrested for theft, to lose his family, and probably go to jail for informing the Ravens of police strategy against them, and where was Paul?

Making love in a cabin in the woods.

"He's in a lot of trouble, Sepia," Paul said. "Can I trust you to—"

"I won't say a thing," Sepia said with a hand to her heart.

Paul told Sepia all about David's misdeeds from beginning to end. Sepia watched as his mood changed and she realized how much of a burden this was on him. She respected his strength of character and his loyalty. He would do anything for his friend.

"Do you think you can help him?" she asked.

"I think I can," Paul said. "That's where you come in."

"Me?"

"I'm trying to make it so David gets the lightest sentence possible. And I have to admit I'm being selfish in wanting to do anything to keep from letting this whole thing rob me of my promotion to detective."

Sepia was still confused.

"The chief of police and the district attorney are the two men who can make all the difference in this. They both know your father, and since I'm doing this favor to them by protecting—"

Paul stopped as Sepia inhaled sharply. She jumped off the bed, wrapping the sheet tightly around herself.

"What?" he asked.

Sepia felt her body shaking all over as adrenaline coursed through her veins. "You used me!"

"What are you talking about?"

"I can't believe you did this." She pointed to the bed as if it were an accomplice. "You thought you could bed me into helping you?"

"Don't be ridiculous."

"I was such a fool." She slapped herself on the forehead, not even trying to stop the tears that were filling her eyes and ready to flood the world.

Paul stood up, not caring that he was completely naked. "No, Sepia. I know what this looks like, but—"

"Are you going to try and say that it's just a coincidence that you just made love to me before asking me to do you and your friend a favor only seconds later? In exchange for this labor of protecting me at that?"

"I was going to ask you before it got to this."

"You just wanted to seal the deal?" Sepia rushed to the dresser, frantically pulling out whatever clothes she could.

"Sepia, you know me better than that." In retrospect, Paul could see how this wasn't the best choice, but there was no way he could have resisted her earlier.

"I know you'd do anything for your friend," she said, slipping her shorts on. "You've made that all too clear, but I can't believe you would—"

"Stop it." He started toward her.

"Don't you come near me!" Sepia grabbed the lamp from off the bed console, ripping it from the socket.

"Sepia, calm down!"

"Let me guess," she said. "You'd like me to get my father to hook you and your buddy up in exchange for you keeping me . . . preoccupied."

"Don't say it like that." Paul was getting angry at her insinuations, but he had to reassure her.

"That's how it is, isn't it?" Fully dressed now, Sepia stood her ground, lamp in hand. Tears were streaming down her hot cheeks. "I was just lying there in that bed, doubting that something this good could be real, but that was too late. I should have known better and saved myself the humiliation."

"It is not," Paul said. "You're being ridiculous. You can't actually believe what happened between us was anything but real."

"I'm sure you got something out of it," she said. "But I don't believe in coincidence either. This is incredibly ironic, don't you think? You couldn't stand the part of me that you seem to suddenly need the most."

"There was never any part of you I couldn't stand," Paul said. "And what you're doing right now is about more than the favor I'm asking you."

She laughed out loud, but her bitterness came through. "Get out of here!"

"I'm not leaving until you calm down."

Sepia threw the lamp at him and Paul ducked just in time to avoid it. It slammed against the wall behind him, shattering into pieces. Sepia slipped into her shoes.

"Fine," she yelled. "Then I'll leave."

"Sepia!"

Paul looked down and realized he was a naked, barefoot man surrounded by broken pieces of porcelain everywhere. He knew his shoes were out in the living room where he had taken them off along with the rest of his clothes.

He strategically tiptoed around the glass until he was safe and rushed down the hallway where he found Sepia in the living room rummaging through his clothes.

"What are you doing?" he asked, approaching her. He sincerely hoped she wasn't looking for his gun.

Sepia could barely think, she felt as if she were choking and ready to explode. "I'm getting out of here."

"No, you don't." Paul grabbed his cell phone from her the second she pulled it out of his pants pocket.

Sepia stood reaching for the phone, but he was holding it up too high. She pushed against his chest and stomach, but she was having no effect on him.

"Give it to me!" She tugged at his arm.

"Not until you calm down and listen to reason."

"I'm not falling for it anymore," Sepia said. "You weren't that good."

Actually he was, and Sepia felt like a fool for falling for it all. And, man, had she fallen!

"No!" Paul wasn't moving on this.

Sepia kicked him in the right thigh. He didn't move, but she saw him wince and he was getting as angry as he had been this morning. "Then I'm leaving!"

Paul tossed his phone away and grabbed her. "No, you aren't. You aren't going anywhere."

"You can't force me to stay." Sepia jerked free. "I'm not accused of anything. I don't have to submit to your . . . protection."

"There is a murderer out there, Sepia."

"I'd rather be on my own than have your protection," she said. "Jeez, I feel like I owe you money."

That stung and Paul's temper got the best of

him now. "You want to leave? Go ahead and get out of here. You're in the middle of the woods and you won't get anywhere without the keys to my car and you're not getting them from me."

"I don't need them." Sepia opened the door. "And I don't need you!"

She slammed the door behind her and Paul cursed out loud. He couldn't let her go even though he felt she deserved a little walk in the woods on her own. She'd be running back soon enough. Only he couldn't chance that, so he got over it and reached for his clothes. He didn't care if he had to drag her by her hair, she was getting back in this cabin.

Sepia almost slipped and fell down the steps being in such a hurry to get away from there. The stairs did not have a railing, so if she fell she would have been in an even bigger mess if that was possible. As much as she wanted to get away from Paul, she had to be more careful.

She was so angry she couldn't stand it. What a fool she had been. Her guard had been down and she could only blame that for her weakness. She was already upset over her encounter with Laurence and she dreaded her next conversation with Louise. Then, when she found out that Paul had not left her for another woman, she was happier than any self-respecting independent woman should have been. Add to it the way he touched her. The mixture of anger and desire he seemed to have for her sent Sepia soaring into the air and into his arms.

She had exposed herself to him in ways she never had before. In making love to him she was more exploring, more giving than with any other man. She had let go completely, making sounds she didn't know she could make. Sounds she didn't know good girls could make. He had brought it out in her and it was all a plan. He knew what he was doing, making her feel as if she were beyond heaven. He was putting her right where he wanted her and she fell for it hook, line, and sinker.

Why in the name of all that was good couldn't Donna Pillant have been there to do the drive-along with her that day? She would never have met Paul Healy and would certainly not be in this situation right now. She would be relaxing in her comfortable home, sitting at her laptop typing away.

Alone. Not to mention the fact that people would still be dying and no one would be safe, so she wouldn't have been comfortable. But at least she wouldn't feel like a fool and kind of easy.

Sepia looked back at the cabin, wishing she could burn the thing down in hopes that everything done there would just disappear in the charred ashes. As she passed his car, Sepia peeked in just to make sure the keys weren't in there already. She didn't see anything. She tugged at the door, almost willing to hot-wire the thing even though she had no idea how to do that. It was locked.

"Who cares!" she yelled out as she kicked the tire.

She bent down to rub her throbbing foot and her eyes focused on the tire she had just kicked, sensing something was wrong. It was low. No, it was flat. A vengeful smile spread across Sepia's lips. That was a nice gift. She relished the look on Paul's face when he would come out and see he had a flat tire. He deserved at least that.

She looked around, seeing the lake in front of her and nothing but woods behind the cabin. She would make her way up the right side of the cabin on the dirt path they had driven down on and hope she could flag a car down. Maybe someone would be nice enough to let her use their cell phone or, if she was really lucky, give her a ride.

Sepia took a deep breath, hoping her feet were up to the task. She would leave Paul to his flat tire.

His two flat tires?

Sepia didn't know what made her look at the other tire, but she did, and it was clearly flat, even more so than the first. She had already had her fill of coincidences. Something was wrong.

In the instant she looked up, a flicker of movement out the right side of her eye caught Sepia's attention. She turned to it and saw something that made her heart jump out of her throat.

Standing next to the house, right on the dirt path, was a man. It was him. He was white and wearing what looked like a T-shirt and jeans. The hair was unmistakable. Jet-black with wild curls.

Sepia blinked, wondering if she was seeing things. After all, how could he be here?

When his arm begin to raise, Sepia saw the gun in his hand and it was pointing right at her. She screamed as loud as she could, her voice reverberating around the woods as she ducked behind the car. She heard the gun shoot before she was out of sight, but wasn't hit. As she leaned against the car, she heard another shot. This one hit the car somewhere, but not her.

On her hands and knees, Sepia crawled to the other end of the car. Just as she was about to scream out Paul's name, she heard the cabin door burst open. She peeked up enough to see Paul, dressed in boxers and gun in hand, rush out onto the porch.

"Sepia!" Paul's adrenaline was on high octane. Where was she?

"Paul!" Sepia waved her arms to get his attention. "He's shooting."

As soon as he saw Sepia hiding by the car, Paul heard another gunshot ring out. The bullet hit the edge of the door, only inches from his head. For a second, he looked to the right of the house to see a man with a gun aimed at him before he jumped over the side of the steps. Another shot rang out, just missing him.

"Stay down!" he yelled to Sepia, hoping to God she wasn't hurt.

What was going on? How in the world could somebody have gotten out here?

Paul peeked above the steps and took his shot. He ducked back down as he heard the man yell out. He'd hit him.

He leaned up again, but had to duck when he heard another shot. This one hit the stairway. He looked to his right and saw Sepia leaning against the tire, staring at him. He jumped up, shooting again, but saw nothing. The man was gone!

"Sepia!" Paul ran to her. "Are you all right?"

She nodded, but she was shaking all over.

"Get inside and use my cell to call Luke. He's one on the speed dial!"

"Paul!" Sepia reached for him, grabbing at his shirt. "Don't go. He could kill you."

"I have to catch him!" Paul jerked free of her just as another gunshot rang out, but it wasn't in his direction and it didn't sound like the other shots. He was very familiar with the sound a particular gun made.

He darted up, seeing no one. What was he shooting at?

"No." Sepia couldn't stand it. "He's still shooting. Stay here."

"He's not shooting at us." He looked down at her. "Get in the cabin and do what I said."

Sepia screamed out again, but Paul was gone. She got up and headed for the stairs to get help. When she reached the door, she heard a car driving off with that noticeable screeching sound as the tires hit the dirt. He was gone!

Sepia ran around the corner of the cabin right into Paul coming back her way.

"I told you to get into the cabin." Paul turned her around and pushed her toward the house.

"But he's gone," she said. "I heard him, right?"

"He's not gone. Get in the car."

Sepia jerked away, spinning around in a circle.

"Get in the car!" Paul yelled, reaching for her again.

She pulled back. "We can't. The tires are flat. Look!"

Paul turned and saw that his two back tires were flat. "Son of a . . ."

He only had one spare in the trunk. He pointed his gun at the car and wanted to shoot, but he might need his bullets. He wasn't going to get the guy now. He turned to Sepia, who was standing at the edge of the cabin, staring at what he wanted to keep her from seeing.

Sepia couldn't tear her eyes away from the man who had tried to kill her twice, now lying in the dirt. He wasn't moving.

"He's dead," Paul said.

Sepia turned around and fell into Paul's outstretched arms. She leaned her head into her chest. "Thank God you got him. He would have killed us both."

"I didn't get him," Paul said.

Sepia leaned away, looking at him, seeing he was strained to his edge. "What do you mean? You shot him."

"I shot him in the leg," Paul said. "He was killed by a shot in his chest."

Sepia remembered the last gunshot when she thought he was still shooting at them, but Paul said he wasn't. "He killed himself?"

"No," Paul said. He hadn't seen a license plate. This wasn't going to be easy. "Someone else did."

Sepia swung around, looking at the path. Someone had shot the killer and driven off! "I heard a car, but I thought it was him trying to get away."

"Let's go call Luke. We can put out an APB on the car. No plates, but I could tell it's an early nineties Chevy. Maroon, I think."

"Why?" Sepia asked. "How?"

Paul approached her, seeing tears begin to stream down her face again. He held her in his arms, her entire body shaking. "Come on inside. Everything is going to be okay."

Sepia wanted like anything to believe that, but she was more scared and confused now than ever.

Nine

Sepia sat in the guarded room of the police station feeling more alone than ever before. After Paul brought her there, he left her in the room promising to come back. That seemed like forever ago. Dunleavy had come in a few times to offer her coffee or something to eat, but as the evening went on, all she wanted was Paul.

At this point, Sepia was willing to defy her better logic and ignore whatever motives she thought Paul had for sleeping with her. She didn't care anymore. If he wanted to use her, he could just use her. She didn't know how she would recover when he had gotten what he wanted and moved on. Maybe she wouldn't ever, but all that mattered was that she could be with him. She couldn't stand any distance between them. Not while this was still going on. She would be dead right now if it wasn't for Paul, and that truth connected her to him in ways she didn't even understand yet, but hoped she would when the shock of it all wore down.

When the door finally opened, Sepia jumped out

of her chair, but her elation was short-lived when she saw it was Louise, not Paul. Still, she rushed to her best friend and they hugged tightly for what seemed like a few minutes before sitting down. Louise held Sepia's hands tight. Tears were streaming down both their faces.

"You're alive," Louise said. "That's all that matters."

"I know," Sepia said. "I keep trying to tell myself that. No matter how horrible things are, we are still alive. But who knows how long before that changes?"

"You can't think that way," Louise said.

Sepia looked at her, speaking with a serious tone. "I can't think any other way now. Not after today."

"You're safe now, aren't you?" Louise asked. "That person that got away, whoever he was, wanted to kill the man that tried to kill you."

"All this does is raise more questions." Sepia had listened in on Paul's phone conversation with Luke as well as the intense brainstorming the two men did in the car after Luke came to pick them up and drive back to the station. "It makes no sense and I don't think for a second that I'm safe yet."

Louise sighed, seeming unable to add anything else. "I asked if I can take you home with me and the officer said no."

"I wouldn't be safe there," she said. "And you wouldn't either and I won't let you be in danger. Besides, I'm not leaving until I see Paul. I won't go anywhere without him."

"Where can he take you now?" Louise asked.

"I don't care if I'm stuck in this room all night. If he's with me, I'll be fine."

Louise leaned back, studying Sepia. "You're serious, aren't you?"

"As cancer," Sepia said. "I love him, Louise, and I can't be—"

"Wait a second." Louise held her hand up. "Since when did love come into the picture?"

"He saved my life," Sepia said.

"So you're confusing gratitude with love?"

"It's more than that." Sepia didn't know if she had the strength to explain. "I was blinded by our differences, but I've felt a connection to this man since the first moment I met him. That's why the things he said to me during the drive-along stung so much."

"But love is a stretch." Louise tilted her head inquisitively. "Did you sleep with him?"

No secrets from Louise. "It was wonderful, but I don't know if he felt the same."

"He's a man," she said. "I'm sure he loved it."

"I don't mean that. I mean, I don't know if he meant it. I think he was using me."

"For what?"

Sepia told Louise about the scenario that had played out in the bedroom that morning.

"I still don't see how you can be sure he used you," she said skeptically. "I mean it's worth finding out the truth."

"Don't get me wrong," Sepia said. "I want to be wrong. Especially now."

"Now that you love him."

Sepia nodded. "I need him, Louise. I always felt like it was such a weakness to admit that about a man, but I do."

"You're scared to death," Louise said.

"You think this will change?" Sepia wasn't sure if that would be a good thing or not.

"I don't know." Louise squeezed Sepia's hands

even tighter. "Your heart will let you know. You're much smarter than I am at that stuff."

The shaky tone of Louise's words hit Sepia in a strange way. She looked at her friend and saw a pain in her eyes that had nothing to do with her own situation.

"What's wrong, Louise?"

Louise began crying uncontrollably as she fumbled through her purse. She pulled out a tissue that was on its last legs.

"Louise." Sepia leaned forward, rubbing her on the arm to comfort her. "What in the world is wrong? This isn't about my situation, is it?"

Louise sneezed into the napkin loud enough to be heard a few floors down before taking a deep breath and composing herself.

"Laurence dumped me."

Sepia gasped. "What happened?"

"He called me and told me that he didn't think it was working out."

"On the phone?" Sepia wanted to slap him even harder than she had. She was racked with guilt, wondering if her pushing had caused all of this. Of course it had.

"I was begging him to get together and talk about it, but he was going on about how I knew things hadn't been good in a long while and how we weren't what each other wanted. Sepia, he's everything I've ever wanted."

Louise was crying hard again and Sepia leaned in close enough to hold her.

"Louise, I think I upset him today. I tried to talk to him like we agreed."

"I know," she said. "He told me and he said that it wasn't necessary because he had made up his mind last night after the book signing. He made love to me that night, Sepia. Knowing he was going to dump me the next day. He can be so cruel sometimes."

"What else did he say to you?"

"I don't want to repeat some of it. I can't stand to hear it again."

"Louise, I don't believe he decided that after the book signing. It was today. He was so upset thinking about his father and what happened last year. He wanted to take it out on someone and you just happened to be in his path. He didn't mean it."

Louise's eyes were bloodshot red. "He meant it, Sepia. It was all the things I was so afraid he thought of me but was never willing to admit. He spoke so badly of people who weren't at his level. Your level."

"I'll talk to him again."

Louise shook her head. "I begged him to get together and talk, but he said it was best if we didn't see each other at all for a while."

Sepia could barely think straight. She wasn't able to figure out what to say to make Louise's pain go away. She could only make promises. "He never really dealt with his pain over what happened to his family. He threw himself into the club to cover it up, but it was going to come to the surface some time."

"And I'm collateral damage," Louise said. "Oh, God, I don't know what I'm going to do."

Sepia leaned back. "Aren't we a couple of sad sisters?"

A smile peeked at the edges of Louise's lips. "Acting a mess over men."

"We're stronger than that," Sepia said. "Aren't we?"

"At least you have an attempted murder to add credibility to your despair."

"We're going to be okay, Louise. We'll just have to figure out how, but we'll do it."

Louise looked desperate. "Sepia, no matter where they take you, you have to take me with you. I need you right now."

"I promise I'll make it happen. I need you too. We fix each other."

"You have to stay alive first," Louise said.

"Easier said than done." Sepia couldn't believe she was laughing at it all, but leave it to Louise and you were bound to laugh at something.

"Girl," Louise said through laughter, "your life is turning into an episode of *Alias.*"

Sepia bent over, her hand coming to her stomach, which was hurting because she was laughing so hard. Both women looked as if someone had just told the joke of the century when Paul stepped into the room. He hadn't expected this to be the scene, but it was better than seeing Sepia crying like she was when he'd left.

"I don't know whether to be happy you're laughing," he said, joining them at the table, "or worry that you've cracked up."

Sepia's heart sang with delight at the sight of him. She wanted to touch his strong, meaningful face. She wanted him to hold her and make love to her the way he had earlier today. It seemed as if it were years ago, but she still felt the heat all over her body when she saw him.

"Louise," Paul said, turning to her, "I need to ask Sepia some more questions if you don't mind."

Louise turned to Sepia. "Remember what I said."

"I won't go anywhere without you," Sepia added

as she hugged Louise one last time before she got up and left.

"Louise has to come with us wherever we go," Sepia said as Paul took the seat Louise had been in.

He leaned over, his arms supporting on his thighs. "I need you to remember something."

"Anything," she said.

"When you and Dunleavy left the club, did he do the regular maneuvering tactics to avoid being followed like I did when we left the book signing?"

Sepia thought back. "You mean driving around in circles, slowing down, and hiding in parking lots?"

He nodded.

"There wasn't any time. He was scared because you were angry. We just shot out of there and came straight to the cabin. He didn't want to take any extra . . ." Sepia realized why Paul was asking her this. "Oh, my God. He followed us from the club. This is all my fault!"

"Don't blame yourself," Paul said. "Dunleavy knows the procedures. It wasn't up to you to remember them for him."

"But if we'd never gone there it wouldn't have been necessary." Sepia felt awful. "Not only did I cause that, but I think I ruined things between Laurence and Louise too."

Paul didn't care at all about Laurence or Louise, but Sepia seemed bothered about it so he pretended to care if only to take her mind off blaming herself. "I'm sure you were just trying to help."

"I can't seem to do anything right. I'm doing nothing but leaving death, heartbreak, and destruction in my path."

Paul wished he could make her feel better, but he was working the case now and he had already gotten into enough trouble merging the two worlds. She was safe now, but she could have been killed all because he had made their relationship personal.

"I can tell you some things," he said, "but I don't want you to tell Louise or anyone else."

Sepia nodded fervently, hungry for anything that might make her feel even a little less confused and frightened. She felt so powerless, helpless to do anything.

"His name was George Krane," he started.

"The man that tried to kill us?"

"He worked at the club, Sepia. He'd been working in maintenance for the last six months."

Sepia couldn't believe it. She had become familiar with most of the workers. She knew the caterers and office personnel the best. Laurence managed all of the maintenance stuff.

"You don't remember him at all?" Paul asked.

"I know what you're thinking," Sepia said. "I never notice the workers because I think they're beneath me."

"I wasn't thinking anything," he said with a soft smile. "He's got a rap sheet."

"Murder?"

"No, petty theft and the like."

"I don't know how he got a job there," she said. "Our security ran background checks on everyone."

"He must have slipped through."

"Laurence is going to be devastated to hear this. He'll blame himself."

"There was something else," Paul said.

"I don't know how much more I can take."

"We found a note in his pocket." Paul hated to

remember the words he read, but this note was one of the strongest clues they had. "It was an angry letter full of racist, hateful words."

"Oh, no." She had feared this. The murders were bad enough, but with the racial component to it things were going to get ugly. The press would make sure of that.

"He resented so many rich black people who were, in his opinion, flaunting it around while he and his white brothers were struggling. He was making a statement to show that, in his words, white people should want for nothing before black people get anything."

"Very unoriginal," Sepia said. "But it doesn't explain who shot him and why."

That was what worried Paul the most. Luke's theory was that this person was more dangerous than George Krane. "We're searching Krane's place now. We'll find something."

"What do you think?"

"Luke thinks that Krane intended to kill you and leave the note."

"Why with me?"

"Possibly you were his last victim. It was getting too difficult for him to continue. However, maybe someone in his racist circle felt he was going to get caught and linked to them."

"So they killed him to shut him up."

"They knew as soon as we caught him we were going to rattle the cages of everyone he knew."

Sepia thought it made some sense. "They didn't know about the note?"

"I'm not sure about that, but Luke and I aren't going to leave here until we figure it out."

There was a knock on the door and Dunleavy entered, standing in the doorway as if waiting. Sepia looked from him to Paul and her heart dropped into her stomach at the look on his face.

"Paul," she said. "I won't feel safe with anyone but you."

"I have to stay here." Paul could never tell her how much it killed him to be separated from her now. He didn't want her out of his sight, but he knew if he appeared uncertain, she would feel even less safe than she did now. "We're taking you to an official safe house, an apartment building in Cromwell with the best security in the city. We'll have Dunleavy and three other officers there. No one will get in without ID and approval."

"But I want to be with you!"

"You can bring Louise with you."

She reached for Paul, but he pulled back and the move tore at her heart. He didn't want to be with her. Her worst thoughts were true.

"You need protection," Paul said. "And I can't do it anymore."

He hated the look on her face, but he couldn't indulge her right now. She had to know this was how it was for tonight. He was a cop, not her bodyguard, and he had to help Luke figure out what in the world was going on. His feelings for Sepia had to wait, no matter how overwhelming they were.

He stood up. "You have to leave and I have to get back to work."

Sepia didn't look at him. She looked down at her hands that were laid stately on her lap. She didn't really have any more tears to cry that day.

"You ready?" Dunleavy asked.

"Let's go."

*   *   *

Luke looked up at Paul as he approached his desk. "You look bad, man."

If he looked only half as bad as he felt, Paul knew it wasn't good. He turned his chair around, leaning against the back as he sat down.

"I haven't been making the best choices lately," Paul said. He grabbed George Krane's rap sheet again, wondering if there was something there that would lead him to these murders he missed before.

"You didn't lead that guy to the cabin," Luke said.

"Not about that." Paul didn't mind telling Luke everything. He knew it would stay between them without evening asking. "About Sepia. I've gotten . . . involved."

Luke looked at him without a hint of surprise. "How long have you been sleeping with her?"

"Just today, but it's been building up."

Luke leaned back, studying Paul. "You feel like your vision is getting clouded?"

"That's an understatement. I can't think of anything but her."

"I need your head here, Paul."

"I'm here," Paul said. "I'm here. I'm with her. I'm with David. I'm everywhere and it's getting to be too much."

"I know you can handle this," Luke said. "You're a smart guy and stronger than even you think, but you've got to keep your perspective and set clear priorities."

"That's easier said than done."

"What isn't?"

Paul smiled. Luke always had a way of getting to the point.

"You want some bad news?" Luke asked.

"You're joking, right?"

"I lost my humor two cups of coffee ago. The bad news is life as a detective is even more demanding than as a cop and you'll have more to deal with."

"What do you do?" Paul asked.

"When the worlds collide," Luke answered, "and I have to set priorities, I sit down with my wife and we talk. I tell her where I am and where I need her to be. She's a great woman and she loves me more than I deserve. She understands when to back off a bit. So do I, but not until I've talked to her."

Paul could only hope to have something like Luke had. Right now, it seemed like an impossibility with Sepia. "I think I love her, Luke."

"You have to make sure it isn't the intensity of the situation."

"When you called and told me that she and Dunleavy were missing, I felt a panic inside that I couldn't relate to anything I've felt before. I was scared to death."

"I heard it in your voice," Luke said. "I knew there was trouble."

"And earlier today when I heard her scream and then the gunshot." Paul felt his entire body brace at the thought of that moment. "The feeling I had at that moment was scarier than anything I've ever experienced."

"You've got it bad, buddy."

Luke took this moment to laugh and Paul didn't appreciate it too much.

"You think this is funny?"

"I guess," Luke said. "I always like to see when another man bites the dust."

"I almost bit the real dust today." Paul tossed the

rap sheet back on the desk. "There's nothing there that tells me this guy is involved with white supremists."

"We're not looking in the right place." Luke's frustration was evident. "We have to start hauling some folks in and getting some answers. I need you, Paul. If sleeping with her is going to be a problem, I—"

"It's not anymore," Paul said regrettably.

"What do you mean?"

"There's not going to be any sleeping together any time soon." Paul explained what Sepia thought of his request for a favor.

"You did it right after sex?"

Paul nodded, thinking in retrospect how bad an idea it was. "Never ask a woman for something after sex. I know the rules, but I was a little desperate. David doesn't have a lot of time and I couldn't think of anything else to help him."

"You shouldn't have been so good," Luke said.

Paul grinned mischievously. "I hate to brag, but how would you know how good I was?"

"When you're real good, they always think you're after something."

"I could do without the teasing." Paul didn't want to talk about it anymore. He and Luke were joking about it, but the situation he was in with Sepia was anything but funny to him.

"Any other ideas about David?" Luke asked.

"Haven't had a second to think," Paul said. "We're both in a bad place."

"I talked to the chief today," Luke said. "He mentioned you."

"In tandem with David, I guess?"

"Why do you think that?"

"If it was good, you would have told me already."

"It's not all bad. He said you're assured the detective role if you roll on David."

"Roll on my partner?" Paul couldn't believe a cop would ask that of another cop.

"He meant more that he expected you to distance yourself from him, because he's going down."

Paul ran his hand over his head, biting at his lower lip. The old saying "when it rains, it storms" came to mind. He was going to lose it.

"It's all coming too fast," he said.

"I'm meeting with the chief tomorrow morning about this case," Luke said. "I can talk to him if you want."

"I need some time."

"You got it. Want my advice?"

"Are you kidding me?" Paul asked. "My head's about to split open."

"My advice is . . ." Luke leaned forward, looking intently at Paul. "You know what to do."

Paul looked at him for a second before nodding. He did know.

"Never turn your back on your partner," Paul said.

Luke winked at him just as the phone rang and Paul's entire body tensed up again.

Sepia joined Louise in the dining room of the spacious apartment they were being guarded in. She had made some hot tea, which was providing a certain sense of temporary comfort.

"Feel any better?" Sepia asked.

Louise shook her head. "I don't think I'll feel better for a long time. How about you?"

"I don't know what I feel," Sepia said. "I mean I feel lousy about Paul."

Sepia had told Louise everything about Paul and what had been happening, only leaving out the information Paul had just shared with her at the station.

"How can you be sure he used you?"

"I'm not sure of anything anymore. I was sure at first, but I think maybe I was just scared to death. Then the way he acted at the station. I don't know what to think."

"You still think you love him?"

Sepia nodded. "It's too sudden though, don't you think?"

"You asking me?" Louise laughed. "I'm the last one to tell you. I've been in a sham of a relationship for eight months. I've been waiting for a wedding ring from a man who never loved me."

Sepia felt for Louise. Not just because of what Laurence had done to her, but because she was just now realizing that she had known it wouldn't work all along and she was feeling guilty about that.

"Even if I don't think he used me," Sepia said, "the way I treated him, he'll blame me if he doesn't make detective."

"You're not going to do it?" Louise asked.

Sepia looked at her, dumbfounded by the question. "Why would I?"

"Because he asked a favor of you," she said. "Whether or not he used sex to get it, the man saved your life. You could hook him up with some contacts. It might make you feel better. You know to close things out between you."

"I don't want to talk about Paul anymore." As Sepia felt the hot drink travel down her throat, she knew she didn't want to close anything between her and Paul.

"Fine," Louise said. "Then let's talk about this hidden driver, second killer."

Sepia dropped her head to the table with a loud moan. "I don't know what in the hell is going on with that."

"You can't tell me?"

"No, but I can tell you I'm not satisfied with what I know."

"Why not?"

The more Luke's explanation of who killed George Krane settled in, the less it made sense to Sepia. If someone wanted to shut him up, they would have killed him before coming out to the cabin. There wasn't a car in sight, so George obviously came up there with whoever shot him. Why would they wait until they were at the cabin to kill him if they wanted to distance themselves from him? It was too risky.

"Oh, my God!" Louise yelled.

Sepia's head shot up, startled by Louise, who jumped up from the table and rushed into the living room where the television was on. Sepia glanced at the set and saw a picture of Richard Sanders on the screen. She followed Louise to see what was going on.

"This just in," an unseen reporter said. "Well-known lawyer Richard Sanders of Cromwell, Maryland, is reportedly coming out of the coma he has been in the last few days as a result of a shooting in his home."

Sepia and Louise grabbed each other, hugging tightly. This was the best news in a while and it was much needed.

"Sanders's shooting," the reporter continued, "is believed to be connected with the recent string of racially motivated murders in the Crawford and

Cromwell area. Channel Four News has learned that a murder in Scully, Maryland, just north of Cromwell, earlier today is related to this case as well. We'll get back to you when we have more details."

"Look!" Sepia pointed to the screen as it switched to the hospital.

There was just a glimpse of Paul and Luke as they entered what must have been Richard Sanders's hospital room. Sepia felt her heart pull at the sight of Paul. She wondered when she would see him again and hoped it would be soon.

"I guess he's talking," Louise said.

"Finally," Sepia said, "we can get some answers."

"Yeah," Louise agreed. "He might be able to tell us anything that guy said to him before shooting him. It might shed some light on his motive."

"Or," Sepia said, remembering Louise didn't know about the note, "if my suspicions were right, it might shed a light on something altogether different."

When Paul entered the hospital room right behind Luke, the first thing he noticed was a groggy Richard Sanders sitting up in his bed. Alone. The second thing he noticed was Mrs. Sanders, whom he expected to be by her husband's side, standing in the corner staring at him. Not really staring, but glaring.

"He just came to," the doctor said to Luke. From the look on her face, she wasn't happy to see the police. Doctors and police could clash at times on when it was the right time to interview patients. "He really needs to rest."

"Is he talking?" Luke asked.

She nodded. "But not very coherently. He's mumbling things. He's apologizing."

"I need to ask him a couple of questions," Luke said.

The doctor reluctantly stepped aside as Luke moved closer to Richard. Richard looked at him, his eyes barely open. He was weak and Paul wasn't sure this man was going to last long.

"Mr. Sanders," Luke said. "I'm Detective Luke Drasutto and this is Officer Paul Healy. We're working your case."

Richard slowly nodded.

"Do you know who shot you?" Luke asked.

Richard nodded, closing his eyes. Paul saw a tear trail down his cheek. That was a red flag if he'd ever seen one.

"Who was he?" Luke asked. He pulled the picture of George Krane out of his pocket, ready to show it to Richard.

Richard looked at him, confused. He seemed reluctant.

Luke showed him the picture. "Was it this man?"

Richard looked at the picture. After a second or two, he shook his head.

Luke turned back to Paul. Paul nodded his head toward the corner of the room. Luke looked in that direction, then back at Paul. He nodded before turning to Richard.

"Mr. Sanders," he said, "who shot you?"

Richard lowered his head again. "I . . . I'm . . . s . . . sorry—"

"Mr. Sanders," Paul interrupted, "we will do all we can for you, but you have to tell us."

Richard looked up at both men. With a grave look on his haggard face, he turned his head and looked directly at his wife. Paul and Luke also looked at her. Gripping her purse tightly, Shelby Sanders stood up and stepped forward.

"I'd do it again!" she screamed. "Cheatin' bastard."

Paul started for her as he reached to his side for his handcuffs.

Sepia had been right again.

Minutes later, Paul lowered Shelby Sanders's head as he escorted her into the police car. Cameras were flashing all over the place. She was crying miserably as if she had been the one who was victimized. As he shut the door behind her, Paul looked into the window at the woman who was sobbing uncontrollably. What disgusted him most of all was that he knew why she was crying. Not because she tried to kill her husband, but because she didn't succeed and now she would be embarrassed, which to a woman like Shelby Sanders was worse than death itself.

Paul tapped the hood of the car and it started off slowly through the crowd of onlookers and reporters. Paul walked over to Luke, who was on his cell phone, and waited for him to get off.

"This messes things up a bit," Luke said. "The chief isn't too happy with this little twist."

"Actually it makes things a lot clearer," Paul said. "Sanders didn't belong in this bunch to begin with. Let's talk for a second. Away from all these cameras."

Ten

Paul's hand hovered above the telephone at his desk. He told himself this would be easy because the purpose of his call was regarding this case, but he'd been lying. He didn't know what to say to Sepia, and he knew that no matter how professional he tried to make the conversation, it would be personal because there were no lines with them anymore. They had all been crossed already.

"Paul?" Sepia was so happy to hear him she almost didn't believe it. "Is that you?"

"Yes, Sepia." He felt himself relax at the sound of her voice. He had been so tense for so long. "How are you?"

"I'm fine," she said, sensing the hesitation in his voice. He had to be tired. "How are you?"

"We're moving along here."

She hadn't meant the case. She wanted to know how he was, but he obviously didn't want to tell her.

"I have to thank you," he said.

"For what?"

"You were right about Sanders," Paul said. "His wife shot him, apparently because she knew about the other woman."

"I gathered as much when Shelby being hauled off in a police car was on every station."

"She said she took advantage of the killings to do it, but had been wanting to for a while."

"This clears things up a bit," she said.

"Yeah, a bit. Now we can focus on the three murders."

"I'm sure you'll find out who's behind this." Sepia sounded like a proud mother encouraging her son, but she really didn't know how to talk to him right now.

"We're getting clues from Krane's apartment. We'll drag somebody in."

There was a silence that seemed to last forever before Sepia spoke again.

"What's next, Paul?"

"We'll see where the evidence takes us." Paul hoped to God she was talking about the case. He wasn't prepared to answer that question about anything else. "It's a little complicated."

"Can you tell me?" she asked, willing to do anything to keep him on the line even though it sounded as if he didn't want to be there.

"I'll let you know what happens when I can."

In other words, no. Sepia got the picture.

"I really don't feel like I'm in danger. I mean, the person who was trying to kill me is dead and whoever is still out there wasn't interested in him being successful in his last attempt."

"It's always better to be safe than sorry."

"I just can't stand being cooped up in here."

"You'll be able to get around with some protection," he said. "Just not tonight. You should get some sleep. It's been a hard day."

"I'm too wired to sleep."

Paul wasn't sure why those words lit a fire underneath him. He felt compelled to talk to her about their situation even though every inch of him told him not to do it. Not now.

"Sepia?"

"Yeah?" For a second, Sepia was afraid he was going to let her go. She didn't want to go. She wanted to talk to him until she fell asleep.

"I'm sorry about this afternoon," he said quietly.

There was a short silence as Sepia searched her own emotions for the right response. There wasn't any, so she just told the truth. "I felt like you were using me."

"I can see how you thought that," he said. "It was the worst timing in the world and if I could take it back, I wouldn't have done it."

What wouldn't he have done? Sepia wondered. Ask her for a favor or sleep with her? "It's okay."

"Honestly, I just remembered my partner when you mentioned him. I promise you I wasn't thinking about him at all while we were . . . together. I wasn't thinking of anything but you."

Sepia smiled, inside and out. "Thanks for clearing it up, Paul."

"Please forget I ever asked you that."

"You don't want me to—"

"No," Paul said. He didn't need this favor between them. There was enough to deal with in their differences. "I'll find another way."

"Are you sure?" she asked. "You're in danger of not getting a promotion."

"I'll get my promotion," he said with confidence. "I'll take care of everything."

He was a hero at heart, Sepia thought. "I would wish you luck, but I don't think you'll need it."

Paul laughed, leaning back in his chair. He suddenly felt better, realizing he hadn't felt good since . . . since making love to Sepia. "Wish me luck anyway. For good measure."

Sepia unwillingly giggled like a schoolgirl and was supremely embarrassed. It was all so crazy, she shouldn't be surprised by anything anymore. She knew this conversation was coming to an end and it killed her. She wanted to be in his arms more than anything.

"Paul, when will I see you again?"

"It's a little crazy around here."

"I understand." She couldn't have hidden the disappointment in her voice if she wanted to. "I'll see you soon, I guess."

"As soon as possible," Paul answered. Anything less than right now wouldn't be soon enough for him. "Good night, Sepia."

"Good night." Sepia hung up. She stayed there, staring at the phone for an amount of time she couldn't figure.

She analyzed everything she said, everything he said, a practice that women so often did even though they knew it usually caused more problems than not. She didn't want to believe the hesitation in his voice was because he wasn't sure how he felt about her anymore. She wanted to believe he only thought of her when they were together. Paul wasn't a liar. He was an honest, good man and that was a treasure. Someone she could trust.

Someone she could help.

Sepia picked up the phone and began dialing. Not hearing a tone, she remembered that outgoing calls weren't allowed except to the station. She hoped she could steal away Louise's cell phone without waking her up.

"Give me some good news," Lieutenant Pitt said as Paul and Luke sat down across from his desk. "You guys have had a whole day. The press is on me and so are the civil rights groups. Now I've got this white supremist group that wants to protest in front of the station because they think we killed Krane."

"How do they know him?" Paul asked.

"They don't," Pitt said. "They just read the paper this morning and decided he's their kind of guy."

"The papers are taking the race slant to the hilt," Luke said. "It's not a good idea."

"What do you expect?" Pitt asked. "That letter got out there fast, and it pretty much laid the groundwork for disaster."

"We need to talk about that," Paul said.

Pitt looked at him. "Shouldn't Luke be the one to talk to me?"

Paul turned to Luke. He had felt the tension from Pitt the second he walked into the office and was sure it was attributed to David. Paul had accompanied Luke into Pitt's office several times to discuss a case and he never seemed bothered by it before today.

"You know Paul works with me," Luke said.

"Do you want me to leave?" Paul asked. He gripped the edges of the chair, ready to get up and walk out.

Pitt looked at him for a second, his eyes squinted. He leaned back, shaking his head. "Tell me what you have."

"We have problems," Luke said.

"That's not what I want to hear," Pitt grumbled.

"Thirty-two-year-old George Krane has no record of racist affiliations," Paul said. "We searched his place, talked to the few friends he had. He never belonged to any group here or in Seattle, which is where he moved here from five years ago."

"Any of his friends?"

Paul shook his head. "All lowlifes, but don't seem to have any racist connections."

Pitt wasn't satisfied. "Doesn't mean he isn't a racist."

"George was married three times," Luke said. "Each lasted two to three years."

"And that matters because?"

"His second wife was African-American," Paul said.

Pitt's eyes widened into saucer cups. "You've got to be kidding me."

That was the same reaction Paul had had when Luke told him the news.

"It lasted two years," Luke said. "I talked to her on the phone this morning. She's telling me there is no way in heaven or hell George is a racist."

"That's a problem," Pitt said.

"There's more," Paul said, tossing onto the desk a copy of the letter found on George. "Notice anything about that letter?"

Pitt looked it over. "In what way do you mean? It's typewritten."

"The grammar is perfect," Luke said. "An English teacher couldn't have phrased it better. He goes on for a while and not a comma or preposition out of place."

"George Krane dropped out of school after the ninth grade," Paul said.

Pitt looked at Paul, the sheet of paper sliding out of his hand. He looked at his desk for a while, not at anything in particular. Paul knew what he was doing. He was figuring out what he and Luke had already figured out.

George Krane was being set up.

"This is the guy, isn't it?" Pitt asked.

"It's him," Paul said. "He's the shooter. The same gun. His blue Volkswagen is parked outside his studio apartment."

"So why would someone set him up?" Pitt asked. "If he's the guy."

"Something went wrong between Krane and whoever it was that shot him," Luke said. "Whatever it was about, Krane wasn't essential. Not anymore at least. I don't think Krane gave a damn who he was shooting."

"It's the victims," Paul said. "They're what matters. We have to go back to them and figure out why anyone would want them dead."

"Do what you have to do," Pitt said. "I've got to call the mayor. The press is going to have a field day with this."

"You okay?" Luke asked Paul as soon as they left the office.

"Yeah," Paul answered. "Don't worry. Pitt doesn't get to me. I can handle him."

"I'm not talking about him. I know you can handle yourself with anyone in this station. When was the last time you saw her?"

"Before she left this station two days ago," Paul

said, the realization bringing back the pain of it all. "I'm focused on solving this case."

"As you should be," Luke said. "But I know from experience, if you're working on a case to avoid something, it only gives that something more power to mess you up."

Paul knew exactly what he meant. The more he had tried to forget Sepia these past two days, the more he thought of her. He was obsessed over what would happen if somehow they could get together and the murders were solved. What then? All he could figure out was that she was worth whatever their differences would put him through.

"I'll call her," Paul said, reaching for the phone as soon as they got to his desk. "I'll be at your desk in a few minutes."

A strong, husky voice came over the receiver. "Hello?"

"This is Officer Healy," he said. "Who is this?"

"Yes." He cleared his throat. "Healy, it's Michaels."

"Who's all there?"

"Just me. Keeping the place clean, you know." He laughed as if that were a joke, but it wasn't.

"Where is Sepia?"

"She's not here."

"I know she's not there! Where is she?"

"She's, uh . . . She went to the club, but she's with two blues. We were told it's okay."

Paul calmed down. "It's all right. Just tell her I called when she gets back."

Paul hung up, not happy that Sepia was exposed without him. He couldn't expect her to say holed up there until he solved the case. Whatever was itching him about this case told him that she probably wasn't in danger, but he couldn't figure out why. What he was more curious about was why

Sepia had chosen the club to go to again. Did she crave being around her own kind so much that it was all she could think of the second she could get away?

Paul couldn't think of that right now. He had a murderer to find.

Sepia was doing her best to let the beautiful scenery off the verandah of the Cromwell Golf and Yacht Club distract her. She could see the beautiful greens of the course in front of her and hear the sound of the water from the lake hitting against the boats docked in it from the side. It wasn't working as well as she had hoped.

Another day in that apartment was much too much for her. Not to mention not hearing from Paul. Since he called her last, Sepia had been hopeful that there was a chance of something between them, but she wasn't so hopeful anymore. Unable to wait for him to call her again, Sepia called the station, asking for him a couple of times. He never called her back. One time she was forwarded to another line and felt the excitement in her heart at finally being able to reach him, but the voice that came over the phone was Luke and it was devastating to her. Luke promised to lengthen the noose on her protection, which made her a little happy. He also told her that Paul would call her as soon as things calmed down. She could tell he was reluctant to get involved even though she sensed he was close to Paul.

Paul hadn't called, and two days later it was more than Sepia could take. She had tried to reach him at home, but he wasn't listed and she wasn't able to get anyone at the station to provide the information for her. Louise, who had returned home by now, offered to help, but there was not much she could do. Sepia couldn't expect her to either. She was dealing with her own broken heart. When she arrived home, she found that Laurence had returned all of the items she kept at his house and taken his from hers, leaving the key behind.

Life goes on, Sepia knew that much. She knew Paul had much more important things to do than cater to her insecurities and she had to get back to the important things in her own life. She had to write. It was the best way for her to escape and feel normal again. It was the way she expressed herself and found peace, something she sorely needed right now.

Permission to go home and write with the protection of two plainclothes officers was the best news she had heard in a while, but the pleasure was short-lived. The silence in the home that suddenly seemed too large for one person unnerved her. She turned on the radio, the television, but they only made her anxious. Upstairs in her office, she was trying desperately to come up with something, her creative juices were interrupted by the sounds of the officers talking and walking around downstairs with the television on. She put earphones on, listening to Beethoven, but nothing was working.

She came up with the idea of going to the club, remembering how she had told Laurence the verandah was a great place to sit and write. It was peaceful and serene, quiet but not too quiet. It was the middle of the day in the middle of the week when she arrived, flanked by her two new best friends. The club was busier than Sepia expected and she thought that was a good thing for Laurence at least.

After a quick lunch, quick because Sepia didn't have an appetite for anything, she made her way to the verandah, which was relatively empty. Just as she hoped. The two officers sat a few tables away, finishing their lunch and reading magazines as she made her way to the edge of the verandah, taking a lounge chair with her. Sepia set everything up meticulously, hoping this would set the stage for a creative eruption. She really needed one.

Except as she pulled up her novel and put her hands to the keys, Sepia had nothing.

"Damn!" Her hands formed into fists. "You can't let a man interfere with your work like this."

It wasn't just Paul. Her near-death experience at the cabin a couple of days ago was still edging at her nerves, but it was Paul that was really getting to her. She thought of him constantly. She played back in her mind every look, every touch, every kiss, savoring it all. She thought of the love they had made and it heated her up, only to lead to despair as she realized how she messed it all up by letting her fear cause her to jump to conclusions. Whatever the case, Sepia knew she couldn't sit around waiting for Paul to call, and she had called enough. Any more and she would seem desperate, which she kind of felt she was. She wouldn't allow herself to act that way over any man, even though Paul wasn't just any man.

"Sepia?"

Sepia looked up to see Elaine standing over her. Caught up in her thoughts of Paul, she wasn't sure how long she had been standing there.

"Hello, Elaine."

"I'm so glad you're coming," she said. "I was told that you probably wouldn't."

"I beg your pardon? Where am I coming to?"

Elaine looked confused. "You're here for the LOD luncheon, aren't you?"

LOD stood for Ladies Of Distinction, a group of well-heeled women in Cromwell who claimed to get together to plan charities, but mostly spent the time gossiping and telling each other what incredible item their adoring husbands had just bought them, whether it be furs, jewelry, shoes, or clothes. A new home in a popular summer spot or in Europe could monopolize the entire two-hour lunch, which took place every two weeks.

Sepia did everything she could to avoid them, but her mother was a regular, and when her mother wasn't there, Sepia was expected to show up to take her place.

"No," Sepia said. "I'm not coming today. I'm here to write."

"Oh," Elaine said as if Sepia had chosen a hamburger over a steak. "That's nice. I understand what you're going through."

Sepia doubted that very much. "Elaine, since when have you been an LOD member?"

"Well, I actually have to thank you for that," she said, followed by a nervous giggle. "It was mentioning you and how you're saddled with my ex that brought it up."

"Who were you mentioning it to?" Sepia cringed at the gossipers.

Elaine clearly hadn't wanted to go down this road. "Well, I . . . Yesterday, I ran into Marlo Collon. You know her, don't you?"

"Yes." The worst gossip of them all.

"She was worried about you and was asking some of the other women how you were. We all heard about that horrible thing out in wherever that was. Anyway, I just offered what I knew."

"And that would be what?" Sepia didn't know why she was being so bitchy at the moment, but she was.

"That you were saddled with my ex. They seemed to really appreciate the update. You know everyone cares about you so much."

"And that led to an invitation to the luncheon?" Sepia smiled as Elaine nodded. "How nice my misfortune can be an opportunity for you."

Elaine frowned for a second, quickly regaining her composure and plastic smile. She looked around. "Is he here?"

"Paul?" Sepia asked. *If only.* "No, he isn't guarding me anymore."

"So it's over?"

"Not exactly." Sepia shared glances between Elaine and her computer, hoping to send the message she wasn't interested in talking to her anymore.

"You got rid of him?" she asked.

Sepia noticed a hint of sarcasm in her tone. "You might want to hurry inside, Elaine. The LOD women hate it when someone is late. It's considered low class."

Elaine was angry now. Remembering everything Paul had told her about his ex-wife, Sepia knew she'd struck a chord.

"The lunch is outside, actually." Her tone was flat, her stone expression deliberate. "You'll say hello to Paul for me next time you see him?"

Sepia only smiled.

"You will see him again?" Elaine asked. "I know he's not guarding you anymore, but that shouldn't prevent you."

"What do you mean exactly?" Sepia knew she should have let it go, but her curiosity got the best of her. This woman probably knew Paul better than anyone, and Sepia wanted to know more about him even if it was from a biased point of view.

"I saw you," she said. "The other night. I saw you kiss him."

Sepia wondered now if there was anyone who hadn't seen that. "I didn't mean to offend you."

"Why would that offend me?" she asked. "Because of my history with Paul?"

History? They were married, for Pete's sake. She made it seem as if they had gone for lunch a few years ago. "I'm not sure, but you seemed determined to mention it, so it has to have some meaning."

"No, Sepia." Elaine's face softened. "I have the life I want. The life I've always wanted. It's not the same as with Paul, but . . ."

Sepia waited as Elaine seemed to smile at the thought of something. She felt jealous for a moment, watching this woman relive a memory of any kind with Paul. She had owned his heart once. Something Sepia wasn't sure she would ever have the chance to do.

"Paul is wonderful," Elaine said. "I was awful to him, but he never returned it in kind. I did love him, but you know how it is."

"No, I don't exactly," Sepia said.

"What I have now is not as good as it was with Paul in some ways." She looked away, showing a moment of emotion. "But you can't have everything, right? I had to choose and I'm not going to look back."

She left without saying anything else. There wasn't much else to say. Sepia knew what she had meant. Elaine had had love with Paul and an okay life. That wasn't enough for her. She chose a rich, social life with Dr. Trent Ryden, but lacking love. It was a choice that a lot of women made. Some of them hoped they would come to love the man they chose for the money, but it rarely worked out that way. Some very fortunate women didn't have to choose, but they were the few.

If Sepia had learned anything in these past couple of weeks, it was what really mattered. A lot of soul searching since she broke off her engagement to Jason and he fled to the West Coast culminated in finding herself. Having your life threatened more than once and seeing people around you murdered cleared a lot of the confusion up. If Sepia could have the chance to choose between love and social standing, she wouldn't have to think twice about it. Not anymore.

The LOD luncheon took over the verandah in mere minutes. As the caterers brought out carnaroli risotto, shrimp, seared tuna, and roasted zucchinis, the women, dressed as if going to a fashion show, gathered around the tables being set up for them. Between a few complaints as to why the table hadn't been set up earlier, many of the women spotted Sepia and came by to hear about her horrible ordeal, which she had no intention of sharing so they could exaggerate their concern. Neither was she interested in reliving the moment, which was causing her nightmares.

Sepia had to go to plan B. Find any other place

she could to write alone and unseen. The club was filling up with lunching buddies and afternoon rounds of golf. One of the two officers following Sepia around suggested the executive offices. Sepia wasn't too keen on the idea. There was no view from her office. It overlooked the driveway to the kitchen, where deliveries were made. Not necessarily inspiring to the creative juices, but still better than nothing.

The officers agreed to sit in the lobby of the offices, where they could at least watch the pretty girls that passed for their tennis lessons and read the magazines that were laid out. One of them had seemed infatuated with the receptionist from the second they walked in. Since the lobby was the only way one could enter the executive offices, Sepia felt fine leaving them there.

The drama didn't stop, and at this point Sepia found it amusing. As she reached her office, directly across from Laurence's, she noticed the cleaning woman leaving his office. She was a short woman, too old to be cleaning anything for anybody in Sepia's opinion. She said she liked for everyone to call her Coco, which Laurence didn't care for.

"You're not going into your office, are you?" she asked as soon as she saw Sepia.

"I was, actually."

"I'm going to clean in there next." She sighed, only adding to the tired look that seemed to engulf her entire person. "Honestly, yours is the last office and then I can go home and see my new grandchild."

"Fine, I guess." Sepia accepted that God did not want her to write today. "I'll just go home, and—"

"Why don't you come in here?" Coco stepped aside, holding Laurence's door open. "As long as you lock it when you're done, because he won't be here today."

"Sounds like a plan. Thanks." Sepia entered the office, satisfied that this would be her last chance. If this didn't work, she would accept that writing wasn't in the cards for today.

Laurence's office was meticulous as usual, and Sepia was determined not to mess anything up. She placed her laptop on his desk and sat down ready to write just as a huge pop-up message appeared on the display. She was running out of battery power.

"For the love of God!" she screamed, before reaching into her bag for the extension cord.

She scanned the room for an outlet, finding one on the left side of the desk. As she knelt down to plug the cord in, she tried to support herself with her other hand on the desk. Only she laid it down on a photograph, causing her hand to slip. Several pieces of paper fell to the floor.

Sepia plugged her cord in and grabbed the sheets of paper. Standing up, she wondered if she could even begin to place them back in the order that Laurence had them. He would definitely notice, but remembering what he had done to Louise, Sepia wasn't going to care about that. She just plopped them down, in no particular order. The photograph she placed back on top. She glanced closer, seeing Laurence in the center of a group of men, holding an award.

Nothing Wasted: Sepia was familiar with the organization that fed the homeless with food unused at fine hotels and country clubs in the area. Homeless people would dine on the same lobster bisque and chicken marsala as some of the richest people in the county.

"So he does have a heart," Sepia said, noticing that Laurence was getting an award for donations, not for volunteering. You can only expect so much.

As she returned to her seat, a knock on the door made her want to curse out loud, but she didn't.

"Yes?" she asked politely.

Gena, the receptionist, stuck her head in. She looked uncertain as she always did when interrupting someone. Sepia told her she would have to be more aggressive if she was going to run this office.

"Ms. Davis?" she asked. "There's a phone call for you."

"Who?" Sepia's first thought went to Paul. Had he tracked her down to talk to her? She was already reaching for the blinking line.

"No," Gena answered. "It's the chief of police. He's been calling you everywhere."

"Oh."

"What happened to your cell phone?" she asked.

"I don't want to talk about it." Sepia wondered how her expensive phone was faring at the bottom of the lake in the woods. Not very well, she assumed. "I'll take it, thanks."

She reached for the phone, hoping she could at least get something done today, if not writing.

Eleven

"I've got something," Paul said as he approached Luke's desk, which looked as if a tornado had run over it.

Paul sat down, opening up his folder. He laid out what the department had gotten on George Krane's finances, including all the bank accounts they knew him to have had. Luke looked at the papers and shrugged.

"This tells us that George didn't have any money," Paul said, "but we know that if he was getting paid to kill, he would have been paid in cash."

"It wasn't in his apartment," Luke said. "Or the car."

"I've been following up on his so-called friends," Paul added. "George was settling a lot of debts. Turns out he's a gambler."

"What is it with you and the gamblers?"

Luke smiled, but Paul didn't. He knew Luke was just kidding with him, but the situation with David was coming to a head and not getting any better.

"Can we get back to the case?" Paul asked.

"You're no fun when you're in this mood. Okay, seriously, this may be in bad taste, but maybe David can help you. Maybe he knows the guy."

"Are you saying he had something to do with this?" Paul was enraged.

"Calm down," Luke said, never losing his cool. "I'm just saying that Crawford is a small town and the Ravens book everybody."

He had a point. Paul wondered if any information David could give would help his own situation. "The point is, Krane had been settling debts with all the people he owed money to. You remember the blond kid that worked at the gas station?"

"He used to live with George."

"George owed him three grand from back rent, and he gave George the Volkswagen after fixing it up and he wasn't paid for it."

"Three grand?" Luke cocked his head to one side. "That's murder money."

"So we at least have strong evidence to show someone was giving him money for something. We've just got to track it down."

"Easier said than done," Luke said. "Krane doesn't come across as savvy enough to have had a bank account in a false name."

"Maybe the person who was paying him was sophisticated enough to do it for him."

"We don't have a way of getting that, so what else do we have?"

"If he hadn't been putting it in the bank," Paul said, "and it's not at his house, we've got to find out where else he went."

"Let's get back to the victims," Luke said. "We've concluded that Elliott Jackson and Dishwana Grimes were very similar. Willis Connor was different and died in a different scene, but forensics confirms it was the same killer."

Paul remembered the country club membership forms. "Again, the first two victims were denied entry into the club, and the third was under consideration."

Luke studied him. "You really think there's something there, don't you?"

Paul couldn't erase that list from his mind for some reason. "I can't tell you why, but something is telling me to go . . ."

Paul noticed the look on Luke's face as something behind him ripped his attention away. Paul turned around and almost fell out of the chair when he saw it.

Sepia had just come out of the lieutenant's office. She was standing in the doorway with the chief of police and Lieutenant Pitt. As a cop, any sighting of the chief of police was a big deal, but Paul couldn't care less about him. He only had eyes for one person.

Sepia seemed to have a glow around her. She looked beautiful in a vintage Audrey Hepburn beige dress that stopped just below her knee. Something inside him felt as if he were seeing her again after months away, but it had only been two days. Two of the worst days of his life.

"What in the hell was she doing in there?" Luke asked.

When he saw her turn to leave, Paul stood up. He wanted to rush to her, but he had to compose himself. He suddenly felt incredibly cowardly for not coming to her, even talking to her in the past couple of days. He told himself that he was too busy with the case and she needed to be left alone to come down from what had happened at the cabin. The truth was he was scared to approach her, because he was scared of her rejection. It made him angry to admit he was acting like a teenaged boy, but Sepia had made him act in ways he wouldn't have thought he ever would. He could honestly say he would rather stare down a Raven right now.

When she saw him, his eyes locked on hers and Sepia vividly gasped. She had hoped, no, she had prayed he would be here and she could see him. She wouldn't ask for him again, because she had done it too much already. Besides, she hadn't come here to see him. He hadn't been anywhere around when she was escorted to the lieutenant's office and she had done the best scanning job possible. Her heart had deflated, because she only wanted to see him. If he didn't want to talk to her, that was okay. Well, it wasn't okay, but at least she would get to see him. She missed him terribly, and seeing him now only made that more real.

Sepia had to control herself to keep from running to him. Her entire body screamed out to fall into his arms so he could comfort her and let her know things were going to be okay. Only when she finally got to him, all thoughts of her own needs were wiped away. He had deep, dark circles under red eyes. He hadn't shaved in some time and that made him look older. Overall, he looked tired and haggard. It was like human nature for her to want to reach out to him and comfort him, make him feel better.

Luke cleared his throat, and stood up, saying, "I think I have to get something in the other room," before quickly sliding away.

"Hello," Paul said, risking a step closer to her.

He was close enough to faintly smell her scented

perfume and it sent sensations through him. He had woken in the middle of the night last night, certain he smelled it. The emptiness of his home filled him with despair.

"Paul." Sepia was praying she could keep it all together. As she looked at him now, the last thing she wanted was for him to be worrying about her. "How are you?"

"Working hard," he said. "We've been caught up in this case."

"How's it going?" Were they actually going to do this? Talk as if they weren't dying inside? At least she was.

"We're making some headway." Paul stuffed his hands in his pockets, trying to keep them from doing what they wanted to, which was to touch her. "How are you doing?"

Sepia looked away for a second. She dug her nails into her palms to keep herself from getting emotional. "I'm doing better now that I've gotten some limited freedom. I thought I was going to die in that apartment."

"I'm sorry I didn't come by," he said. "I've been—"

"It's okay," she said, even though it wasn't. At least he bothered to mention it. "I know you've been busy."

Paul smiled, hoping she meant that. "Still, I should have—"

He was stopped by her touch as she reached forward and gently touched his arm. It was meant just to reassure him, but it did so much more than that.

"It's okay, really," she said, feeling an emotion for him that she would only expect after loving someone for a long time.

The compassion in her touch, in her eyes, awakened Paul to his own emotions. The gesture itself moved him in ways he hadn't been moved before. After everything she had been through, everything he had put her through, here she was with no judgment, only comfort.

He loved this woman.

"I want to be alone with you," he said, stepping closer. He took her outstretched hand in his and squeezed it tenderly as he looked into her eyes.

Sepia had to step back as the intensity of his look, his words ripped through her. She wanted this man more than anything. She could never resist him, never deny him.

"Come with me," Paul said.

"Yes," she said, her voice cracking.

Just as he turned to lead her somewhere they could be alone, he heard someone scream his name across the room.

"Healy!" Standing in the doorway to his office was Lieutenant Pitt, waving him over. "Get in here."

Yeah, right. "Not right now, Pitt. I—"

"The chief wants to talk to you," he said. "So, yeah, right now."

When he turned to her, Sepia could see the regret on his face. She knew he didn't have a choice. "You can't turn down the chief of police."

"What does he want?" Paul hadn't asked her why she had been in the office. He had been so overwhelmed with seeing her, he'd forgotten.

"I wanted to do something for you," she said.

Paul couldn't believe this. "You didn't have to, Sepia. I told you I—"

"I know what you told me," she said. "And I appreciate you for rescinding the favor, but I wanted to do it. After all, you saved my life."

"Sepia." Paul searched for the right words. "Do you remember when we met?"

"How could I forget?" she asked. "I thought you hated me."

"I never hated you," he said, "but I did think you were a stereotype. An image of what I thought you were, sprinkled with a little bitterness from my past. You've done nothing but prove me wrong since that moment."

Sepia bit her lip to keep from crying. Now wasn't the time to tell him how much his words meant to her. She wouldn't tell him at all. She would show him.

"I don't think the chief wants to be kept waiting," she said, "but I don't mind."

"I don't know how long I'll be. David's in a lot of trouble."

When Luke returned, he made no attempt to hide that he was listening in. "Why don't you wait at Ray's? It's across the street."

"No way," Paul said. It was a police hangout and it was loud. "That place is a dive. It—"

"I don't mind," Sepia said. "I really don't."

He believed her and that gave Paul all the strength he needed. "I'll be there as soon as I can."

"Healy!"

Paul headed for the office. He would be eternally grateful to Sepia for whatever it was she had done, but he still had a lot to do if he was going to help David or himself.

"You okay?" Luke asked.

Sepia hadn't moved from her spot. There was a peaceful smile on her face as she turned to him. "Yes, I'm just fine."

Luke smiled, understanding the hidden meaning. "Good, because he's going to need you. No matter what the decision is, it isn't going to be pretty."

Anxiety cooled Sepia's thoughts of passion. "What

about his promotion? I don't want him to lose that."

"He's more concerned with David than himself," Luke said.

Sepia knew that and it was why she loved him. "He must believe David is worth it."

"David is his partner," Luke said.

Sepia realized Luke wasn't going to say any more about that and she assumed that was all that was necessary to say. She didn't know the details of blue unity, but would have to learn quickly if she was going to support Paul in the way he needed.

"Check it out," one of the officers said, pointing to the television mounted high on the wall. "It's Superman."

Sepia smiled as Paul appeared on the screen, walking with a very reluctant, rather angry brunette woman into the police station. The reporter voiced over the scene.

"Police have been pulling in all known associates of George Krane, who was known to be a white supremist."

Luke sighed. "They just have to put that in there, didn't they?"

"He's wasn't?" Sepia asked.

Luke shook his head, putting his finger to his mouth to indicate that this was still a secret. It made Sepia believe there was progress being made and that was good news.

". . . day and night," the reporter continued. "Channel Four waited outside the station to talk to one of Krane's associates, who tried to avoid our cameras, but finally gave us a few words."

It was the brunette again, decked out in denim with blue eye shadow to match and bloodred lipstick. She stared into the camera with an angry look on her face.

"George wasn't no racist," she said. "He'd been in trouble before, but he wasn't like that. He was a cool guy. What the heck would a white racist be doing living in Crawford anyway?"

"But the police say they have evidence to prove he was the killer," an off-camera voice said.

"What evidence?" she asked. "They wouldn't tell me anything. Look, I don't know what was going on and I know he had come into some money and stuff, but he wasn't a bigot and he wasn't a killer. He was a giving person."

"Giving?" the off-camera voice said. "How so?"

She had to think awhile on this one. Considering the man was a cold-blooded killer, it would take some thinking or some lying. Finally, the brunette's eyes lit up and she remembered something.

"Oh, yeah!" She pointed her finger at the camera as if accusing it. "He volunteered at that food place. You know, Don't Waste It."

"You mean Nothing Wasted," the off-camera voice said.

The brunette nodded. "Yeah, that. It proves that he wasn't all bad."

The screen was suddenly filled with a photo of George Krane, obviously a mug shot taken when he had been booked for another crime some time ago. The sight of him sent chills up Sepia's spine and made her turn away.

"You don't need to see or hear this stuff," Luke said.

He was writing something down on a sheet of paper. Sepia thought it was something for her, but he folded the paper and put it in his pocket.

"Let me walk you out," he said.

"That's okay. I'm fine." At least as soon as she could get away from that photo, she would be. She knew the man was dead, but it scared her to death to even see his picture.

"No," Luke said, already leading her out. "I'm on my way to check something out. I'll take you to Ray's. You don't have to be a cop to get in there, but they like to see you at least know one. Although I sincerely doubt any of those guys will have a problem with you."

Sepia smiled at the compliment. "What's good there?"

"Nothing," he said. "The place is a dive, but it's ours. Owned by a former cop."

"Thanks for giving me credibility."

Luke winked at her. "Just do me one favor."

"Anything." She was really getting to like this guy.

"I know you and Paul have a lot to talk about, but when you see him let him know he needs to call me on my cell. After you guys talk, of course."

Talking wasn't really what Sepia had in mind with Paul, but she would help Luke out as best she could. As they exited the station, Sepia had the feeling that she had forgotten something and it irked her. Maybe it was just leaving without Paul. She would remember it if it was important.

Sepia didn't know what Luke was talking about. As she dug into her cheeseburger, she thought it tasted great. She had been sitting in the café for the longest time with no intention of getting a bite, but after the waiters kept passing by her with plates full of food, she gave in and ordered the cheeseburger. It was greasy and she was certain her arteries were cursing her, but the food was good. She was enjoying it enough to miss Paul coming in until he slid into the booth across from her. Embarrassed, she quickly grabbed a napkin to wipe her mouth.

"Sorry," she said, certain she looked like a grazing cow.

Paul laughed. "Don't be. I like seeing a woman take her food on like that."

"I couldn't help it," she said. "I just got my appetite back and I'm starving."

"I know what you mean," he said.

"Here." She slid her plate toward him.

Paul saw the woman beyond this beauty, with a speck of mustard on her cheek. Just in small gestures like this, she was giving. She was obviously hungry. The way she had been eating, Paul was a little afraid to disturb her. Still, she was offering her food to him. She was caring and giving, something Paul had forgotten a good woman could be.

"How did it go?" she asked. She didn't want him to think he was obligated to share with her out of gratitude.

Paul sighed, his voice and his head lowering. "I can't say good, because that would be a lie. It went the best way it could. Thanks to you."

"I'm glad I could help if only a little bit."

"David's going to have to quit the force," he said, picking at the food. "He's going to have a record, so he'll never be able to be a cop again."

"I'm sure that kills him."

"He's also got to give up everything he knows about the Ravens' gambling unit to help them prosecute."

"Isn't that going to be dangerous?"

"They're going to have to move, leave Crawford and most likely the East Coast, which might be a good thing."

Sepia had remembered everything Paul told her after they had made love in the cabin. "They need a fresh start, right? I hope he can work that out." She reached across the table, placing her hand gently on his. "I know you'll miss him, but at least you saved him from jail and you'll get your promotion."

"Things are going to be okay." Paul entwined his fingers into hers, looking at her with tender eyes. "But not because I'm getting my promotion. Because of you."

"Me?"

"You have to know this by now," he said. "I love you."

Sepia's heart sang with delight and she was consumed with a blissful happiness.

"I needed you," he said. "I needed you in my life to help me let go of the baggage I held from my divorce. I was blaming this group of people for seducing my wife away, and I was determined to make you one of them. Only you proved me wrong. You're a giving, loving, smart woman with a strong head on her shoulders. You made me accept the truth, which was that I married the wrong woman and that mistake was mine. Once I realized that, I was able to let it all go and forgive myself."

Sepia felt the tears well in her throat, but she didn't want to cry. Not because they were in public, because honestly everyone had disappeared the second he entwined his fingers in hers. She just didn't want Paul to think she was anything but happy.

"I love you too," she said, loving the way his eyes seemed to jump in response to her words. "It's amazing how God works. He brings people into your life so you can get to the place you need to be. After Jason, I was at a loss as to who I was and what I had always used to define myself. I was trying to meld the stuff that mattered with the stuff that didn't. If you hadn't come into my life, I would still be there. You helped me find my heart and myself."

"I'm happy for you," he said. "As long as finding yourself doesn't mean you don't need me anymore."

"Not for a second," she said, knowing she would never stop needing him.

They met each other halfway, leaning across the table. Their lips connected and Sepia was filled with a sense of relief and hope. Not to mention a hunger that had nothing to do with food.

The whistles and hollers around them finally got their attention enough for Paul and Sepia to reluctantly separate. He smiled at her, seeing that hint of desire in her eyes that he felt in his entire body.

"Let's finish this someplace else," Sepia said, hoping he had another uniform shirt, because she was going to rip this one off him the first chance she got.

"I'm way ahead of you."

Sepia let out a moan as Paul pulled out of her. His mouth came down on hers with a possessiveness unlike any she had felt before. That kiss told her that he knew she was his and always would be. She could have told him that already. The noises she made as they made love twice should have been enough. This was as good as it got and it was better than she had ever expected to have.

More familiar with her body now, Paul did more to please Sepia this time around. What he got out of touching her, caressing her, tasting her was heaven in itself. The end was just all the more reason for him to know that this woman was his and he was hers.

He placed himself beside her, holding his arms out so she could nestle into them. They were both wet with sweat, but it didn't matter. He wouldn't have had it any other way.

"I like your place," Sepia said, feeling as if she could stay in this position forever. No food or drink, just Paul's arms.

"You're kidding, right?" Paul asked.

"No," she said. "It's you. Very conservative, but strong and understated. It's masculine, but not overbearing."

"Thanks for the compliment," he said, "but I get the idea that you're thinking of ways you can soften it a bit already."

Sepia laughed. "Well, since I'm going to be spending a lot of time here, it's only fair that it reflect my taste as well. Besides, I want any woman that comes here to know that someone has already staked her claim."

"Possessive, huh?" he asked.

"With you I am."

"Well, you don't have to worry, because there is no other woman and there never will be."

Sepia warmed at his words even though he hadn't needed to say them. She knew she could trust Paul. Finally, trusting a man. "Still, it could use a little softening."

"This place is too small for the both of us," he said. "It's a bachelor pad only meant for women who stay the night and leave before morning."

"How crude." She dug her elbow into his chest.

"All I'm saying is that isn't who you are, so we need a bigger place."

"My place is big," she said cautiously. "We can spend a lot of time there, if it doesn't bother you."

"Why would it bother me?"

"Some men can be touchy about that stuff. You know, their woman having a bigger house or a nicer car and stuff like that."

"Not me," he said, knowing she was fishing for a sign that he was okay with the differences in their economic status. "I have an ego, but nothing that brings us together could hurt that ego. You have a ton of money and it would be selfish of me to make you pretend like you didn't just so I could have some false sense of manhood. There are other ways to take care of my woman."

Sepia snuggled in closer, knowing exactly what he was talking about. "And you definitely know how to do that. I'm completely spent."

"That's good to hear," he said. "Because if you had anything left, I would have to get back to work. I wouldn't want anything wasted."

Sepia looked up at him, wondering how in the world she could have forgotten. His words brought it steaming back into her mind.

Paul looked at her as she sat up, wondering what he just said to get such a reaction.

"Did I insult you?"

"No," she answered, "but you made me remember something. When they were talking about George Krane on the TV earlier, a friend of his mentioned that he had worked at Nothing Wasted."

"Yeah?" Good, Paul thought. Any place George went, he could leave a clue.

"I remembered it because I'd seen it before."

"What do you mean?" Paul sat up, seeing the conflicted emotions showing themselves on Sepia's face.

"It couldn't mean anything, could it?" She looked at him, wishing she didn't know what she knew or wasn't thinking what she was thinking.

"Tell me, Sepia."

"Laurence is involved with that organization," she said, the words struggling to come out of her mouth. "I don't know how, but they gave him an award. I saw the picture on his desk."

"I'm a cop," Paul said. "I don't believe that much in coincidences. How is it that Laurence, who supposedly does background checks on all his employees, had an ex-con working for him that also volunteered at the same place he does?"

"But Laurence couldn't possibly have known him," Sepia said. "I know it's awfully rude, but Laurence wouldn't consider George a person worth noticing."

"I've got to tell Luke," Paul said, getting out of the bed.

Sepia slapped her forehead. "I forgot. I'm sorry. He wanted you to call his cell after we finished . . . talking."

"I'll call him now. Where is my cell?"

"It's probably in the living room with your pants."

As Paul rushed out of the room, Sepia pulled the covers to her chest. She couldn't believe that Laurence would have anything to do with this. It had to be a coincidence. After all, Cromwell and Crawford were like brothers who hated each other but couldn't stay away. If one paid attention, there were probably a lot of things that brought citizens of one to the other.

Besides, Laurence had no reason to kill anyone. He certainly didn't run in the same circles as Elliott Jackson, Dishwana Grimes, or Willis Connor. He would have no beef with them. He wouldn't even bother to acknowledge their existence. She remembered how upset he was when talking about the attack on Richard Sanders, but then remembered just as suddenly that Richard wasn't one of George Krane's victims.

"No, no, no." She got up, with the sheet wrapped around her, and paced the bedroom remembering everything that could tie Laurence to this case or set him free, which was what she preferred.

Sepia remembered it was Laurence's writing on his membership form suggesting further consideration of letting Willis Connor join, which he wouldn't have done if he wanted the man dead. It didn't make any sense.

"He saved me." She needed to talk out loud to hear herself over her own thoughts. "When George threatened me, he saved me."

And no matter what she thought of Laurence's character, Sepia felt certain he wouldn't hurt her. Whoever had been paying George Krane to kill someone had paid him to kill her, and it wasn't Laurence Weaver.

"Paul," she said as soon as he returned to the bedroom, "I've got this all wrong. There's no way he could have—"

"Before you say anything," Paul interrupted, "I just talked to Luke. George kept a locker at Nothing Wasted. They said some of the regular volunteers there store some things. Luke busted the lock and it had about five grand in cash inside."

"So someone was paying him," she said, noticing that Paul seemed apprehensive about continuing. "What else is there?"

"A list of names," he answered. "Jackson, Grimes, and Connor were the first three."

"Oh, my God." Sepia sat back on the bed, feeling her knees weaken. "Was I on that list?"

"No," he said. "I told Luke what you said and he couldn't find anything at the charity to trace George to Laurence. We already searched his work locker at the club, but we don't have anywhere else to look."

"Would we if we had that picture?"

The picture! It was a start, but . . . "I can't ask you to do that. I can see how much this is upsetting you already."

"I'll do it," she said. "I'm certain Laurence isn't behind this and I want to get this cleared up right away."

"We have to think about this." Paul had a bad feeling about Laurence and he didn't want Sepia near him.

"There's nothing to think about," Sepia said. "I'm the only person that can get in there and take something that could be used in court. If you have to wait for evidence to get a warrant, you could be waiting forever. You need a judge to get a warrant, don't you?"

Paul nodded.

"Well, Laurence is a very important person and his father was a revered judge. What judge will give you a warrant against the son of the man who was probably his idol?"

Paul knew she was right. "Can we get into the club tonight without being noticed?"

"I think we might now, but we better hurry.

There's a benefit for prostate cancer going on tonight."

"Sepia." Paul flipped up the shade to his bedroom window. "It's tonight already. We've been here making love for three hours."

Sepia looked at her watch to confirm that. "This makes it a little harder."

"Are you invited to that benefit?"

"Yes, but I hadn't planned on . . ." Sepia saw a smile form at the edges of Paul's mouth and it excited her. "You better have a tux, or they won't let you in no matter who you come with."

Sepia immediately noticed a change in the level of security at the country club when she and Paul entered. There was hardly any at all. It was amazing how things began to come back to her now that Laurence's guilt was in the picture.

"It might not mean anything," she said to Paul, "but I remember when I came here with Dunleavy. Laurence seemed adamant that the club didn't need the security it had anymore. He was upset about the cost."

"How would he know it was all over?" Paul said. "Luke said that list had five names on it."

She had spent the drive out there explaining to Paul that Laurence wasn't capable of killing anyone, but when Paul asked her why, her own responses wouldn't hold up. He had come from a good family. So did a lot of bad people, unfortunately. He had been to the best schools. Paul reminded her that the Unabomber graduated from Harvard. He reminded her that Ted Bundy and some of the worst criminals in history had a college degree. Laurence belonged to all the best men's clubs whose members were leaders in finance, politics, and business. The country club prisons were full of those guys, Paul reminded her.

"I would know," Sepia said. "We weren't best friends, but I knew him well. Especially since he started dating Louise."

"What do you think she can tell you?"

"No way. I'm not saying a word to her about this until we're sure."

"She might be able to help the case," Paul said. "I know you want to spare her feelings, but Luke is going to call her in as soon as possible now that I told him about the charity."

"Are you sure you don't just want Laurence to be guilty?" she asked.

"Why would I want him to be guilty?"

"Because he's a snob and was a jerk to you." Sepia waited for a response, but Paul only stared at her. She knew him well enough to know he was a better man than that. "Sorry."

"It's okay," Paul said as they entered the open lobby where everyone seemed to be gathered. "Dinner hasn't started yet?"

"It's over," she said. "They're mingling now. As soon as the band begins playing, they'll go back into the dining hall and dance."

"These people dance?" he asked. "Isn't that a little barbaric for them?"

Sepia grabbed his arm, pinching some skin. "Enough of that."

"There he is." Paul pointed.

As he stood at the far end of the lobby, surrounded by a group of young women who apparently were aware he was again available, Sepia saw Laurence in a different light. She saw his smugness and his facade of perfection. She was biased now because of what he had done to Louise and she wanted deeply to believe this was why she was even considering Paul's suggestion of his guilt.

"Charming the room," Paul said, grateful for the gaggle of women around him. "Looks like he'll be preoccupied for a while, which is a good thing. At least to keep him here until Luke can get here."

"He'll never get a warrant that fast," Sepia said as she led Paul past the lobby toward the executive offices.

"But the chief will give him permission to bring Laurence in for questioning if we can find that picture." It irked Paul that they would need permission to bring anyone in for questioning, but he understood how it was with people in power. They had to be delicate, because any rush would come back to bite them.

"Hello, Jim." Sepia nodded with a nervous smile as they passed the security guard who stood outside the offices' reception area. "I need to get into my office."

"Yes, ma'am," he said. "You look lovely tonight, Ms. Davis."

"Thank you."

As Sepia passed, the security guard turned to Paul. "Good evening, sir."

Paul nodded, realizing that to this guy he wasn't a cop or a working man. He was a member of the upper crust and there was almost a dip in his head when he greeted him.

As they reached Laurence's office door, Sepia tugged at the knob.

"It's locked," she said. "I don't have a master key. Only one to my office."

Paul looked back. They were out of Jim's sight. He knelt on the floor, ruffling through the inside pocket of his tux jacket.

"What are you doing?" Sepia asked.

"This." Paul pulled out a tension tool lock pick, used to open all types of locks. It worked with just a few turns. "If anyone asks, the door was open."

"Who would ask?"

"I'm thinking about the lawyer down the line."

Sepia smiled. "You're thinking like a detective."

"Don't make me want to kiss you right now. We're too busy."

"Later." Sepia turned on the light.

"You can count on it." Paul winked as he made his way toward the same file cabinet Sepia had shown him the last time they were there. "This guy has a thing with neatness. That could be a sign."

"Since when is neatness a sign of psychotic behavior?" She hurried to the spot where the picture was.

"An obsession with perfect order has led a lot of people to murder," he answered as he found the file he was looking for. "Some people are willing to kill if it means things will be . . . neater."

He looked up, noticing that Sepia was staring at him with a blank look on her face.

"What did I say?" he asked.

Sepia felt a chill run down her spine as a motive for murder entered her mind. Never, she thought. "Nothing. Here's the picture."

She held it up and Paul squinted for a look even though he couldn't see anything. "Look to see if you can find something else."

Sepia turned back to the desk, shifting through papers, trying to distract herself from her own thoughts.

"What is it, Sepia?" Paul knew something was wrong. Without even looking at her, he could tell she was upset.

"I was just thinking about what . . ." She looked at the picture, then back at Paul. "When I told Louise about seeing George Krane, she said she only told her mother over the phone."

"You think she told Laurence?"

"No, but she and Laurence have been spending time at each other's place. He might have overheard her telling her mother."

"We're definitely bringing Louise in first thing tomorrow."

"Paul, that's not all." Sepia's hand went to her stomach as she suddenly felt a little queasy. "When I came here to talk to Laurence about Louise the other day, I told him I was going back to the safe house. He knew where I was. That's how George got out there."

"Then why would he kill George before George could kill you?"

Sepia didn't know the answer to that one. "Are we sure it was Laurence?"

"If he's any part of this," Paul said, "I'd be pretty sure he's everything. Is there a copy machine close by?"

"It's down the hall, but I'd have to warm it up. Why?"

Paul pulled out a couple of sheets of paper. "I'll just take my own notes. The other two names on George Krane's list were declined entry to the club as well. It looks like Laurence was adamant about a Steven Redding."

"Ugh," Sepia said. "He's an awful lawyer. He's a proponent of shortening sentences for criminals based on race."

"Why?" Paul noticed Laurence's notes were sharp and square, Paul's experience telling him that they were written in anger.

"He believes that because they're black or Hispanic, living in a country that oppresses them, they can't be held as responsible for the crimes they commit. So, to give them the same sentence as, let's say, a white or Asian person who commits the same crime is racism."

"Sounds stupid," Paul said, "but grounds for murder?"

"That guy hated Laurence's father. About five years ago, the judge convicted a man of murdering his wife. He gave him life without parole."

"Redding was defending this guy?"

She nodded. "He suggested that the man's wife, who was white, calling him the N-word, which he could not prove actually happened, should have commuted the sentence to manslaughter."

"Don't look now," Paul said, as he leaned over a console table to take his notes, "but you're putting together a case."

"Maybe the character I'm writing about should be a detective instead of a cop."

The second Sepia turned around, a flash of light passed the front door, which was half open. Something told her to look at the floor, and in less time than can be measured a dark movement slipped away. A shadow.

"Oh, my God!" Sepia stepped back.

Paul looked up. "What's wrong?"

"Someone is out there," she said, pointing to the door. "I saw a shadow. I saw something."

"Calm down." Paul put the file folder down and hurried to the door.

He looked down the hallway, both ways, and saw

nothing. He closed his eyes and listened for any vibration, any sound. Nothing. He returned to the room.

"No one is out there."

Sepia sighed. "I guess my nerves are just getting the best of me."

"Where do you keep the financial records?" Paul asked.

"I can't tell you. Laurence is the CFO as well. He writes all the checks."

Paul reached inside his jacket for his cell phone. "We shouldn't risk it. We've got enough to bring him in for questioning. I'll call Luke and . . ."

"Your phone?"

"I don't remember where I put it." Paul's hands clenched into fists. Some detective he would be. "I can't believe I came in here without my cell phone."

"Well, mine is at the bottom of the lake, thank you very much." Sepia smiled at his smirk. "Use the office phone."

"They'll be able to trace it and know that I was in here, and I'd rather not let that out."

"Right," Sepia said. "The lawyers. Ask Jimmy."

"The security guard?"

"He's got a cell phone. I saw it on his hip. Don't let him hear you though. Laurence is his boss."

"All right," he said. "Let's go."

Sepia looked around. "I've got to tidy this place up a bit. Even I can tell someone has been here and Laurence is nuts about this stuff."

"I don't want to—"

"It'll take five minutes," Sepia said. "Go. I'll meet you back at the party."

* * *

As she locked the door to Laurence's office behind her, Sepia felt such a heavy heart. There was still a flicker of hope that she was completely wrong, but it was dimming. Something in her gut told her that Laurence was a killer and she couldn't believe she had pushed her best friend toward this man. She thought of Louise and what this would do to her and she thought of all the fine families of Cromwell, and how this would devastate them.

As she headed down the dimly lit hallway, she saw Paul standing in the reception area, his face hidden in the darkness and only the white of his tuxedo sash guiding her toward him.

"Sepia."

Sepia gasped, panic rushing through her as the face behind the darkness was illuminated. It wasn't Paul. It was Laurence and the look in his eyes reminded her of the way he had looked the other day when he spoke about his father's mistress. Hate and pain.

"Laurence." Her voice cracked. "What are you doing here?"

"That's what I came to ask you." He stared at her with the intensity of a wildfire.

Sepia swallowed, knowing that Paul would come for her if she didn't show up at the party. He'd better be quick. "I had to get something out of my office. Some personal items I needed for the weekend."

He looked down at her, seeing only a tiny purse. He didn't appear confused at all. "What about Paul?"

"What about him?" she asked.

"You came back here with him. I saw you two walking past the party. What is he doing here?"

Sepia had to think quickly. From the way he was

looking at her, she was certain he didn't believe a word she'd said so far.

"You got me, Laurence." She smiled, throwing her hands in the air. "You caught me, but you can't tell anyone."

"What are you talking about?" There was only a hint of confusion for the first time.

"I'm so incredibly embarrassed." Sepia fanned her face. "Paul and I were back there . . . we were making love."

Laurence's smile slid across his mouth like a snake. "Sepia, I'm surprised. How very . . . low class of you."

She glared at him for a second, unable to stomach insults from this man.

"You're angry with me, aren't you?" he asked.

"Why would I be?" *Perhaps because you're a murderer.*

"Because of Louise of course."

"I am, Laurence," she said. "And I really can't speak about that right now."

"I knew you before she did, Sepia. We are the same kind of person."

Sepia couldn't control herself. "I'm nothing like you."

Laurence's lips pressed together, but returned to their smile as he stepped closer to her. "So you do hate me."

"I don't hate you, Laurence."

"Good," he said, holding his hand out. "Then you'll dance with me."

She recoiled at the sight of his hand. She could pretend she didn't know he was a killer, but she couldn't touch him. Not now. "I really have to find Paul. You see, he left before me so people wouldn't see us together, and I—"

"I deserve this dance, Sepia."

Sepia didn't have a response for that. She just looked at him, seeing a different person than she had ever seen before. He was crazy.

"You would be dead if it wasn't for me," he said calmly.

Sepia felt her entire body shaking even though her feet were frozen in place. Was this really happening? As Laurence took another step toward her, Sepia stepped back.

"Paul is calling the police," she said. "Right now."

"I saw him come out here," he said. "He didn't see me, but he was pretty upset that Jimmy wasn't here. He ran off somewhere, but I sent Jimmy outside, so I don't think he'll find him for some time. Why was he looking for him anyway?"

Unsure of where Paul might be, Sepia realized that she was on her own. There was no more stalling. This was it. With a burst, she rushed past him and ran as fast as she could toward the lobby. Toward people.

She felt his hand grip her arm and pull her back with a jerk that took her off balance. She was only held up by Laurence, who had a strong grip on both her shoulders. He was facing her, his eyes straining, his face a letter of desperation.

"Just listen to me, Sepia."

"Let me go or I'll scream. I don't want to embarrass you, Laurence. I know what all of those people out there mean to you."

He smiled. "You certainly know my weakness, don't you?"

"Yes, I do. Now just let me go."

"I want to make a deal with you."

"I just made you one. You let me go and I won't—"

"You care about Louise, don't you?"

Sepia's eyes widened. "If you hurt her, I'll—"

"I wouldn't," he said. "But I know she loves me. She calls me all the time, asking to talk to me. I can make her very happy. If you keep your mouth shut, I'll take her back and give her the life that she always wanted."

Sepia was certain now that he was incredibly mad. "You expect me to keep quiet about the fact that you're a murderer and hand my best friend over to you?"

"George is the murderer," he said. "I'm more of a mastermind. You talk about those people out there. I did all of this for them. For you, and if you let me explain I know you'll agree that keeping quiet is the best thing you can do."

"How can you say that you did this for them?"

"Those people were dirtying our image as a group," he said, his tone sounding merely annoyed. "Our race. They were a complete embarrassment."

Sepia jerked away, but Laurence's grip was tight.

"Embarrassment is too polite a word for Elliott Jackson," he continued. "He threatened to sue when I told him he was declined membership. Despite his disgusting lifestyle, he was becoming pretty powerful and he could have won. We can't let that type of black person in power, Sepia."

"What are you . . ." Sepia couldn't even find the words. She didn't know whom she was talking to. This man hated his own race.

"You can't stand Dishwana Grimes, Sepia. If you'll be honest with yourself, you'll tell me that you're not happy she is gone. After what she was doing to the reputation of black women? She was degrading you all and you know the white media is more than happy to give her as much publicity as possible."

"What about Willis Connor?" Sepia asked, even

though it didn't really matter. "He wasn't like either of them."

Laurence blinked, showing a second of regret. "I didn't have any choice. You know how I feel about that kind of music. It's so . . . and he moved into Cromwell and was trying to get into the club. He even offered to have his band play at the opening gala. Could you just imagine the look on those people's faces if that music started blaring here?"

"Please, Laurence." Sepia tried again to pull away, but nothing was happening.

Laurence ignored her pleading. "I was pressured by the others to reconsider him, but there was no way. Then I found out, because he so proudly told me, that he was going to perform for the vice president. That would've been on national television. Can you imagine that? Not our black opera singers, blues, jazz, or even R and B. No, some crap like that. It is our responsibility to control the images of black people to the world."

"They were human beings!" Sepia ripped away from him, her anger giving her the strength this time. She was too upset to be scared now. "They had families, children! They had nothing to do with you and they weren't responsible for what anyone thought of you. How could you become such an animal?"

"You don't know the whole story," he said. "You'll be quiet about this because I saved your life."

"That whole scene outside the restaurant?" she asked. "That was staged, wasn't it?"

"After I told George that you had spotted him, he wanted to kill you. I told him I was going to talk to you and make sure everything was okay. He must have followed me. If I hadn't seen him approach you, he would have done it. I promised him I could control you and I intended to call everything off. I was running out of ways to steal money from the club to pay him anyway."

"Then what was he doing at the cabin?"

"He was giving me a hard time. He wanted to snip all the ends, but I knew he had to go. The weak ones always do. So I used the media's suspicions and set him up. I followed you from the club. That cop was speeding so fast, but I found out where you were, and I told George I would take him there to finish the job."

"And you killed him too, right?"

"He can't possibly matter to you, Sepia."

"You're not as smart as you think," she said. "All of your supposed superiority has betrayed you. When you left him there, you told everyone that he wasn't alone. They're completely on to you."

"It's all circumstantial. Nothing leads him to me."

Sepia didn't want to mention Nothing Wasted. She wouldn't give him the pleasure of knowing. Let him wonder. "They have enough. They have me."

Laurence sighed. "You hurt me, Sepia. You're a well-educated woman. You know the situation our race is in. It is a crisis. The best of us are being pulled back by the worst of us."

"You're crazy." Sepia turned to leave, but Laurence grabbed her arm again, swinging her around.

"You won't give me up," he said. "Because you know that it's up to us to move our race forward. No race, in the history of mankind, has ever made it to the next level without sacrifices. If we wait to bring everybody over the bridge, we'll never get there."

"Look at you," she said, disgust obvious on her

face as she looked him up and down. "You talk about how bad all of those people are, but you're a murderer. You're worse than all of them and what you've done will do more to hurt the *best of us* than all of those people you had killed combined."

"Not if you don't tell." Laurence appeared more like a helpless boy now. "I'm untouchable, Sepia. My father was the most respected judge in—"

"What about your father?" she asked. "What if he was alive now? You would kill him out of shame because of what you've done."

A metamorphosis came over Laurence's face that Sepia would have sworn only movie special effects could do. She was seeing the real Laurence Weaver, a man whose damage went far beyond anything that had happened to him in the past year. There was something about his father that triggered him and Sepia had set it off.

Sepia let out a scream that was stifled when his hands came to her throat. She felt the pressure begin to halt her breathing, making her want to panic. Adrenaline ripped through her body like gas fueling a race car. She began kicking and scratching at him, struggling with all of her might. Her foot connected with his groin and his hands loosened. She pushed away and fell back to the floor. She looked up just in time to see Laurence scream as Paul jumped on him and dragged him to the floor.

"Quit fighting," Paul said, sitting on his back. "There's no point and you know it."

He grabbed his tuxedo sash and created a quick makeshift tie around Laurence's hands, which he held behind his back. He tightened the cloth until he heard Laurence scream out in pain.

Two security guards came running to the scene,

confused as to who was who and what was going on.

"I'm a cop," Paul said. "Get cuffs quick."

He looked at Sepia, who was standing up.

"Are you okay?"

He had come back there prepared to yell at Sepia for not doing as he said, but when he saw Lawrence's hands on her throat, Paul was filled with a rage he didn't know he was capable of. He had to work hard to remember he was a cop. If it hadn't been for the crowd of partygoers that began to gather, Paul wasn't sure he wouldn't be beating Laurence to a pulp right now.

Sepia nodded, her hand coming gently to rub her sore throat as someone helped her stand. "Did you get Luke?"

"Yeah," Paul said, reaching into his pocket for the cell phone. "I found Jimmy on his way outside."

"Laurence sent him away," she said.

One of the guards returned with a pair of handcuffs and Paul got off of Laurence as he took over. Paul was using Jimmy's cell phone, telling Luke what was going on.

Sepia scanned the crowd of all of Cromwell's finest staring in shock and awe at the scene. She heard the whispers. One of their own. What could he have possibly done? Someone as fine as Laurence treated like a low-life criminal? It was a travesty.

When Paul got off the phone, Sepia ran into his arms and squeezed tight. "I thought I was gone."

"Not on my watch." He leaned back, looking into her eyes. "Besides, it looked like you were handling yourself pretty well. You might want to consider being a cop."

"No way," she said. "I'll stick to just writing about them."

As the security guards worked together to get Laurence standing, Sepia glared at him, but he avoided her stare. He avoided everyone's glances. He was embarrassed, and Sepia didn't have the heart to find the irony in that.

"His warped desire to do what he thought was lifting his race up caused the lives of innocent people," she said.

"Taking the burden of an entire race would make anyone crazy," Paul said.

"It runs so much deeper," she said. "I just don't see how I couldn't tell. How can you know someone so well and not know them at all?"

"There was no way for you or anyone to tell. Some people tell lies, some people live them." Paul looked at Laurence, feeling pity for a man he had wanted to beat the lights out of just moments ago. "Either way, the result is only more pain."

He wrapped his hand gently around Sepia's head, bringing it to his chest. Sepia felt the warmth of his love and she knew she was where she belonged and would stay forever.

Epilogue

"Nice to see you, kid." Richard Sanders winked at Sepia as she passed. "It's nice to see you here again."

"So nice to see you again, too." Sepia waved, not planning to stop until she got to her destination.

Here referred to the country club. It had been three months since Laurence was arrested for the murders of Elliott Jackson, Dishwana Grimes, Willis Connor, and George Krane. The effect on the club as well as everyone who knew Laurence had been devastating. No one believed it at first, but the evidence that Luke and Paul gathered in tandem with the district attorney's confidence began to convince them. He was denying it all and had hired a group of the most expensive lawyers in the country to defend him, but Sepia wasn't concerned. Laurence was going to pay for what he had done.

In that time, Sepia hadn't been at the club even once. She had spent most of her time with Paul and they were growing closer every day. She had hoped that with the excitement of the situation over, their passion wouldn't dissipate. Not only did it not dissipate, it grew stronger and more overwhelming. Even her parents liked him despite their attempts not to. Sepia knew he would win them over. Paul was irresistible to anyone who gave him a chance.

She had also been a shoulder for Louise to cry on, happy to repay the favor given to her after her breakup with Jason. It turned out that Louise was a lot stronger than even Sepia had given her credit for.

Everything was coming into place, and as Sepia reached her table in the main dining hall of the club, she smiled from inside out.

"For me?" Paul asked, as Sepia held out a tiny cupcake with a lit candle on top. "It's not my birthday."

Sepia leaned over, kissing him on the forehead before sitting next to him. "I know, but you did get a promotion, Detective."

Paul smiled, loving this woman more and more every day. She was so strong and independent, yet she always made him feel like a king whom she needed and loved. She would be by his side through thick and thin and he would do the same for her.

He took a bite before handing it back to her. "You should take a bite too."

"Why?"

"I forgot to tell you that Margo called for you this morning. You were in the shower, so I told her I would take a message."

"What did she say?" Sepia asked pensively.

"Relax, honey, you know you're great."

"You know," she said. "And I know, but . . ."

"She said the first five chapters were fantastic. She read them twice, and she can't wait to get the rest of the book. This cop character is going to be a big hit."

"That's because it has a real, gritty feel," she said. "And that's thanks to you, my consultant."

They both turned as the next piece for auction came up. It was an antique Chinese glass vase, donated by Dr. and Mrs. Davis. Tonight the Cromwell Golf and Yacht Club was holding a gala to raise money for the family members of Laurence's victims. It was part of the recovery of the group that was so hard hit by the deaths. It was a way to give back, and Sepia thought some of them felt guilty even though they weren't.

"Your parents are willing to part with that?" Paul asked.

"I threatened them if they didn't donate something nice."

Paul looked around as guests began offering incredible prices. "You know, I had these people all wrong. Well, not maybe all wrong, but they're good folks."

"I told you," Sepia said. "As for you and me, we keep the good and stay away from the bad."

A waiter approached, handing Paul a tall glass of beer. "Your drink, sir."

Paul accepted the drink, thanking the waiter. He lifted his glass to Sepia. "This is the good, and I could really get used to this life."

Sepia laughed, but she was really impressed with Paul. He was a man of principle, but he never denied her any of the nicer things she wanted. This was going to work. It was going to do better than work. This was going to last.

"There's more to high society than being served, you know."

"I know," Paul said. "For example, the emphasis

these people place on education is something I haven't seen before. Really strong, and it's encouraged me."

"Are you planning on getting a degree in something?" Sepia took a bite of the cupcake after blowing out the candle.

"Not me," Paul said. "But that kind of environment is going to be good for our kids. They'll know from the start how important education is."

Sepia almost fell out of her seat. She tried to maintain her composure. "You said our kids?"

Paul looked at her as if it were all just a simple afterthought, although his heart was racing right now. "Yeah. You do want kids, don't you?"

"Well . . . I . . . of course I do. You mean with you?"

"Who else were you planning on having them with?" He put his glass down, leaning into her.

"No one," she answered. She couldn't imagine anyone other than Paul.

"So we'll have a baby, then."

"I'd love to." She smiled, as he stared at her. Waiting. Waiting.

"Now, I'm not a piece of meat, Ms. Davis." He gently cupped her chin, bringing her face closer to his. "I demand respect. You'll have to make an honest man out of me before any baby, you know. That means marriage."

"If I must," Sepia said, a happy tear trailing her cheek.

Their lips connected with the promise of forever and never separated.

ABOUT THE AUTHOR

Angela Winters is a national bestselling author. Her first romance novel, *Only You*, was published in January 1997, followed by *Sweet Surrender, Island Promise, Sudden Love, A Forever Passion, The Business of Love, Know By Heart, Love on the Run, Dangerous Memories, Saving Grace*—the third installment in the Hart family saga—*High Stakes* and *A Class Apart*. Angela's first short story, "Never Say Never," appeared in the Mother's Day anthology Mama Dear in May 1997. Her second short story, *Coming Home*, appeared in the holiday anthology Season of Love in October 2002.

Angela's novels have received strong reviews from *Romantic Times, Romance in Color, Affaire de Couer* and *The Romance Reader*, among others. An aspiring screenwriter, Angela has adapted many of her novels for the screen, written original screenplays and spec scripts for television series.

A native of Chicago, Angela received her bachelor's degree in journalism from the University of Illinois. She currently resides in the DC metro area. She is a member of Romance Writers of America, Washington Romance Writers and The Organization of Black Screenwriters. You can reach Angela via e-mail at ajw827@yahoo.com. More information can be found at her Web site at www.tlt.com/authors/awinters.htm.

BOOK YOUR PLACE ON OUR WEBSITE AND MAKE THE ARABESQUE ROMANCE CONNECTION!

We've created a customized website just for our very special Arabesque readers, where you can get the inside scoop on everything that's going on with Arabesque romance novels.

When you come online, you'll have the exciting opportunity to:

- View covers of upcoming books

- Learn about our future publishing schedule (listed by publication month and author)

- Find out when your favorite authors will be visiting a city near you

- Search for and order backlist books

- Check out author bios and background information

- Send e-mail to your favorite authors

- Join us in weekly chats with authors, readers and other guests

- Get writing guidelines

- AND MUCH MORE!

Visit our website at
http://www.arabesquebooks.com